MONTANA TWO-LANE

— B. R. Riggs —

ISBN: 979-8-218-14924-6 (paperback)

For Joan, as promised.

His arm hung from the crushed SUV like a mouse tail dangling from an owl's beak. I took out my pocketknife, ready to slit his veins from wrist to elbow if I detected a pulse, but didn't feel the slightest throb. Good luck mitigating bad luck had been the hallmark of the past five days.

TUESDAY

The anxiety hit where Interstate 90 squeezes through Hellgate Canyon. Not the fear of an unlocked door or water left running in the sink—more like a box of high explosives left next to a pile of burning garbage. Deserting my family while we were under siege was perceived as traitorous and felt that way too, but we'd have nothing worth saving if not for Marie. I had to see her.

Nine hours later, Red Bend appeared as an angular scab on the smooth horizon, its silver grain elevator turning fluorescent orange and glaring back at the setting sun. I veered off the highway, took the shortcut into town, then waited at the only traffic light in the county. Marie was nineteen miles from the ranch where she'd put out the welcome mat for death, but a covert departure had proved to be the one thing she couldn't make happen simply by putting her mind to it. Suicide would've been cheating, God refused to intervene, and she ended up in town, waiting for death to slowly, painfully reel her in.

Parking in front of the one-story hospital sprawled at the end of Box Elder Avenue cemented the reality of Marie's demise and diluted the anticipation of seeing her. The disease had won, closed in for the kill, and she'd been too out of it to talk on the phone lately. I hurried to her room, stepped quietly around the nearly closed door, and suppressed a scream as Karl hauled me into a bear hug. He took his time setting me back on my feet then stood there beaming as if he'd conjured me out of thin air.

"Damn! It's good to see you, Lynn!"

"Good to see you too, Karl. Even if you did scare the bejesus out of me."

"Sorry."

His joyous grin negated that word. Then came a flurry of questions.

"How the hell have you been? How was the drive? How're things going over in your neck of the woods? Dang! You just missed Darlene. She's really looking forward to seeing you. Walter and Becky are putting us up. You staying at the Cottonwood or the Wagon Wheel?"

"The Cottonwood."

"Good. It's closer."

Closer? How could it be closer? Nowhere in Red Bend is more than a laid-back minute from anywhere else, but I smiled and nodded. Wanting to please Karl is an old habit, effortless as antagonizing his brother Walter. With blond hair disappearing faster than graying and skin too transparent to hide the bulbous veins bracketing his forehead, Walter is nothing like his sibling in looks or temperament. He remained ensconced in the mauve vinyl recliner, and only after he'd entwined his fingers over his paunch and crossed his legs did he disturb his frown long enough to speak.

"Hello, Lynn. Long time, no see."

"Hi, Walter. Has been quite a while, hasn't it."

I turned away and stared at Marie. It stung to see her bold, bright presence emaciated and mute, cognition submerged in the steady stream of drugs flowing through the port in her chest. She'd hated the thing ever since it was implanted it to ease the long months of chemo infusions. Getting rid of it had been the single upside when she'd learned the poison it dispensed would only kill the cancer by killing her. But a nurse had warned her she'd be glad to have the device when her veins collapsed, and it stayed under her skin. She'd called me that night, first time I'd been allowed to give rather than receive solace, first time I'd heard despair in her voice.

"Ain't good, Lynn. Been handed a number and left standing in the slow line to death's door. And it looks like I'll be taking this goddamn hunk of plastic to the grave with me."

It seemed she'd been right—as usual. I wanted her to open her eyes, wanted her to know I'd made it there to see her, wanted her to speak to me, but she couldn't oblige. Karl picked up on my frustration.

"Mom's not waking up much anymore, Lynn. And when she does, the pain gets so bad they gotta dope her up again. Did you know Rimrock County has the highest rate of liver cancer in the whole damn U S of A?"

Uncomfortable with delivering bad news, Karl shifted his weight and ran both hands through his thick hair, wavier than I remembered. Aging had added muscled bulkiness to his frame and ruggedness to his exotic, soft brown, monochrome coloring too. Enjoyable observations that ameliorated his troubling words, but my question still contained more outrage than curiosity.

"What in hell could cause that here? You don't have any pollution."

"Yeah, we do. Just ain't hanging over our heads like it is over your way. It's in the water."

"The alkali?"

"No...from the goddamn oil drilling. There's a good chance it's contaminating the aquifer."

"No way!"

"Yup. Got it straight from our head engineer the night of his retirement party. Showed up three sheets to the wind and kept right on sucking down the booze. Didn't take his better half long to get fed up and leave him there. And guess who got elected to drive his drunk ass home? Yup, me. I got to talking about Mom, and that's when he let the cat out of the bag."

This could not be. Not in the untainted, safe, sane side of the state. Walter, blue veins bulging across his temples, didn't like what he'd heard either. Karl shot him a challenging glance, but his brother kept schtum.

Karl understood the oil business better than anyone in the county, maybe in the whole state, and certainly better than anyone in that room. He'd signed on at Shoen Creek, an oil field sixty miles west of Red Bend, right out of high school. It was backbreaking work, sixteen hours a day, seven days a week, often a month at a time without a day off, but it paid multiples of the going wage. Promotions came fast, and Karl made district superintendent the year he turned thirty-five.

He'd always be Walter's kid brother, though, and they must've been getting on each other's nerves after spending so much time together in tight quarters. Marie made an effort to get along with their wives and left it at that. It was her sons who stood vigil— and I needed them gone.

"Why don't you two take a break. Get away from here awhile."

Karl rewarded me by attempting to squeeze the air out of my lungs again.

"Thanks, Lynn. You're a sweetheart!"

Walter pushed himself out of the recliner. His eyes, the flat blue of a number two billiard ball, had lost their habitual cynicism and betrayed something close to gratitude as he delivered his provisos.

"Okay, Lynn. But you have to promise to let us know right away if anything changes with Mom. Or if she happens to wake up."

"I will, Walter."

But Marie slept on, her breathing shallow and erratic. I smoothed the unrumpled bedding, inspected the room for absent bits of garbage, fussed around her bedside, then checked the flowers herded onto the sill of a long, low window to see if they needed water. They didn't. Above the blossoms, my reflection suggested I'd walked the entire five hundred miles from home. Standing straighter, finger combing my short hair, and tugging down the legs of my wrinkled jeans didn't help much, so I switched off the overhead light and replaced my image with the orderly cottages across the street.

Their open drapes revealed flickering TV screens, nightly rituals, and peace. Mesmerized, I jumped a foot when Marie let out a croaking, phlegm-clearing groan, and, as I whirled around to rush toward her, my elbow sent a vase of daffodils crashing to the floor.

"Karl?"

Before I could respond, Marie's papery eyelids descended. Willing her to stay awake, I leaned over the bed rail and rubbed her arms. Then she repeated her question.

"Karl?"

"No. It's me, Lynn. Hey...I'm here. I made it!"

"Lynn?"

"Yeah. Yeah, it's me. You okay? Want some water? Can you have water?"

As I wet her lips with the green, sponge swab thingy on her bedside stand, a short, spiky-haired nurse came in to suss out the noise.

"You're awake!"

Seemingly intent on rectifying that situation, she marched toward the IV stand. I stood aside, but Marie bristled.

"No. No. Want...want to talk. Gotta...sit up."

The nurse raised the head end of the bed. But withholding drugs went against her training, and she wasn't inclined to grant the implied request. She watched me pick up the pieces of broken vase and sop up the water then, voice coated with skepticism, looked at Marie and delivered her demanding question.

"Promise you'll let me know as soon as the pain gets worse?"

Marie nodded. The nurse took a few steps toward the door but, wary the stranger might be influencing her patient, positioned herself so Marie couldn't see me and pressed her for confirmation.

"You're sure about this?"

"Yes, yes."

"Don't wait too long, Marie. Okay? Remember, it's easier to *keep* the pain under control than it is to *get* it under control."

Even then, she wouldn't leave until she'd braced the door wide open. I waited a second to ease it closed, and Marie reached for me with tethered arms. A year of rest couldn't erase decades of toil, and her cold hands were rough as the bottom of a dog's paw. But her cheeks, like the prairie wind that had wrinkled them, were soft and warm against my lips.

"Lynn, ain't you a—"

Her brow furrowed, and she drew a slow, shaky breath.

"—sight for sore eyes. How's my favorite god-daughter doing?"

I was her *only* goddaughter. The silly old joke had been ours since that first summer together, when I turned six, and how could I not laugh before answering her question.

"I'm okay. Better now that you're awake."

"Hate sleeping away what little time I got left. The boys?"

"Talked them into taking a break. I'll let them know you woke up. Promised I would."

Marie didn't like the sound of that any more than I did.

"Okay. Tell them don't hurry, though. So we can talk."

I did as instructed but knew full well they'd rush back anyway and resented them for shortening my time with her. Every word counted now, and how surprising and gratifying to have her pick up where our last phone conversation had ended three days earlier.

"So, Lynn...what's the verdict? Better bite the bullet and do something PDQ. Or the regret will chew on you like maggots on a wire-cut sheep for the rest of your life."

"Yeah, I know. You're right. I've finally faced facts. Phil too. We're done being the end birds on a wire, giving way till they lose their perch. Besides, a promise is a promise. And we're going to keep ours. Whatever the cost. But this isn't the time for you to be worrying about my nightmare."

"Yeah, it is. Kinda takes my mind off my own. And don't you worry. You and that ex-husband of yours are doing the right thing. Goddamn social services people weren't any help."

"No. You got that right. And we were crazy for turning to them."

Marie nodded and managed a misshapen smile as she tried to move her body into a more endurable position.

"Are you okay?"

"It'll pass."

It visibly did not. Numbers on the monitor moved in unhealthy directions, and the steady beeping developed a stutter. Even so, I didn't have the heart to sic that nurse on her. Rekindled hatred of all things bureaucratic had put a gleam in Marie's eyes and spirit in her voice.

"No sense feeling foolish, Lynn. Ain't the first to find out going to officials is like jumping naked into a pond full of leeches. Higher-ups to peons...crooked, useless, or both. Always have been. Always will be."

Around Red Bend, the worst thing you can say about a person is that they'd make a damn good politician. Mistrust of all things governmental had sprouted on *ne Stap* in the Ukraine when Russia repealed the guarantees of anonymity that had lured Germans to her bedeviled outpost, and it flowered in 1918 when the United States reneged on its promises of liberty and banned all use of the German language in schools, papers, and churches. That mistrust is self-sowing now—passes in our DNA—and an endless supply of political bullshit produces good crops.

Marie dealt with the absence of integrity in government the way she did the rest of life's injustices. She planned accordingly, distanced herself whenever she could, and never used it as an excuse for failure. I'd always admired the brave, rational way she lived, would've done anything for her, but could only moisten her lips again and smile you're welcome for the thank you in her eyes.

"When you heading home?"

"Saturday morning."

"Good. Still be here...for my funeral. Did ya know Daddy and Grandpa helped build that church?"

I shook my head and delighted in watching her talk.

"Yup. They sure did. Same year I came into this world. Mamma wanted it ready for my christening. Told Daddy, if one woman could create a baby in nine months, they could build a church in seven. They did...and I was. Got married there too. Guess I'm closing the circle."

Familiar voices echoed in the hall, Karl and Walter closing in on us. There'd be no time to lie and tell Marie her funeral was a long way off. No time to thank her for the letters holding a stick of gum with a dime slipped under the wrapper. No time to thank her for the summers that left me determined to emulate her and not my alcoholic parents. No time for anything but a quick kiss goodbye as her pale hands, hands which should've been tanned by the middle of May, slipped out of mine while she whispered a plea.

"Promise? Promise you'll take the gun. Just in case."

"I promise."

I refused to cry. But tears threatened, unwanted and uncontrollable—the mad woman beating her fists against an attic window. I hurried to the door, jerked it open, and collided with Karl as he charged into the room. There's no give to that body of his. I'd have hit the floor if he hadn't caught me around the waist. Then, in two long strides, he was at his mother's bedside. I stopped in the corridor, just outside her door, and pressed my back against the cool wall.

The floor gleamed under the bright lights. No intrinsically dirty carpeting here. Hospital-clean still meant something in this little outback of the Medical Establishment. No need to slip a mickey of feel-good drugs to postop patients then hustle them out the door before some institutionally bred infection did them in. An assuaging observation, a better distraction would've been figuring out how to get Marie's gun from her house or re-examining Phil's plan. My ex had come up with a good one for sure, but any plan is only as good as its backup. We didn't have one—and there was Walter, hobbling embodiment of things gone wrong.

He'd incurred the injury on his twelfth birthday when his horse stepped in a gopher hole. His shifting weight had torn the heel off one of his worn-out boots, letting his foot slip through the stirrup, trapping him in the saddle, and bringing the mare down on his leg. His ankle took the worst of it, and left him unable to walk. Marie fashioned a crutch from an old board, then, believing Walter would heal on his own, she'd waited too long to have a doctor look at him, and his ankle never did heal right.

Although it's a sure bet mother and son would never broach the incident in private, Walter didn't shy away from talking about his misfortune if conversation led to it. He enjoyed pointing out how small-town high school is just hell without the flames when you can't play sports, and he'd bare the dent in his ankle if you asked him to. The outline of a stirrup is unmistakable. Marie's one contribution to his recital of events never varied, and her voice never held a trace of remorse.

"If I'd a took those boys to the doctor every dang time they got themselves hurt, they wouldn't a had a roof over their heads or food in their bellies."

Marie's life was built on tough choices, and she didn't waffle. I'd have to be just as strong over the next few days and began by leaving her and walking down the hall. I stopped when I met Walter, but, for him, hurrying is akin to gaining speed in a car with four flat tires. He lumbered on by and talked over his shoulder.

"Told Becky and Darlene you'd head over to our house as soon as we got back."

His voice would've garnered attention in a rowdy mess hall. I'd nearly saluted, "Yes sir!" and felt guilty for the few seconds it took to reach the front door.

Air is never sweeter than when you walk out of a hospital. Add the smell of new grass, enlivened soil, and something blooming in the darkness, and it's ambrosia for the nose. The cab of my truck didn't smell so sweet, though, and every part of my body protested being behind the wheel again. I lowered the windows, and, ignoring Walter's directive, headed straight for the motel. Reservation or no reservation, I wanted the room key in my hand.

The Cottonwood Motel's namesake can be seen from anywhere in town, and the arboreal gatekeeper was promenading its new leaves halfway across the narrow entrance. Their piquant aroma brought to mind the thrill of crawling out on a cottonwood branch hanging over the Milk River then stretching out belly-down to study the churning water. The only thing I'd missed about home during my summers with Marie. And replenishing that sweet memory compensated for the indelible, rust-colored resin those shiny leaves had smeared across the driver's side of my truck.

Careful not to brush up against the sticky mess, I got out and walked into a fresh-smelling, tidy, well-maintained lobby decorated with non-plastic, healthy plants. Sadly, the man behind the counter possessed none of those qualities. His false teeth didn't fit any better than his fake tortoiseshell glasses, dandruff had collected on his shirt collar below the recliner-rooster tail on the back of his head, and his body wafted the odor of an unreliable bladder. Yet, somehow, he'd retained the confidence and manners of a hardworking rancher.

"Daughter and her husband took in the grandson's track meet in Wibaux. I'd of gone too...just ain't up to those long drives anymore. Got a new hip put in last winter. And, Katy, their regular help, she's in the hospital having a baby. So I came on in to hold down the fort. Anything you need...you just let me know."

"Thanks. I sure will."

Taking the proffered key from his arthritic fingers, I edged out the door before a second monologue ensued, although listening to him sounded better than dredging up the energy to visit Becky and Darlene. The only place I wanted to go was my room, but could only drive by it and look forward to returning. I'd be able to park right in front of my door too—no hiking across a parking lot, no climbing stairs, and no trekking down a hallway. I'd be staying at an actual motel, not a hotel being passed off as one.

My pet peeve never failed to cause Phil's recruitment-poster face to wrinkle into a smile. And why hadn't he called? Had something already gone wrong? I wanted to find out before getting tied up with Becky and Darlene and checked my phone. No message. He called a block later, though, and I pulled over in front of the high school, away from the houses with small lawns and large picture windows.

"Hi, Phil. I was starting to get worried."

"Makes two of us. Jill took her sweet time returning my call. I thought maybe we'd been wrong about her jumping at the bait."

"But did she?"

"Oh yeah. That conniving bitch can't wait to hear what has me so concerned about you. Meeting's set for Saturday afternoon at three."

"Where?"

"I've got the perfect place. Watching it for a guy who's out of the country. Can't be seen from the road, and the closest neighbor is a quarter mile away. And get this...it's due south of the Colonial Inn on Wedding Drive. Justice can't get any more poetic than that."

"No, it can't. And it has to be a good omen, right?"

"Course it does. She's going to lose everything right where she stole it. Trust me, Lynn. All she has to do now...is show up. Say, before I forget, how's Marie?"

"Convinced I'll still be here for her funeral. And she's probably right."

"That bad, huh? I'm really sorry, sweetie. Know how much you'll miss her."

"I'll be lost, Phil. Without that flawless logic of hers, how will I know what to do when right and wrong are too damned mercurial to pin down?"

"Don't worry. You will. You couldn't forget what she taught you even if you tried. It's who you are."

"Hope so. And it sure is good to see her. But what if things get worse at home? I'm so far away I'll be useless. Has me worried sick."

"Now you know how it's been for me ever since you learned why that evil bitch latched on to our son."

"Far away maybe. But you've never been useless."

"I don't know about *that*."

His tone of voice told me he'd put on the crooked

smile that won my heart many years before, the one that defies his determination to keep a straight face when he's praised.

"It's a fact, Phil."

"Oh...well...uh...anyway, at least you have a solid reason for being out of town. And no one would think anything of it if things go sideways and you have to swing over to Helena to help me out. But, trust me, that won't happen. So relax."

I didn't have to ask how Phil was coping. He's a pro, happier with things set in motion, first domino on its way to the next. We said goodbye, and facing "the girls" appealed to me even less than it had. What in the world would we talk about?

One of Becky's Christmas letters had mentioned their new house being "at the very end of Short Street," presumably ending in a grain field sooner than all the others. I located it on the other side of the Red Bend Badgers football field, and, if not the shortest, it's the oldest street in town. It runs between overgrown Siberian peashrub hedges, rusty swing sets, sagging outbuildings, old cars, and unsold tractors from the farm auctions held in the dirty thirties. The only indicators of the houses still being occupied are shiny new pickups and freshly plowed gardens.

Walter and Becky's two-and-a-half-story home, with their surname, Taylor, arching high above the driveway, looms over the dusty Lilliputian street in a cartoonish fashion. Their house would've blended right in where I lived. Missoula suburbs were crammed with these wannabe castles—rooflines resembling shingled mountain ranges and moats of unkempt plants lapping against fake rock siding. But, as a row of Quasimodo-like pines escorted me to the house, I nursed a sober envy for the unembattled lives sheltered within its walls.

Four carriage-style garage doors glowed sickly yellow under the sodium yard light, and everything else lay in darkness, including the house. All the excuse I needed to vamoose, but shifting into reverse seemed to trigger a silent alarm. Down-lights, up-lights, walkway lights, and house lights came on everywhere. Then Becky appeared, pointing toward my truck with one hand, motioning toward the house with the other, and hollering.

"Just leave it right there and come on in."

She kept it up until I got out of the truck and trotted toward her.

"Sorry, Lynn. Didn't think to turn the lights on till I heard your truck idling. Good to see you."

I followed her to the front door, through a great room—like most, more room than great—then down a narrow, poorly lit hallway to a kitchen so bright it made me blink. Large, plain, and practical with lavish, indiscriminate whitewashing to keep it cheery, the room perfectly reflected the woman overseeing it day and night.

"Figured you'd be hungry when you got here, Lynn, and fixed you a bite to eat. Darlene will be down in a second. She grabbed a quick nap. Have a seat."

A linen placemat, heavy silverware, and an expensive stoneware plate holding a paper towel folded into a napkin marked my spot at the breakfast bar. After wrestling a wooden stool into position on the tile floor, I fought to get my butt on the high, slick seat and tried to shake the feeling I'd accomplished it with all the poise of a pig climbing on a swing by shifting my attention to the marble backsplash tiles in need of re-grouting, the protruding finishing nails in the garden window, and the white sink faucet that wasn't. Then I reminded myself I hadn't been invited for free real estate advice.

Walter's trophy house would always be Becky's home, and she wouldn't want it any other way. While her attitude and dress are somewhere left of Harriet Nelson and right of Jane Fonda, her style is squarely Aunt Bee. Quick and efficient as a truck stop waitress, she filled my cup with coffee as she placed a sandwich in front of me then added half the contents of her commercial-sized fridge. Ceasing at last, she pulled the towel off her shoulder, wiped her hands, and surveyed each pitcher, plate, tub, jar, and plastic container to be sure of my answer before asking the question.

"What else can I get for you, Lynn?"

"Absolutely nothing, thanks. It's way more than I'm used to...and then some."

The sandwich of ham, cheddar cheese, and lettuce between thick slices of moist, homemade bread had my mouth watering. Becky got it right. I was starved. But, just as the cool lettuce caressed my lips and the first delectable bite touched my tongue, Darlene walked in. She took in the feast then gave me a knowing wink, and I choked trying to chew, swallow, and laugh at the same time.

Tall, trim, and pretty, with her usual fitted shirt tucked into tight jeans, silver barrel racing buckle, cowboy boots, and quick perfect smile, Karl's wife is rodeo queen material and owns the look. She coaxed one of the contrary barstools into position and glided onto the seat. Then, in a voice as smooth as the silk scarf missing from her neck, she asked those polite, inescapable questions.

"How was your trip, Lynn?"

"Oh, you know me. Any mile away from the mountains is a good mile."

"And there's a lot of those between Missoula and here."

"Yes there is."

"How're you and the rest of the family doing, Lynn? And what about that grandson of yours? He's about a year and a half now, isn't he? Right at the age when they're getting into absolutely everything."

I cleared my throat, straightened my spine, and, except for agreeing with her about Bryan being at an inquisitive age, began layering pearly lies over the galling truth.

"Yeah, he is. And he sure keeps Jill and Mike on their toes. They're doing great, though. Same with Amy and Paul. And I can't complain either. But, hey, how're things going around here? Must be difficult having Karl and Walter at the hospital with their mom most of the time."

Becky had finished adding sourdough to next morning's pancake batter and brushed away my attempt to change the subject. Legs splayed, fanny braced against a cupboard door, one hand in her pocket, the other hauling in snacks from the lineup on the granite countertop, she began scratching away at my lustrous story.

"I'll bet you were knocked for six when Mike, such a confirmed bachelor, got married and made you a gramma before Amy did, huh, Lynn?"

"I sure was."

"Don't recall Marie saying Mike got engaged. He know Jill very long?"

"No. Kind of a whirlwind romance."

The prodding continued until Darlene interrupted and threw me a lifeline.

"To answer your question, Lynn, things have been okay with us. For the most part, anyhow. Marie being in the hospital kinda stirred things up for sure.

But we help each other out as much as we can. And you must be pretty darn busy. Seems like Montana's become the cure-all for whatever ails a body these days."

"It sure does, Darlene. Wolf down every bit of propaganda put in front of them. Too bad what they're running from sticks to their lives like dog crap on the bottom of a tennis shoe. Doesn't take them long to discover moving to Montana only changed the scenery. Trouble is they don't go home. They dedicate themselves to creating some utopian hybrid of where they came from and where they are. And the hell of it is, they're good at it. They know how to cram their half-baked ideas and starry-eyed agendas down our throats whether we like it or not."

Becky peered into her box of pretzels, judged it tainted by the distasteful happenings on my overrun end of the state, and exchanged it for a sack of potato chips.

"How can you put up with a bunch of strangers moving in and telling you what to do? We sure couldn't!"

"You don't have to worry, Becky. Mountains are what they're being sold, and mountains are where they want to be. For now anyway."

Both women snickered, unable to entertain the possibility of people invading their overlooked half of the state. When it happened, they'd be done for. They take pride in being apolitical and wouldn't have to be elbowed out. They'd simply freefall into dispos-session. Such a troubling vision I took a big helping of bread pudding and didn't spare the cream.

"You sound pretty frustrated, Lynn."

"Downright disgusted is more like it, Darlene. Have to admit it, though. These awful winds of change sure are blowing in the buyers. Couldn't ask for a better time to be building and selling houses."

"You still thinking about heading over our way?"

Had Darlene made an extremely perceptive supposition, or had Marie relayed my malcontent? Missoula got worse every day. Western Montana's boom invoked crime, from teenagers dabbling in drugs and petty theft to individuals who'd pursued their evil bent to PhD level—Jill being a prime exam-ple. But, god willing, no one around there but Marie would ever know the truth about my daughter-in-law.

"Well to be honest, Darlene, the business is keep-ing us so busy I haven't really thought about it much. Not for the past year or so, anyhow."

Becky pointed a potato chip at me.

"Sympathize with you, Lynn. We been burning the midnight oil too. And we harvest for a guy who lives in California...neighbor of ours runs the place for him. So I know all about those out-of-state folks."

How could she if a neighbor ran the place? But I gave her a break. Maybe she didn't understand deal-ing with rude, demanding immigrants, but she un-derstood business. Custom cutting wheat probably yielded as many troubles as fuel bills every year, and she validated my conjecture.

"Things got so hectic around here last year, we up and drove to Billings to get a computer. It helps out some. If you don't count the time I wasted figuring the blasted thing out. Say, Lynn, you think they'll really all quit working after New Year...cuz it'll be 2000?"

"Nah, Becky. Just hype. They've got too much at stake to let that happen."

"Walter says the same thing. That it ain't nothin' to worry about. Hope you're both right. Anyway, the new mobile phones are the contraptions I'd miss. They're the real blessing. Save scads of time when we got somebody broke down out in the middle of nowhere...long as they got coverage. Bet they're a boon for your building outfit too, Lynn. Even if your help ain't spread from hell to breakfast like ours is."

She eyed the chip she'd been holding then popped it into her mouth.

"Yeah, Becky, they do save us a lot of time. Downside is...you can never, *ever* get away from the damn things. And you feel guilty if you turn them off."

"That's true."

Becky dismissed my offer to help clear away the food in a way that said she had no use for amateurs messing around in her kitchen, and Darlene didn't even bother to volunteer.

"There's cake. Want a piece, Lynn? It's chocolate."

"Really tempting, Becky. But no thanks. Already ate more than I had room for."

"Okay...if you're sure."

Becky frowned as though I'd doomed myself to certain starvation, shook her head, and re-cloistered the cake. Had it been at all possible, I'd have eaten a piece just to make her happy. I had to decline her next offering as well, this time from an old-fashioned coffee percolator, and put a hand over my cup for the third time. How did these people ever sleep? After re-filling Darlene's and her own mug, Becky scavenged a handful of animal crackers from a circus train box then, returning to her locus, braced her butt against a cupboard door and picked up the thread of our conversation.

"A mobile phone would've been just the ticket for Marie if she'd had coverage out there. Huh, Darlene?"

"Sure would've."

Darlene swept back her long, dark hair, picked up her coffee cup, and let Becky elaborate.

"Every time she didn't answer the phone we got all stirred up wondering if something had happened. And we went right on worrying, too, till she felt like checking her machine and calling us back. Ain't nothing else we could do, though. Couldn't drop everything and run way out there every time it happened. Just had to wait and hope she was okay."

Darlene jumped in then, with a surprising amount of agitation in her voice.

"But, Becky, that's what Marie wanted. To drop dead out there on the ranch before she got any worse. And who could blame her? She might've too... if Walter hadn't paid her that surprise visit and found her passed out on the floor next to the bed."

Walter was destined to be a source of consternation for his mother, even when he was trying to be kind.

"You know, you guys, I was thinking about that when I first got into town tonight...how much Marie wanted to die at home. How it was about the only thing she couldn't make go her way. Think of all the blue ribbons she won at the fair every year. She did it all. Canning, baking, gardening, sewing. And her flowers. Can't forget those flowers."

Becky gladly took up a new topic.

"No, can't forget her flowers. She loved them. And won as many ribbons for them as she did for all the other stuff she entered. Do you remember when she started pinning the blue ones on the dining room wall, Darlene?

"Nope, not really. It's covered with them now, though."

I mentioned that I'd always wondered how Marie had accomplished so much in one day—and found out they didn't have a clue either.

"We never could fathom how she did it all. Could we, Darlene? Ran the ranch single-handed too, after Otto died. Told folks it got easier with him gone, didn't she?"

Darlene nodded, then we chuckled and agreed Marie would've believed it even if it hadn't been true.

"Well, you two were around her all the time, and I wasn't. But she seemed perfectly happy to me. Never acted like she needed or wanted anyone to take care of her, did she?"

They shook their heads. We'd run out of words, and the kitchen had been quiet for some time when the bird clock above my head emitted a loud electronic squawking. I jumped to my feet, Darlene caught my barstool as it toppled over, and, after a millisecond of silence, we burst into laughter. The perfect time to leave, but the motel room had lost its appeal. Friendly chitchatting rarely happened in my life anymore, and it had gone to my head faster than a cold beer on an August lunch break. The banal talk contained insight, these two were old friends, and my life was the way I'd painted it for them.

"Can't believe it's ten already! Better get going. Had a good time. Thanks for all that delicious food, Becky."

"You are more than welcome."

She untied her apron, tossed it on the counter, then took off down the hall, and, after she had a firm grip on the front door handle, asked me where I'd be resting my head that night.

"Sorry we can't put you up, Lynn. We would've had enough room, even with Karl and Darlene here, if Susan and Steve weren't living with us right now.

They oughta be back pretty soon. Went out to his mom and dad's spread south of Hammond today. Said to say hi, by the way."

Relieved of inventing excuses for staying at a motel, I was grateful for Becky's full house. She was not.

"They'll be here till the new place is ready. And you can bet your boots that ain't gonna be till September. Even if that builder stays on schedule. And they never do."

I ignored the slight—true for the most part anyway—and let Becky moan.

"It's gonna be a long summer with the pair of them and two little ones underfoot. They didn't want to stay with us. Meant storing all their stuff for one thing. But they got a good offer from some folks in an all-fired hurry to move in and figured they best go ahead and take it. What do you think, Lynn?"

I thought she should be thankful her kids hadn't unwittingly brought a genuine, longer-lasting misery into her life but smiled and answered the question.

"They made a good decision. Bird in the hand... and better in the long run."

"Not for me, though."

Becky sighed, opened the door, and walked out of the house. Darlene and I followed single file to more easily negotiate the frost-heaved mudstone walkway narrowed by aggressive perennials and their wild counterparts. When the incandescent white blossoms of coyote tobacco caught Becky's attention, she stopped, pulled it out of the ground, and dropped it where it had grown.

"I've been after Walter, for I don't know how long, to take care of this mess or hire someone. Say, I'll bet Susan and Steve would do it for me while they're here, wouldn't they?"

She'd spied the silver lining in her dark cloud and smiled at us before setting off again at a faster pace. The two women waited at the edge of the driveway as I walked over to my truck, and, instead of getting right in, I stood on the rocker panel, calling out and waving to them over the roof of the cab.

"Thanks again, Becky. Goodnight. See you both tomorrow."

Red Bend lay as quiet as the wheat fields surrounding it. I took my foot off the accelerator and felt a little less obtrusive coasting along at fifteen miles an hour. But, at the motel, engine noise ricocheted off the rooms encircling the parking lot, and it was a relief to turn it off and hear only the tick of cooling metal and restless insects.

I grabbed my old duffel bag off the back seat, and the memory projector rolled scenes of Marie and me walking hand in hand down the road on a moonless summer night to let the house cool down. The pictures disintegrated too soon, and I stopped to stargaze, a telescopic experience compared to spotting a few lone beacons in Missoula's sky, obscured even from a mountaintop.

How had I ended up in such a place? I'd never meant to stay. It just happened. And the kids were waiting there for me to call. I unlocked the door and switched on the lights but only stared at the phone. I wanted to live the lies I'd told Becky and Darlene a little longer, and, besides, there was a gift waiting to be opened.

Amy had surprised me with a "don't open it till you get there" present that morning. My daughter's way of saying she understood my leaving and things were okay between us. Being forgiven for deserting our war with Mike's wife didn't end it, though, and god only knew what fresh hell she'd delivered.

In no hurry to hear about it, I unzipped my duffle bag, lifted out my present, plucked off the blue velvet bow, tore away the silver wrapping paper, opened the box, and found a pretty cosmetic bag. Dumping my toothbrush, toothpaste, lipstick, hairbrush, and various travel-sized bottles of toiletries from a tattered zip-lock plastic sack onto the bed, I tucked everything worth keeping into the silky, red pouch. Then I carried it into the bathroom—the bathroom of my second-grade dreams.

Outlasting the American Motor Company, The Beatles, and the Berlin Wall, that little room had completely and perfectly conserved its 1950s decor. It was all there: the beveled safety-glass shelf oozing green light, the aerodynamic chrome fixtures, the metal-flaked linoleum, the charcoal-colored, skylark

Formica countertop, and the all-important carnation pink, tub, sink, and toilet trio.

I was standing in *The Modern Bath* my seven-year-old self had pined for. The one I'd carefully cut from a magazine ad and carried around till it fell apart—because I'd detested outhouses. Your feet dangled far from the floor, your hands were all that prevented you from falling in, and what would happen if they slipped? A fate so grotesque my mind's eye hadn't been able to stop staring at it.

Envisaging that scenario to such a degree, at such a young age, must've been a premonition of what Jill would do to my life one day. I imagined pushing her through one of those outhouse seat holes and reveled in the space-age, Technicolor, bathroom finally right there before my eyes. I longed to strip, step into the tub, close the sliding pebbled-glass door, flip the rocket-shaped handle into position, and let that sublime shower drain away life's parasitic realities. But I wouldn't have been able to enjoy it. The promise to call home was circling like a shark with a belly full of bad news. I found the calling card Amy had insisted I use to reduce roaming charges and spun the dial on the chunky, black phone holding down the desk.

"Hi, Mom. How was your trip? How's the motel?"

My shoulders dropped and my jaw unclenched. Amy sounded relaxed and what passes for happy when you're battling through each day.

"Trip was good, thanks. The motel's great. Quiet too...I'm the only one here. And you wouldn't believe this bathroom!"

Patient as always, she listened until I gave up trying to share excitement over something from my childhood.

"Hope you'll have enough hot water, Mom."

Amy is as pragmatic as she is patient, like her father.

"Hadn't thought about that. Things are okay at home, then?"

"Wonderful! Didn't hear from Jill all day. And neither did Mike...last I knew anyway. He stayed for dinner but went home right after. Paul and I are watching a movie. Nice being able to really relax for once."

I could visualize it so clearly—Paul with his arms around Amy and her sprawled over him, leaving one side of their reclining love seat all but empty.

"I can see you snuggled up to Paul in your favorite yellow pjs."

"How'd you know!"

We laughed. Paul had purchased the terrycloth pajamas at the new Victoria's Secret store in the mall. He'd sworn never to set foot in the place but, hoping to find exactly what Amy wanted for her birthday, went there anyway, and she's had an ongoing supply of their trademark pink sacks ever since. She often uses them to send things home with Mike, and he razzes Paul about spending so much money there. Amy's husband professes to find women bewildering but demonstrates an unerring knowledge of how they want to be treated. Coupled with Amy's easygoing, practical nature, their marriage is able to withstand trouble—even the kind Jill dished out.

Paul and Mike's friendship survived Jill's malicious attacks, too. Buddies man and boy, they'd hung out at our house all through their school years. Amy's feelings about her big brother's sidekick had run the gamut from puppy love, to envy, to animosity and back again, then settled on indifferent acceptance. That pivoted one hundred and eighty degrees when she'd agreed to accompany him to his cousin's lavish wedding.

The reception, romantic to the nth degree, had featured low lights, flowing champagne, and a band playing love ballads. Amy and Paul danced to them all. By the end of that night they were head-over-heels in love, a little embarrassed, somewhat confused, and completely surprised. Mike and I had been nothing but happy about their new relationship. The four of us grew even closer in the following years, and things were better than any intelligent person would ever have expected. Then Jill shot into our life, like a poison arrow we couldn't remove.

"Jeez, Mom, how could today, just an ordinary day, be pure heaven?"

When most days are pure hell was the answer, but I didn't want to spoil the mood.

"You deserve every minute of it, Amy. Say, before I forget, how's Third Street going?"

"Right on track. Do you know if we can incorporate those old radiators into the new heating system yet? Without pricing ourselves out of the market, that is."

"Yeah, Amy, we can. Those cast iron beauties are still in good shape. Might have a buyer lined up too. Get ahold of that Allwest agent who showed it last week, would you. See if you can find something out."

"First thing tomorrow, Mom. Oh, and how's Marie doing?"

"Not good. Liver cancer is one horrible way to go. Don't think she'll be suffering much longer, though."

"Poor thing. We're glad you went to see her, Mom. So is Mike. Just that...with the way things have been with Jill...we were sort of gobsmacked when you told us you were leaving. Oh, and we're still going up to the cabin on Friday, just like you wanted us to."

"You have no idea how relieved I am to hear you say that. I'll be up there on Sunday anyhow, and you guys need to get away."

"That's for sure. We do need some time off...specially Mike. He bought the cutest little pair of insulated coveralls for Bryan. He's big enough to sit in front of us this year. No more baby backpack. And it'll be cold getting up there on the four-wheelers, even this time of year. I can hardly believe it. We're actually going to have some fun for a change."

"Yes you are. No road in, no cell coverage, and no way for Jill to screw things up."

Phil had chosen the coming Saturday to meet with Jill because the kids would be together at the cabin for Memorial Day weekend. And, unlike mine, fate hadn't churned their right-or-wrong certainties into a soul-dampening fog of morality versus duty; they'd be able to enjoy their unexpected respite from her.

"Mom, being up there at the cabin, where it's impossible for that miserable excuse for a human being to get at us, will be wonderful beyond words. Even if it is only for three days."

"I'm hoping things stay quiet a lot longer than that, honey."

"Yeah, maybe there'll be a miracle. Jill will just drop dead and disappear off the face of the earth."

"Sure would be nice, wouldn't it? Well, I'll let you two watch your movie. Should check in with your brother before it gets any later. Tell Paul I said hi."

"I will, Mom. Enjoy your awesome bathroom."

"Can't wait to get in there."

Though welcome, the unprecedented break in Jill's bombardments worried me, especially when both Mike's cell and his home phone went unanswered. Resisting a masochistic game of what-if, I unpacked my sweater and laid it in a drawer then clipped my black dress slacks to a hanger so gravity could take out the wrinkles.

With nothing else to do and no callback from Mike, my newly acquired sense of well-being faded fast. And there's something disconcerting about being alone in a motel room at night—a disconnect that invariably draws me to the window. This one was hiding behind pleated drapery with a lewd Hawaiian flower print from the same era as the agate bola tie and snap-button western shirt worn by that old rancher in the office. Probing the folds of nubby, gold-flecked cloth, I located the frayed cord, pulled slowly, and the drapes opened with a fingernails-on-chalkboard squeal.

In spite of Phil's good advice about relaxing and knowing him to be nothing if not dependable, the peace so evident on the other side of the glass eluded me. It had been lost a lifetime ago, little Bryan's lifetime to be precise. My grandson's birth had relegated any pervasive, taken-for-granted, contentedness to the future, reduced it to a shimmering mirage on a bad patch of life's highway. Even the tranquil parking lot held specters of failure, and I remained at the window—guarding my ground.

Three feet from the glass, the truck's grill displayed a collection of detached legs, less identifiable bug parts, and shimmering, body-less wings. Beside the motel room doors, cone-shaped light fixtures projected crescent moons onto the cratered stucco walls, and the wagon wheels protecting a sparse lawn had dissolved into their own crisp shadows. I turned the brown Naugahyde chair to face the window instead of the television and settled in to wait for Mike to call.

There were no good reasons my son wasn't answering the phone. He stayed home at night whenever possible so his wife couldn't track him down and create a public scene. She never tired of performing her one-woman act of the devoted mother who'd toiled to locate her baby after his uncaring, neglectful father had spirited him away. We'd twigged to the fact Jill wanted Mike known as a bad parent, but we hadn't come close to puzzling out why. Unable to conceive of her insidious motive, we'd mistaken each clue for a sign of her cruel nature.

＿

When Bryan came into the world, Jill wouldn't even consider nursing him, and the seven days Mike stayed home to help her out she spent at the gym, the tanning salon, or the mall. Her behavior, though odd, didn't prepare him for what he came home to after his first day back at work.

His newborn son had been left cold, wet, hungry, and crying pitifully upstairs in the nursery while his mother spent the entire day in the basement family room. She told Mike, yes, she knew she couldn't hear the baby from there; that was the point. And, yes, she'd given him a bottle, and, yes, only one, but he wasn't going to starve to death in a few hours was he? Said she didn't intend to be at the beck and call of a baby all day, and, if Mike had a problem with that, maybe he should hire someone to take care of *it*.

Jill seemed far too cheerful for postnatal depression to be the problem, but Mike urged her to see a doctor anyway. She laughed at that. Told him he just needed to find someone to take the baby off her hands and everything would be fine. Not a nanny, though. She didn't want a stranger in the house. She'd have no privacy, and the baby would still be around, bawling and making it impossible for her to sleep in or enjoy having friends over.

So Mike took another week off work and searched for someone willing to care for a newborn in their own home. When he located a retired teacher who fit his model of the ideal sitter to a tee, he became optimistic and said we just had to think about the thousands of working women handing newborns over to a daycare.

Amy and I fostered his rationalization and hoped for the best, but Jill's next move had us questioning her sanity. She stormed into the sitter's house the first day Mike left Bryan there, ranting about how she couldn't understand why her husband would want to hire someone to watch their son, then demanded the woman hand him over and left. The angry, bewildered sitter called Mike to say she didn't know what was going on between the two of them, but she wanted no part of it and good luck finding someone who did.

Mike rushed home that night hoping his wife's maternal instincts had finally kicked in and she'd had a change of heart. But, when he found his son wet and hungry in his crib and his mother watching TV two floors down again, hope imploded and comprehension filled the void—Jill possessed no maternal instincts and had no heart to change.

The following day, and for weeks to come, Mike took Bryan to work with him. Everyone enjoyed having a baby around, and I helped out as much as possible. Only a stopgap measure for a long-range problem, though, and no one had to explain that to Mike. He lost weight worrying about it.

Amy was the glaring solution. She worked from home as office manager and bookkeeper for the family business. However, work is work no matter where it's done, and, after what Jill pulled with the first sitter he'd found, Mike worried about how she'd react to Amy being the one to care for Bryan and how disruptive she'd become. A fear that squelched his every intention to ask his sister if, after he'd hired a nanny to be there too, he could bring Bryan to her house five days a week. He was still summoning the nerve and seeking the right place and time to make his monumental request when Amy called and asked him to come over for lunch.

Mike braced himself to explain the receipts he'd recently handed in and had no inkling she wanted a face-to-face talk for something far more important than his indecipherable notations. He returned from lunch nothing like the man who'd handed me a car-seat full of sleeping baby, switched a diaper bag from his shoulder to mine, and trudged off to his sister's house.

I'd have given away a house to see the look on his face when Amy had *offered* to watch Bryan. The cause of his elation brought the same questions from me he'd put to his sister, and he had ready answers. Amy really did *want* to watch Bryan. Paul really was okay with it. Yes, it would be for as long as he needed her to. And there was more good news. While grateful for Mike's offer to hire a nanny, Amy wanted to care for Bryan herself. They would add a bigger office on the east side of the house, turn the current one into a nursery, and hire a bookkeeper. That way, the wages and building expenses would be deductible, and having an employee around might ward off trouble from Jill. Amy had it all figured out.

Mike thought he'd outsmarted Jill when she phoned Amy the next day not to bitch but to say thanks. He was wrong though, and, because no good deed ever goes unpunished, Amy would suffer as much as he would. Jill had played us all while she was pregnant and pretending to be the perfect wife. She'd befriended Amy long enough to gather information, including the fact she couldn't conceive, and Amy's desire for a baby went into Jill's heavy-artillery arsenal. Her mistreatment of Bryan had already ensured we'd have done anything to keep him away from her, but she increased that weapon's range and impact by maneuvering Amy into becoming Bryan's surrogate mother.

Neglecting Bryan had been the first volley in Jill's war against us, but we were too busy keeping our heads down to see it for what it was. Mike's marriage had propelled the family down Alice's rabbit hole to our own inescapable wonderland. We wondered when Jill would strike next. We wondered how in hell she could repeatedly, systematically outmaneuver us. We wondered how much more we could take, and, most fervently, we wondered how to escape. The only roads out exacted heavy tolls, and Bryan's well-being was the only accepted currency.

When I'd learned the full horror of where we were, Phil engineered a bypass. It wasn't straight and narrow, but it would get us out. We still needed that backup plan though, and I was trying to tease one out of the ether when Mike called.

"Wait a minute, honey. I'm going to hang up and call you right back on the motel phone."

I reached for the black phone, noticed the woman in the mirror above the desk looking haggard and worried, and put a smile on my face. But it wasn't easy to keep it there while dialing an endless string of numbers on an old rotary phone.

"Sorry, but you know how your sister is. Everything okay?"

"Yeah. I just didn't hear—"

"That's good. Started to wonder if Jill was on the warpath again."

"Nope. Read Bryan a story after his bath and put us both to sleep is all. Had a nice meal with Amy and Paul. Then came home and took Bryan for walk. Don't know how he finds so many things to be fascinated by...but it's a lot of fun watching him do it."

"Sure is. I already miss him. So glad you had a good day. Say, how's the Third Street job going? Did the inspector ever get over there?"

"Yeah. Showed up this afternoon. We're green-tagged and good to go. Couldn't say enough about how he liked our retrofit for the radiant floor heat. Man, that Wirsbo PEX pipe is nice stuff to work with. And you'll be glad to hear the old lath and plaster walls you wanted to save came through with only a few hairline cracks. Crew did a phenomenal job of replacing those rotten beams."

"Great. We'll schedule the flooring and get the place listed."

"Yup. How was your trip, Mom?"

"Blissfully uneventful. And the scenery made it even better."

"Until you got past Bozeman, you mean."

"No. *After* I got past Bozeman. Off those damn rocks covered in big trees, little trees, dying trees, scraggly brush, and knapweed everybody loves so much and out on the prairie. The perfect blend of earth and space that earned Montana its nickname. But we don't have time for our favorite debate tonight."

"Damn sneaky way to get the last word in, Mom."

"Wasn't it, though."

He chuckled as we said goodnight and sounded a little bit like the old Mike, the one whose voice didn't carry sadness and consternation even when he laughed. He'd always been attracted to women with a little fire. But Jill had burned his world to the ground—doused him in gasoline—then catapulted him onto the hot coals.

It was dead open and shut he'd extricate himself one way or another before long, and the lull in the fighting couldn't have come at a better time. One niggling thought dampened my optimism. Whatever Jill had found more important than harassing Mike could also prevent her from meeting up with Phil in Helena. Massacring that fear before it penetrated, I peeled off my clothes, left them where they dropped, and ran into the bathroom for another dose of 1950s starlight romance, satellite dreams, and atomic expectations.

Thankfully, the water heater didn't date from that era, as Amy had intimated it might, and it took a gloriously long time to run out of steamy, softened water. A non-standard, luxurious mattress provided another treat, and I drifted off within seconds of my head hitting the pillow. A blissful and unusual event. Jill had pummeled the contentment out of my life, and getting to sleep normally required at least an hour of imagining ways she could die.

WEDNESDAY

Sounds bled through the heavy drapes, a semi's Jake Brake, dogs barking, and sparrows disputing the day's pecking order. Shocked to see I'd slept till eight o'clock and inexplicably embarrassed to see my clothes strewn all over the floor, I threw them on the bed then peeked out the window. The sunshine scouring shadows from the parking lot confirmed a morning in full swing. My cellphone would've disturbed me, long before, if it hadn't been on the desk with a dead battery. As soon as I plugged it in, it beeped about messages and Karl's came up first.

"Um...uh...just wanted to let you know. Mom passed away a little while ago. And, uh, call me back, please."

Oh no. Marie, gone so soon? What if I'd been later getting to the hospital? What if she hadn't woken up and we'd never had that precious, final conversation? I phoned Karl expecting to get voicemail, but he picked up on the first ring.

"Hi, Lynn. You got my message?"

"Yeah, and I'm really—"

"Hey...Mom woke up for a few minutes. About three this morning. And, strangest damn thing, she made me promise to do something for her."

"What was it?"

"She was dead set on me going out and looking things over at her place today. Like she knew I wouldn't have to be with her at the hospital. Something else too...she made me swear I'd take you with me. Ain't sure what that's all about. But I'll be damned if I'm going to break the last promise I'll ever make to her. Walter's gonna take care of everything here. So, will you come on out to the ranch with me this morning?"

Even in her last hours, Marie had worried about me being able to get that gun of hers. I'd never done anything to deserve such devotion and wished, as I had nearly all my life, that there'd been more I could've done to repay her.

"Of course I will, Karl. Maybe she just wanted to make sure I got to see the place one last time. I'm going to miss her. Miss her so very, very much. Can't even imagine how it'll be for you. Feel awful for the rest of the family too. Not for your mom, though. She was going through pure hell."

"Yeah...kinda feel the same way. Time to let her go. Our turn to suffer. Acourse, watching her die like that was no picnic either. Not by a long shot. Okay if I pick you up around ten?"

"Sure. See you then."

I called Amy, let her know what happened, told her I'd be without coverage most of the day, and asked her to pass it on to the rest of the family, including her dad. They'd feel bad about Marie, but their mornings would go on as usual. Phil's were a mystery, but Mike would've already had a quick breakfast and taken a sleepyhead Bryan to Amy's. She'd be trying to cajole the little guy into believing eggs taste good, and her husband would be halfway through his early morning rounds of the houses we had listed.

Paul and I catch flak for being worrywarts, but we got that way for a reason. A young, hotshot real estate agent had showed one of our new houses and left without looking the place over. Someone he had in tow, kids we thought, had left the patio doors open in the master bedroom, and, of course, that would be the night we got a storm. When the shyster wouldn't own up, we ate the repair costs rather than file an insurance claim. The incident sparked the ritual of Paul checking our listings every morning and me doing likewise after work, and I had come to enjoy strolling through the empty houses. It made going home all the better.

Mike couldn't even enjoy the simple pleasure of being home after a long day. Jill made their house ground zero and disfigured our world in ways that would remain long after she vacated it. Marie had left her marks too, but good ones. Every wise move I'd ever made could be accredited to her. And, as Phil had prophesied, her advice hadn't died with her—I heard her coaching me.

"Cry all you want to...ain't gonna change a damn thing. And you better eat. Can't tackle anything on an empty stomach."

I dug out my travel-worn teabags, heated water in the miniature coffee machine, and made a cup of something not quite coffee or tea, but definitely bad. It helped wash down the granola bar I'd stashed underneath my clean socks, though, and I took it into the bathroom to sip on. But the Styrofoam cup clashed with everything in that retro room, and the disgusting brew went into the garbage can.

After spending more time in front of a mirror than I had in a long while, I put on a clean pair of Carhartt jeans, a long-sleeved tee shirt, and the many-pocketed hunting vest I'd commandeered from Phil on our honeymoon. Then I coaxed the drapes open and kept an eye out for Karl while tidying up the room. He showed up in a big flatbed Ford and had to swing wide to park broadside behind my Sierra 2500 HD, looking distinctly less Heavy Duty in front of his big F350. A full thirty seconds passed before he opened the truck door, settled a boot on the pavement, tilted his head, and followed his hat into the sunshine. I glanced at my diminished truck and left the motel room feeling like I was ditching a trusty companion.

"You travel light."

"Yeah, don't think I'd hold much sway over the crew if I carried a purse around. Not even if it had DeWALT or Makita stamped on the side."

Karl grinned and opened the passenger door. I'd assumed he needed something from that side of the cab then realized he was holding the door open for me and tried to hide an odd mix of discomfort, amusement, and pleasure by shielding my eyes from the sun. My voice gave me away when I thanked him, though.

"What's the matter? Don't they know how to treat a lady over on your side of the state anymore?"

"Not sure most of 'em ever did."

A minute later we were on the narrow paved road that will take you all the way to Gillette, Wyoming if you let it. Iconic cowboy country that whispers the world is basically okay. But everything about being in the passenger seat felt wrong. I shoved my hands in my pockets and watched green chenille fields of pubescent grain furrow into a blue organza sky.

"What's so interesting out there?"

"Pretty much everything. Haven't been here since you and Darlene got married in '79. Twenty years ago, come September. After that, your mom and I just met up in Billings whenever we could."

He ran his open palm across the nape of his neck and shook his head.

"Dang, has it really been that long since you were here? And let's see, Dad had already been gone for seventeen years by then. That means Mom was on her own for nearly half her life."

"She had you and Walter, though. And living alone suited her. She liked her independence."

"You bet she did!"

"And your mom never stayed cooped up."

"Nope. Always going someplace or other. Never wasted any time getting there, either. Drove like a damn teenager."

I smiled, recalling those long-ago trips to Red Bend in Marie's pickup, clutching the armrest with both hands around every corner, certain sliding across the vinyl seat and bumping into her would send the truck flying off into the sagebrush. But, when we left the oil, Marie's term for running out of pavement, Karl held his speed to sixty. It's the usual, inadequate concession to gravel roads where distances are long and there's always someone waiting for a ride, machine part, dose of medicine for an ailing critter, or a helping hand.

"Hey, Lynn, did Mom ever tell you about my first summer out at Shoen Creek? How I cut an hour off the trip home by taking those cow path, backroads?"

"Oh yeah. One of her favorite stories. She could see your dust when you were still five miles out and have a meal on the table by the time you walked in the door."

"Those were the days. Had that big old '64 Wide-Track Pontiac. Just pointed that chrome V on the hood between the dirt tracks and kept my foot in it. Shortened some bunchgrass and cactus. Never took out an oil pan or got stuck when it rained, though."

"Musta been some wild rides."

"They sure were! Just a dumb kid though...risking my neck to get home a little earlier. Acourse, days off were damned few and far between back then."

Karl's thoughts drifted to his past, and I sought out familiar landmarks. The way to the collection of old buildings Marie called home had persisted over the years like a catchy tune, and I knew her lane would appear ten miles past the deserted farm where she spent her childhood. My mom and dad grew up nearby but hadn't stayed and returned only four times for their parents' funerals.

Why my mother married a man like my father and traded a saddle for a barstool, couldn't be comprehended. She hadn't gotten pregnant; they'd been married five years before I came along. Her choice had baffled Marie too. She and my mother, best friends until Mom moved, had shared ranch life, a country school, a church, hard work, and fun. Marie loved reminiscing about their epic horseback rides just to get to a dance.

"Karl, how far do you think our moms rode to get to those dances over at the Iron Butte grange hall?"

"Damn. Had to be twelve miles, give or take a couple. Helluva ride cross country for sure."

"Your mom said they'd leave as soon as they finished the milking, dance all night, and still make it home before morning chores. You'd have to be working awful damn hard to call that playing, wouldn't you?"

"Sure as hell would."

He chuckled, and feeling so good about making that happen bothered me.

"And the crazy thing is, Lynn, until she got sick, Mom still packed more into a month than Darlene and I did in a whole year. Got to more square dances than we did too."

"Did your mom still wear her turquoise outfit with the flared skirt and all those crinoline petticoats? She looked so pretty in that color."

"Yup, the very same one. It still looked good, though. And so did she."

"Her turnoff's right up there, isn't it, Karl? Right before the top of the next rise?"

"Dang, Lynn. You didn't forget!"

"Nope. Probably never will."

I loved every prickly pear cactus, alkali seep, and clay-packed wash on Marie's place. I'd never seriously considered moving somewhere close to her, though. Not until some Pollyanna part of me began reasoning like the dissatisfied people rushing into the western end of the state, and I got the crazy idea that putting most of Montana between my family and Jill would save us from her. I'd pictured the business thriving too. We'd be local and would corner the machine shed, barn, and elevator construction jobs in the area. I'd have been in for a big disappointment on all fronts. Marie could've told me why if I'd asked, but I hadn't, and the idea died in the light of careful consideration anyhow.

When Marie's rusty, hail dented mailbox came into view, my heart beat faster. The barbed wire gate was open. We drove on through and, for nearly a mile, jostled in and out of the deep, wind and sun hardened ruts recording successive struggles through wet clay. Marie had cussed her lane, nothing more than twin grooves driven into the prairie, yet considered my offer to put in a graveled road a complete waste of money—she'd gotten by all these years and could get through a few more, couldn't she?

Just as the farm buildings and house came into view, we dropped into a gully, crossed the narrow, hell-built-for-stout bridge over Lame Johnny Creek, then climbed into the deathly still farmyard. Karl got out, came around to open the door for me, and slipped my troubled, complicated thoughts into a few simple words.

"Sure as hell feels lonesome out here now, doesn't it?"

I could only nod.

"I'll go on inside and turn up the heater...take the chill off."

I stood transfixed beside the wooden gate. It still scraped the ground, still needed paint, and still made the funny, eerie sound of a door opening in a B rated thriller. But where was Marie? Why wasn't she there holding it open with one hip so she could use both arms to engulf me in a fierce hug? I touched the gate where it had been smoothed by her hand then swung it open, waded through my grief, and stepped reverently into the house.

The glass dome I imagined building over Marie's ranch to preserve it forever shattered when her phone rang. Karl answered it with a curious hello, and I was grateful for the opportunity to linger out in the porch. It hadn't doubled as a milk room for over seven years, and the cream separator had been evicted. But, by standing motionless and breathing slowly through my nose, I caught a whiff of the machine's warm motor and the fresh milk gushing between its stack of steel cones.

Marie swore her cream and egg money had "kept the bankers out of her pockets" during hard times. She could've proved it too. Since her marriage in 1944, she'd penciled each sale on a calendar hanging in the milk room, and every New Year's Day it went into a box underneath her bed with its predecessors. More and more memories rained down, and Karl's voice drifted through them as muffled and irrelevant as the present.

"Well, you know Mom...with her dying breath she made me promise to check on the place *today*. And I wasn't about to break my word. Walter said he'd handle the funeral arrangements, and Darlene and Becky will take care of the rest. Did I tell you Lynn's here? She rode out with me. You must remember her...spent summers with us when she was a kid."

There was a long pause then a self-conscious laugh.

"Yes, *that* Lynn. Stay where you are. Be up in a few minutes."

Karl hadn't heard me come into the house and rushed into the porch at full power. Trapped beneath an avalanche of memories, I'd no hope of getting out of his way, and, once again, he had to catch me in his arms to keep from knocking me off my feet. His words were teasing, but his voice was husky and serious.

"Dang, Lynn. We have *got* to stop meeting like this."

I backed away, before I wouldn't be able to, and spoke from the other side of the room.

"Yes, we do. But thanks for saving me again."

"My pleasure. Hey, that was Roger on the phone. He's fixing fence up on the bluff. Saw my truck and went home to call me. Wanna take a ride? I'm gonna hop in the Jeep and, if the damn thing will start, go on up there and BS with him for a little while."

"Sounds like fun...but I think I'll stay here. Take a last look around."

"Okay. Coming down to the shop with me, though, aren't you?"

"I sure am."

I'd never miss a chance to visit that dugout. As a girl, I'd pushed against the locked chain till I could squeeze through the gap and risked getting caught in there because, even when the thermometer topped a hundred in the shade, it stayed cool under that sod roof. It housed fascinating things too: naughty calendars, a welder stickered with dire warnings, and maybe a tractor or truck spilling its guts.

We walked the hundred feet or so down the road to the dugout, then Karl slid the key from some crevice above the door I still couldn't have reached, opened the padlock, and pulled the chain from one handle. As the heavy plank doors swung open, sunlight erased a world never seen and only heard for the split second its tiny inhabitants dart for safety. Awareness of their realm is fleeting and faint, like extrapolating Jill's dark intentions from the damage patterns left in her wake. I made up my mind not to let thoughts of her taint that treasured space, but, the very next second, she showed up in the shiny, black floor—filth packed to a glossy surface.

"What did you say, Karl?"

"I said, you liked hanging around the shop with us, didn't you?"

An understatement, I couldn't get enough of being where work had lasting importance. The house had vague problems with varying solutions, and hours of accomplishment vanished in minutes. Anywhere outside had offered better, but the shop was best because broken things got fixed there.

"Are you kidding, Karl? I loved being in here. Would've loved it even more if your dad hadn't made me promise not to ask 'even one single, solitary question' if I wanted to stay."

"Dang, Lynn, Walter and I were flabbergasted he let you in here with us at all. Hay-baling old farm machinery together had a way of bringing out the worst in Dad."

"Yeah, I remember. And your mom always told me, 'You'll forget everything you hear out in that shop if you know what's good for you.'"

"Hope you took her advice."

"Tried, but some of those words come in handy from time to time."

He grinned, traded his hat for a dusty, web-covered Powder River Feeds baseball cap and whacked it against his thigh before pulling it on back to front. Then, with a purposeful grace acquired on horses, football fields, and oil derricks, he vaulted into the front seat of the open-topped Jeep like he had as a teenager. After pumping the gas pedal exactly four times, he turned the key and gave me an exaggerated look of surprise when the engine fired.

"Mom must've been using the cantankerous old beast more than I thought. Make yourself at home, Lynn. Won't be long."

"Don't hurry on my account."

Karl waved goodbye as the Jeep roared away from the shop then shifted into second and exited behind the shelterbelt trees. Seeing Roger would be comforting for him. Like Mom and Marie, they'd known each other since they were babies consigned to the same quilt at dances and pinochle parties. They'd been gifted with a lifelong friendship and an imbued sense of belonging that comes to you in childhood or eludes you forever.

Being an outsider gradually came to my attention during those summers with Marie, and it might've been the true reason I hadn't found the time to make it back for so many years. I'd have forever to regret the memories never made, though, and set off to rejuvenate the ones I owned. The path to the barn had been used for so long even the fanweed hadn't managed to encroach. And the door to the milking stanchions opened with the same wooden latch I'd turned all those years ago. How could something so inconsequential still be around, but not Marie?

Inside the barn, dust motes glistened, and the smell of cows, cats, desiccated manure, and scraps of musty hay rejuvenated the last-best-dream standing. My desire to own a ranch like Marie's had flourished when lesser dreams were strangled by neglect or felled by practicality but quickly withered under the shroud Jill spread over my life. Marie had warned me about it.

"I'm damn proud of you for protecting your kids, Lynn. Even now that it's got to be more than you bargained for. Just don't forget the promise you made to yourself."

"It isn't important right now."

"Yes it is, damn it! Person gets old before they know it. It's like setting off horseback on a beautiful, sunny day worrying about some fool thing you don't have a snowball's chance in hell of changing. Then... just when you finally got that figured out and start enjoying the ride...a storm blows up and all you wanna do is hightail it home."

She'd been right of course. And I felt the dream greening a little here, in the place where I'd watched Marie milk cows and listened to the rhythmic music of milk squirting into a metal bucket slowly change from a clear, crisp bell-ringing to a plush, cello crescendo. I could still hear it, and an old routine drew me to the hayloft.

Halfway there a ladder rung broke underfoot, but the one below it held. Heart still racing, I stopped there, eye level with the rotting floorboards, and observed—nothing. My loud approach went unnoticed, no mamma cat moving kittens into hiding, no mice scurrying for cover, no barn owl taking flight through the open hoist door, nothing but a deep, final silence.

Backing cautiously down the ladder, this time with my boots on the thick, unworn edges of the rungs, I continued searching for the past. Surely Karl wouldn't be back for a while yet. There'd be time to get Marie's gun. At the other end of the barn, the tack room door had swollen shut. I put my shoulder into it, and it banged open, rattling bridles, curry combs, and draft horse harnesses, their burnished white beads like cherries underneath a crust of grime. This was the room, filled with the lovely scent of horses and old leather, where Marie had paused beside the saddles to give a grownup's answer to a ten-year-old's question.

"Do you think I'll be able to have a ranch like yours someday?"

"Ain't gonna sugarcoat it for you, honey. You got a lot stacked against you."

Her candor prevented me from hamstringing myself before I could outrun my destiny. But it wasn't at all what I'd wanted to hear, and I negotiated for a brighter future.

"It's what I really, really want, though. More than anything in the whole world. I'll work hard and save all my money. Honest."

"Sounds easy now, Lynn. But pretty soon you're gonna get interested in boys. And the kind interested in you ain't gonna have a pot to piss in. Likely be drinkers like your dad too. Won't be any of them hanging around that's worth a damn...less they're up to no good. Nope. If you want a ranch and not end up like your folks, you're gonna have to wait till you're older and can find a guy with something to offer.

"And a guy like that...one who's willing and able to see past your circumstances...ain't gonna be easy to find. Might never show up. Don't settle for anyone else, though. No matter how much they say they love you. Or how much you think you love them. Be better off on your own than settling for some deadbeat. No matter how lonesome it gets."

A deluge of bad news, but it came with love. I heard it in her voice and saw it in her eyes.

"Then that's what I'll do. I promise. No matter what. And, anyhow, I'm used to being lonesome. Cuz we move so much, and nobody likes new kids. And there's nobody but grownups at the bars."

Each birthday had revealed more of the truth underlying Marie's advice. She'd been right about the kind of boys showing any interest in me and right about me being lonely. A misery made worse in the eighth grade when we moved "too far away to visit Marie" and my summers with her ended when I'd needed them most. Her letters saved me. They'd provided hope, someone to pour my heart out to, and prescient counsel to counteract the fairytale mentality that gets teenage girls into trouble. And those letters swept away the thoughts of suicide that multiplied in the days between them.

Without Marie's long-distance ministering, I couldn't have held out for Phil, that guy with something to offer but willing to see past my situation. And I learned being with a man like him is even more important when the marriage falls apart. He hadn't let our divorce ruin the good life we'd created, and he wouldn't let Jill take a wrecking ball to it either. So much owing to Marie and no way to repay her now, except to win, and then I remembered the gun.

I have my own firearms, but when Marie heard I'd be coming to see her, she'd insisted on me taking her old pistol back with me because it was untraceable and "you just never know." A good point. However, what drove me to take the gun home was the fact I'd told her I would, and my death, not hers, would be the only reason to break my final promise to her.

Wiggling and tugging, I finally got the warped tack room door shut then ran outside, but too late. The Jeep had already rattled through the yard, and Karl was locking the shop doors. When we met at the end of the path, he put his arm across my shoulders and we walked to the house side by side.

"Did you have a good look around, Lynn?"

"Yeah...bittersweet though."

"I'll bet it was. Sure ain't looking forward to clearing out Mom's things."

I wanted to scream that her house couldn't be left empty and uncared for. Wanted him to promise the ranch would stay the same forever and be a memorial to Marie. Wanted to beg him to hold me until I ran out of tears—words too volatile to utter.

"Damn it all to hell, Karl. It's—"

"It's tough. Damn tough, I know. How 'bout we go in and see if we can rustle up some lunch."

Countless haphazard improvements had given the exterior of the house a homey, crazy-quilt sameness. Only the bedroom addition retained the original brown, brick-patterned, asphalt material. Deemed "still okay" in 1958, it hadn't been replaced with the *safer*, fireproof asbestos siding being installed on the rest of the house. Those white slates carried a rusty tracing of every lawn watering since they had been nailed up, and every section of the hand-poured sidewalk displayed a different shade of gray. Long gone was the saggy, wooden walkway that had sent me sprawling hard enough to gash my knee.

Long gone, too, the white scar it left, a cherished, tangible remnant of my summers with Marie, and I'd wept when it faded away. Now it looked as though I'd never see the old place again. But, considering how things were at home, I was lucky to be there at all. Karl took his arm off my shoulder then ushered me through the gate, into the house, and on into the kitchen. He dropped his hat on a hook by the phone then looked lost, running a hand through his hair as if unsure what to do without Marie setting food on the table. Contemplating all the hours she'd spent cooking, baking, and canning in that room made my legs ache.

"How did your mom tolerate this floor all those years?"

"We did talk her into getting new linoleum."

"I see that. Still not much cushioning with concrete under it, though."

"I know. And we thought about Pergo or carpeting. But she wouldn't hear of it. Swore the concrete didn't bother her."

"Well, you never know, maybe it didn't. She was tough as nails."

"Nary a truer word spoken."

I got busy making a pot of coffee with water from one of the plastic jugs on the counter, and Karl hunted through the jumbo-sized chest freezer on the other side of the room.

"Look what I found, Lynn...kuchen."

"Yay! You found kuchen!"

Marie made the German coffeecake the way it's supposed to be made, sweet dough molded into a pie pan, filled with cinnamon-sprinkled custard, then baked. It came from the microwave wafting the same heavenly scent it had when, potholder in each hand, she'd slid it out of the oven two pans at a time. Sharing only smiles between bites, we savored our memories and the treat in silence. When we'd picked the last crumb from our plates, I took them to the sink, turned on the faucet, then covered my nose with my hand.

"Worse than you remember, isn't it?"

"Yeah. Lots worse."

"Yup. Even Mom had to quit using it. Course she always did collect rainwater for washing her hair."

"Yeah, I remember that."

"Knowing what I do now, I feel bad about working for the damn company that might've killed her."

"But, Karl, your mom wouldn't want you to feel that way. And you quitting wouldn't have changed a thing."

"You're right there, Lynn. Petro products create, preserve, or transport most everything we use anymore. They can do whatever they damn please, and who's going to stop them? The S.O.B.s who're supposedly keeping tabs on how they do things have their snouts in the same trough and are just as interested in keeping it full."

"Yeah, Karl. And the public likes hearing everything's okay cuz we're hardwired to make things better for ourselves. But if we weren't, we'd still be going through life naked with nothing better to do than scavenge for food till we dropped dead."

He smiled at that and defaulted to his upbeat self. Or as close as he could get to it on the day his mother died.

"Guess that's true, Lynn. And burying dead people musta been one of the first bright things we came up with, huh?

"I bet it was. Watching them rot away or get eaten by scavengers would've gotten kinda depressing."

We looked into each other's eyes and laughed at that scrap of black humor till we were wiping away tears.

"Well, Lynn, guess I'd better give the old place a quick once-over before we go. Wouldn't surprise me if it's been ten years since anyone's set foot upstairs."

Karl had to tiptoe up the child-sized steps and turn his shoulders sideways to squeeze through the opening to the attic. Floorboards groaned overhead, closet doors whined open then thumped closed, and rusty springs screeched when he sat on his old bed then complained again when he got up. As he walked, stopping and starting, to the other end of the attic, I watched the soapy water run out of the sink and pined for the old one.

It was a stained-beyond-bleach behemoth filled with a red hand pump and emptied through a waste pipe running outside via a hole in the wall. Three times a day, I'd stood beside the old sink and dried the last dish while staying alert for Marie's hand to reach for the plug. When it did, I would toss the towel on the table and race outside to watch the dishwater flow over to her prized yellow rose bush, and the screen door would slam an exclamation point behind her unfailing instruction.

"If you're that bored, pull some of that quack grass while the ground's wet!"

Sad to think of the old sink and kitchen pump landing in the junk pile east of the house, but Marie hadn't seen it that way. Even pointing out that the pump might come in handy when the electricity went out and add charm to the kitchen hadn't swayed her. Shabby chic sounded as oxymoronic to her as good government or honest politicians. The kitschy painted cupboards were gone too, replaced by fashionable oak cabinets. I hated them. But Marie's best, never-to-be-used, neatly ironed dishtowels were still kept in the bottom drawer next to the fridge, and they still smelled of frying bacon, pickling spice, and Raid.

Their embroidered helpfulness perturbed me. If life was so goddamn simple—Monday laundry, Tuesday iron, Wednesday mend, Thursday shop, Friday dust, Saturday clean, and Sunday church— why was I rummaging through them for a gun? I found it, along with a box of shells, underneath those very towels. Marie had wrapped them in a piece of used freezer paper, and *Beef Roast 11/1/97* was scrawled across the top in the nearly illegible hand-writing I'd come to cherish.

I slipped the revolver and ammo into the pockets of Phil's vest designed to conceal them, added the folded freezer paper, then stood up and gasped as if I'd seen Marie standing in the doorway.

"Karl! Jesus Christ! You scared the hell out of me!"

"I take it you forgot all about the stairs on the other end of the attic."

"Yeah. But I never will again."

He laughed, and, if he'd seen what I'd been doing, didn't let on. He just turned around, leaned against the doorjamb with his arms crossed, and stared up at the metal heat grate covering a square hole in the center of the living room ceiling.

"Walter and I slept up there from the time we could negotiate them stairs till we left home. Froze all winter. Damn mice were better off. Ain't noth-ing stopped them from sneaking downstairs where it was warm. And, come summer, we damn near baked. Beat sleeping outside and getting ate alive by mosquitoes, though."

"Kids wouldn't even be allowed up there nowadays."

We'd blurted it out at the same time then laughed and agreed we sounded like a couple of old fogies.

"It's all changed, Lynn. So goddamn fast too. Roger and me were just talking about how rough things were back then. And how we didn't think anything of it cuz nobody else had it any better. Now people think things are bad if they ain't living in a five bedroom house."

"Too true. I see it all the time. Couples won't even consider buying the two-bedroom, one-bath houses their parents were proud to own. Every kid has to have their own bedroom now. And, my god, master bedrooms are almost small apartments."

"I blame TV, Lynn. Most shows have gotten to the point where they're just long ads between short ads."

"I hadn't thought of it that way, Karl. But you've hit the nail on the head. Those programs make people feel like failures if they don't buy big houses they don't need and can't afford. Makes it a great time to be in real estate, though. There's a joke going around the offices about that."

"So, c'mon...tell me."

"Okay, here goes. Do you know why the cops in western Montana ask to see your real estate license when you get in trouble?"

"No. Why?"

"Because not everybody has a driver's license."

He laughed that sexy laugh again then walked over to the big propane heater and turned it off. Time to leave. I walked out of the kitchen still wondering if Karl had actually seen me taking Marie's gun and surveyed the porch before stepping over the scarred threshold. Then Karl shut the door behind me, hard, and leaned into it to make sure the latch had sprung. He could do no more. Marie's back door never did have a lock.

Out on the treeless lawn, blooming yellow tulips filled a blue and white striped tractor tire, and the retired separator had cat-faced pansies spilling from its huge steel bowl and a blanket of creeping phlox warming its iron feet. Karl waited by the gate till I'd finished admiring the flowers then hooked the chain over the post and secured it with baling wire the way Marie had when she wanted to keep out loose stock.

I couldn't leave without snapping photos, especially of the geriatric yellow rose bush on the west side of the house near the kitchen window, and Karl stood patiently by the well house until I finished. When he came over to the truck, he smiled for the camera as he opened the passenger door and gave my arm a squeeze of understanding as I climbed in. Then he eased us away, past discarded sickle mowers, plows, spring-tooth harrows, discs, dump rakes, hay wagons, and a coral-colored 1959

Rambler station wagon. And somewhere out there in the grass waited the old porcelain sink and cast-iron pump I still couldn't save.

We'd already rumbled over the bridge and crossed the frothing creek—full of itself and mockingly unhesitant. Karl stopped out on the main road to shut the gate and empty the mailbox, and, when he leaned over to put a handful of envelopes in the jockey box, he was way too close and smelled way too good. The provocative blend of bleached white tee shirt, healthy man sweat, the outdoors, and machinery affected me in ways hard to hide.

I hoped to hell he wouldn't notice and sighed with relief when he got out of the truck, then started fretting again because he didn't say a word when he got back in. He just wrapped his hands around the steering wheel and tapped his thumbs against it while staring out the windshield. Long seconds passed before he put me out of my misery and spoke.

"Thought maybe we might as well check on the cows while we're out here. How about it?"

"Nothing I'd like better."

A lie—and I worried Karl had sensed what I would've liked better. But revisiting Marie's "government land" came in a close second, and I couldn't wait to see the two sections she leased from the BLM. Being forced to do business with them for more grazing land didn't sit well with her, of course. But she only owned five sections, and even Marie couldn't have made a go of it on 3,200 acres of the driest ground in Rimrock County. Karl had always been proud of his mom's ranching ability and sounded sadder than he had all day.

"Not much of a herd anymore. Mom ain't bought replacement heifers for the past five years. Sold a few head, too. Shoulda let 'em all go. But she just couldn't stand the thought of it."

"Look, Karl! The coal banks. Only about three more miles now, isn't it?"

"You really haven't forgotten much, have you?"

"I come here a lot."

"What!"

"Not actually...but you know what I mean."

"Yeah. S'pose I do."

He wouldn't allow me to open the gate when we got there. So I slid across the seat, drove the truck through, then got out and followed him over to the stock tank. The water it holds, sweet and clear as any in the state, is pumped from a deep well by an outdated windmill. *Monitor* could still be read on the tail vane, but the ornate black lettering wouldn't survive many more dust storms. Naked or not, the blades would continue ticking, pinging, and moaning softly, their fleeting, entrancing shadows falling to the ground as they sliced through the sunshine.

"Say, Karl, did your mom ever tell you she came out here when the pain got real bad? Kept a sleeping bag and pillow in her truck so she could turn off the engine and still stay warm. Said being out here listening to the old windmill lulled her to sleep."

"No. She never told me. Wonder why."

"Probably afraid you'd try to move her into town if you knew how sick she was getting."

"Fat chance of pulling that off."

Karl looked down and flipped a rock into the air with the toe of his boot. It arced over the cow-tracked mud encircling the tank then fell silently into a thick patch of sagebrush.

"Darlene says you've been busy, Lynn. And Mom told me all about Mike getting his master plumber's license."

"It made such a big difference. And Paul, Amy's husband, got his electrician's license two years later."

"You're set up real good, then."

"Yeah. The business is doing okay."

"How about you, though? What've you been doing, besides working?"

"Not much. Keep a pretty tight rein on myself. Life's simpler that way."

"Maybe...but dang it. You and me both know that's the fastest way to ruin a good horse. And it ain't gonna do you no good either."

"Things should be different when I get home. I'll be able to slow down long enough to change gears."

"Better do that, Lynn. Life's short. Don't spend it waiting for the right time to enjoy it."

"That's what your mom said. And speaking of enjoyment, three years ago, we built a house for a ranch couple who live a few miles from a sweet little town called Opheim. It's west of Scobey. Anyway, this rancher and his wife had kids at the university. Saw a remodel we did on one of those big old houses and liked it enough to pay what it took for us to travel clear across the state to build them something similar. Three-story house with forty-two hundred square feet, plus full finished basement...that far off the beaten track...it took a while."

"I bet it did!"

"On one trip, when I could stick around for a few days, I did some exploring. Liked what I saw."

"You thinking serious, then, about getting out of Missoula?"

I nodded. The first overt sign of my intention.

"Well that's good. But why move clear the hell and gone up there? Why not buy a place around here?"

His question was loaded as a 12 gauge shotgun, and, despite having mulled it over for the past few years, I had no answer for him.

"You ever spend any time up in that corner of the state, Karl?"

"Yeah...funnily enough. Just last fall. Some geologist published a paper about the Bakken oil shale reserves. And when the company bigwigs wanted to go sniffing around up there, I got hornswoggled into nursemaiding them. More like a tax-deductible hunting trip far as I could see."

I shifted to a dryer patch of mud and smiled, enjoying the timbre of Karl's voice, the unhurried tempo of his words, and that eastern Montana man body language.

"Did they have any luck?"

"Didn't need any. Some rich, east-coast friend of theirs owns a place in the Missouri breaks above the CMR. Runs just enough cattle to legally hay the elk. Bastards shot 'em from a damn tower! Bad thing is, as soon as the shooting's over on that posted land, the elk move right back onto it and stay there till hunting season's over. Then they move right back off, and the ranchers adjacent to that posted land are feeding five head of elk for every head of cattle. Can't do it for long. Fish and Game ain't happy with the situation either."

"That's something at least."

"Yeah, even the government can see how bad it's getting. Anyhow, after those guys filled their tags, we left for the oil fields, and I chauffeured them around for damn near a week. We passed through Opheim to get there. And you're right. It's impressive country... and damn sure empty. Even makes our neck of the woods seem kinda crowded."

"You got it, Karl. And the trees don't stray far from the riverbanks up there. It's just grass, wind, and miles and miles...of miles and miles. Backcountry's only about twenty minutes from anywhere you happen to be. Drove it for hours on end without seeing another soul. Crossed in and out of Canada too. Didn't even know it though. Not until I happened on a boundary marker. Just a flat piece of concrete sinking into the sod."

"You saying it ain't the end of the universe, but you can see it from there?"

"Yup. And that's a very good thing in my book."

He shook his head, laughed, ran a hand through his hair as he slid off his hat, then clamped the brim between two fingers and rested the hat on his thigh by hooking his thumb in the watch pocket of his jeans. What makes men like Karl different, I couldn't quite pinpoint, but having them around is another good thing about the prairie.

"Believe me, Karl. Somewhere the locals are outnumbered by livestock instead of out-of-staters... that's exactly where I want to be. Will it stay that way, though? What's the deal with the oil around there?"

"There's a few working wells. Not many. Production's pretty much centered in the Williston Basin."

"North Dakota?"

"Yup. In Nodak...behind the iron curtain."

North Dakota gets called that because it and northeastern Montana, once nicknamed the red corner, were socialist in the early 1900s, and the movement had endured somewhat in North Dakota as the Nonpartisan League.

"You think the drilling will stay there?"

"Most likely not. Fracking chemicals and other techniques for getting oil out of shale are improving. Sooner or later the oil lobby will buy up enough politicians to get their startup costs subsidized then start drilling like mad. Helluva boom coming before too long."

He had just poisoned the last dream standing. I wanted no part of an oil boom after months and months of warring with Jill, just peace and more peace.

"Jesus, Karl! That's the last thing I wanted to hear. Some huge influx of people ruining everything about the time I get settled in."

"Not something you'd like being in the middle of, Lynn. That's for goddamn sure. Bad 'uns pop up in those boomtowns faster than weeds in a plowed prairie. Every damn bit as thirsty, aggressive, and good-for-nothing too."

"How far will the new drilling reach into Montana, do you think? What if I stayed west of Highway Twenty-Four between Glasgow and Opheim? There's not much but rez to the east."

"Might be okay there. At least you'd only be on the fringe of it. And Glasgow shouldn't get hit too hard. But I don't reckon you'd be running into town all that much anyway."

"About a trip a month would do me just fine."

"Well, there you go then. And if a boom does hit... ride it out. They never last long in the Bakken."

"Well that's good news."

"Any plans for when you're gonna do this?"

"Can't say. Salable land is scarce as hens' teeth up there. The couple we built the house for, they're sitting on forty sections. That's over twenty-five hundred acres tied up right there. Then there's a corporation and at least one other rancher who own more than they do. Add a million-plus square miles of BLM, and it'll soon take that many dollars to buy a small place. I could get priced out before too long."

"Dang. Sorta hope you do. Maybe then you'll think harder about moving here. Darlene and I have just about decided to buy out Walter's half of the ranch. Plan to retire there. Sure would be nice having you closer."

"Thanks. It's something to think about. And I sure am glad to hear you'll be taking over your mom's place."

"Yeah, important to keep it in the family. Remember that summer we were right here moving the herd off the BLM? A month ahead of schedule... cuz we had such a dry spring?"

"I could never forget that day, Karl! I'd always had to leave before you brought the cattle home. Your mom said I must've prayed harder that it *wouldn't* rain than the folks praying it *would*."

"And she let you ride Babe...her favorite cow horse. Cuz she was riding that papered gelding. She traded a good bull calf for that Quarter Horse...on account of Babe getting a little long in the tooth. The old mare could still move right out, though. Sure enough had you grabbing leather."

"I hoped you were all too busy to notice how many times she spotted a straggler before I did...and just about left me in the dirt."

"And Mom made you ride drag with Walter!"

"Yes she did. Ate a lot of dust. But couldn't have been happier."

That day of chasing cows had become my holy grail. But moving cattle is an exercise in containing trouble—some kind, somewhere, sometime—same as dealing with Jill. An automatic comparison that defiled the memory.

"Well, Lynn, reckon we better go see if we can find Mom's cows."

I jumped over the puddle in front of me and came down scrambling for footing.

"You look like a newborn foal on a patch of ice. And you can't blame that one on me."

Karl, big grin on his face, crossed his arms and leaned back against the truck. I fixed my attention on keeping both feet on the ground, slipped in the mess between us a few times, but made it back without falling.

We didn't drive around just hoping to stumble across the herd. Karl made an educated guess as to where the cattle would be that time of day, and we discovered them bedded down below a south-facing outcropping of scoria. Venturing out on that rocky slide would've brought trouble. We stopped short of where we wanted to be, Karl blew the horn, and calves scattered from their crèche to run circles around each other while mamma cows begrudgingly heaved themselves off the ground. Then he quickly counted them, easily identifying cow-calf pairs in the blur of red hides.

"How'd you do that? It would've taken me all afternoon."

Karl patted my shoulder and grinned.

"You saying that ranch of yours is gonna come with one helluva learning curve?"

"Afraid so. But, if I found a place around here, I bet you and Darlene might help me out."

"No doubt about it."

"Thanks, Karl"

He patted my shoulder again then moved his hand back to the steering wheel, and I suddenly felt cold.

"Well, looks like they're all fat, sassy, and accounted for. Wish I could let Mom know."

Karl shifted into reverse, and, harassed for no reason they could discern, the cows continued to stare at the truck as we rolled off the hillcrest. I stared back with empathy—Jill polluting my thoughts again, but a meadow lark's sweet call erased her. He was advertising his availability from a weathered fence post and looked unusually serene in his unruffled feathers.

The wind had failed to come up with the sun as it normally did, and we were driving through a still-frame landscape. I opened my window and basked in the warm sage-scented air. What unimaginable luck to be there on the kind of day that moves a gruff old rancher to try his hand at cowboy poetry. The kind of day that breathes life into dying dreams.

Your true self is invisible, out of sight and out of mind, until something or someone has the power to reflect it. For me, it's Karl. I'd always felt the same easy closeness with him as I had with Marie. Not through time spent together, it was minimal, but from shared beliefs and attitudes formed by the same point of view. I wanted to look into his brown eyes again, but he'd given his full attention to avoiding badger holes and oil pan busters. Hidden perils making me think about the carnage Jill intended to inflict on us and wonder if we'd actually be able to stop her.

I opened my mouth to confide in Karl, but an inner voice screamed, "Bad idea," and I summoned the restraint to heed it. Relating Jill's iniquities wouldn't have provided him with even a glimmer of the hell she put us through during the past eighteen months anyway, and it highlighted the genius of her strategy. The more you tried to explain what she'd done, the crazier you sounded. Karl could never have understood unless, like Marie, he'd been receiving the battlefield reports.

"Lynn! Hey, Lynn! Where'd you go?"

"Sorry...what?"

"I said, you wanna take the long way back?"

"Oh sure. Sounds great."

We shared stories about the amazing woman we lost that morning and passed through five gates as we worked our way over field roads to the highway. We hadn't been on the pavement a mile before Karl's phone rang.

"Darlene says everything's going okay. Funeral's tomorrow at ten. Said to let you know we're all having supper at Walter and Becky's tonight. About six, but to come on over earlier if you can."

Minutes later the steeple cross on Marie's church came into view, a beacon of stark white reality. But, as we drove into town, Karl cheered me up.

"Look over there, Lynn. At the Sunday school classrooms. I kissed a girl there once. Bravest thing I've ever done."

I smiled at the memory and the fact he hadn't forgotten either.

"Oh, Karl. That's where you gave me my first kiss. We hung around after class and you offered me a chair then knelt down in front of me...with the strangest look on your face. And, for a second, I thought you wanted to pray."

Karl laughs like he means it. And you can't resist joining him.

"I even had a speech memorized, Lynn. But couldn't say a word."

"Your lips said plenty."

"S'pose they did."

I'd always remember our first and last kiss. A week after it happened, I went home, Karl started high school, designed for guys like him, and any notion of *us* ended with that last summer on Marie's ranch. Before we could do any more reminiscing, we reached the motel parking lot and Mike called, mad as hell. I whispered, "See you later," to Karl, hopped out of the truck before it came to a complete stop, then ran to my room door, unlocked it, and stepped inside as my son shouted his question for the fourth time.

"What in the hell am I going to do, Mom?"

"Calm down. You've got to calm down...and tell me what in blue blazes is going on."

"That goddamn bitch. That miserable, no good, rotten, goddamn bitch."

Mike had run out of air and needed a long, deep breath before he could continue.

"That bitch went over to Amy's and made off with Bryan!"

"Oh my g—"

"I've been calling all afternoon, Mom! Amy said you wouldn't have coverage. I kept trying anyway and—"

"Jill took Bryan? This can't be happening again. Especially right now."

My slip of the tongue didn't escape Mike's attention, and I didn't need to be with him to see the questioning look in his eyes.

"What do you mean, right now?"

"Just that...I'm gone and everything."

"Yeah. Does make this a damn sight worse."

"For both of us, Mike. Now, please tell me exactly what happened."

"Okay...it was about an hour after lunch. Amy heard someone at the front door. And when she opened it, Jill shoved her out of the way...about knocked her down. Then wouldn't tell her anything. Just yanked Bryan out of his crib and ran out. And what could Amy do? Not a goddamn thing...that's what!"

"No she couldn't. Jill's his mother, and the law's on her side. Whether we like it or not."

"And don't I know *that* too damn well. Anyway, I headed right home. Praying she took him there. But she didn't. So what in the hell am I going to do? You think that bitch is pulling the same thing she did last summer?"

"I don't—"

"Wait, Mom! Someone's calling. It's Amy! Call you back."

He hung up and left me to curse Jill's latest sub-version. It would jeopardize Bryan, maybe permanently. Because, if it siderailed Phil's plan, Jill would be free to steal everything she wanted, poison what she didn't, and go on using her son to torment us like she had the previous June.

Mike and I were sitting outside Clark Fork Water Supply. He'd asked me to come with him to look at a new line of lavs, a sure sign he had something he wanted to get off his chest.

"I can't live like this anymore, Mom. Reasoning with that woman is impossible. I might as well be talking from the far side of the moon."

"Bryan's only six months old, though. What if she gets custody?"

"Can't let that happen. And I won't. Our roofer, you know, Stan, told me about a lawyer who's supposed to be phenomenal at getting sole custody for guys like me."

"But, Mike, do you honestly think he could cut through Jill's smoke screen? She's in tight with everyone who's anyone in this town now. And does her best to convince them you're an asshole and she's an angel."

"That's okay. I guess this guy has no problem playing dirty either."

"Well it's a helluva risk. So he better be as good you say."

"Charges like he is. Wants five K up front but... whatever it ends up costing...it'd be worth it a hundred times over to get shed of that bitch and still keep Bryan."

"Yes it would. And you know your dad and I will help out."

"Yeah. And thanks, Mom. You guys shouldn't

have to shell out for any of it, though. Would hope to hell my savings covers it...damn sure ought to."

I had no idea Mike had saved that much money. He surprised me every once in a while.

"This whiz kid have a name?"

"Dan Blake. You heard of him?"

"No. But that's not necessarily a bad thing. Maybe he's okay."

"Hope so, Mom. It's one helluva gamble...I know. But things can't go on like they are. And Dad always says the best defense is a good offense. I've got to *do* something. And what else is there? I can't just up and take off with Bryan. They'd call it kidnapping...and then what kind of shit life would he have?"

"You're right. And running away wouldn't work, anyhow. Jill's got enough money to track you down. She'd have the authorities on her side too. And if they found you, you'd be lucky to ever lay eyes on Bryan again."

Then Mike asked the question I'd been dreading, the one that leaves a parent shouldering the blame when things go bad and receiving no credit when they go well.

"So, Mom. You think I'm doing the right thing?"

"Yeah...maybe trying to get a divorce is worth it if you think this lawyer can get you sole custody. Like you said, you can't go on living like this."

"No I can't. But I won't go ahead with it unless this guy convinces me he's really that good. Promise."

Mike envisioned a lifeline because he needed one but only had hold of a straw. His appointment was noon the next day, and Jill must've heard about it before he walked out of Gould, Bormann, & Blake's office building. She showed up at Amy's house about two o'clock, drove off with Bryan, and didn't answer her phone or come home that night.

Mike couldn't report her missing before the required twenty-four hours. After they'd elapsed, minute by long minute, Mike called the police again. We all listened in on the speaker, and when the desk clerk asked Mike to repeat his name then instructed him to hold for a detective, our intake of breath was audible. But the guy only passed on a message.

"Jill thinks you need time to come to your senses. And, by the way, she has every right to take her son wherever she likes."

The detective severed the connection before Mike could react, and, although the rest of us were too overcome with relief to see it, Phil pointed out the vile implication. Jill had climbed farther up the power chain than we'd suspected, so far up she could, directly or indirectly, have a police detective delivering messages for her. That staggering fact broadened our worst fears and deepened our despair. I found excuses to work with Mike all week, and, when Jill finally called that sunny afternoon in hell, I heard every word she screamed.

"Get your ass over here. Take this brat home. I'm sick of listening to him bawl. He just never—"

"For chrissake, Jill, where are you?"

"I'm in Remount. You'll see me."

She hung up, Mike turned the truck around, and we took off to get Bryan. I phoned Amy to fill her in before we lost coverage then kept my mouth shut until we were out of the sharp curves outside Bonner where big-horn sheep are prone to wandering across the highway.

"Why in god's name would she go to Remount, Mike?"

"Dunno. She did mention it once, though. Something about a family friend owning a big chunk of the Rocky Mountain Front around there."

"And I think I know who."

"Couldn't be him, could it?"

"Bet it is, Mike. Sucking up to people in state government is what famous people do when they move here. It's how they get backing for all their hare-brained projects. Her parents had pull too...lot of media coverage when they retired."

"Jill doesn't have any use for her mom and dad. Calls them dimwitted do-gooders."

"I wonder if they have any idea what their daughter is really like."

"Dunno, Mom. But it could explain why they retired where they did."

"Yeah, it could. Can't get much farther away than Australia."

The highway owned Mike for the rest of the journey. Torn between getting there safely and getting there before Jill had second thoughts, he drove stiff-backed, hands clenching the wheel, thoughts on what lay ahead.

I kept lookout for deer and envisioned Jill's body floating in the river, hanging from a tree, or splattered all over the highway. It made covering the one hundred and thirty-five miles between us and Bryan bearable. Mike overtook nineteen vehicles as he raced up the Blackfoot through traffic flowing steady as the river we shadowed. Then I lost count. The Continental Divide didn't slow us down as much as it should've either, and we made the trip in less than two hours, in a pickup, which must've set a record.

Remount has a post office, general store, lodging, a few bars, and a hundred or so homes and sells itself as The Bob Marshall Wilderness Gateway. Yet it hangs on to its Old West ranching persona with the tenacity of a bronc rider and still hosts the biggest one-day rodeo in Montana. In the middle of seventh grade, my parents and I moved to a ranch only thirty minutes away. What a letdown when they'd refused to take me to the event everyone at school was raving about.

We hadn't even made the nightly trip into town that Sunday. They waited till the following evening, and we'd been amazed to find the street curb-deep in empty beer cans. What fun when Dad had plowed right on through them, crunch, crunch, crunch, then turned around and drove through them again so he could park directly in front of the Mint Bar where he always did. We moved away in 1964. Now, after managing to avoid the town for thirty-five years, I'd returned.

"There she is, Mike! Parked in front of the Trading Post. Straight ahead, on your right."

A split second later, Jill threw open the door of her mud-spattered Lexus LX 470 SUV and jumped into the street like a bull into the ring. I was ready for an all-out fight, ready to bail Mike out of jail, ready to end up in jail, ready for anything except what happened. Jill stomped off toward the store without giving any indication she'd seen us, and we never could decide if she had or if she'd just left Bryan there to wait alone.

I'd rejoiced to see Jill walk away—Mike knew her better.

"Oh god, Mom! What if she locked the doors?"

But she hadn't. Mike unstrapped his son, handed him to me, threw the carseat and diaper bag in the back, and we were gone before the door of the Trading Post banged shut behind her. Poor Bryan couldn't be consoled and cried so hard his little body quivered. Tears left tracks on his dirty face, his clothes were filthy, and Jill must've had the AC blasting because his clenched fists were like tiny snowballs.

I cuddled him against my shoulder, he calmed down enough to identify us, and his strange wailing changed to a familiar, expectant cry—hungry—time to feed me. I got hold of the diaper bag and hauled it into the front seat. There were masses of clean disposable diapers but only two bottles, both empty, not a single jar of baby food or juice, and we didn't even have water with us. Stopping in Remount would've been a fool's choice; Jill had just stormed into the only grocery store in town. But Bryan needed milk, the truck needed fuel, and we'd never make it back over the pass, much less to the gas station in Lincoln, on what we had. So we headed for Simms, turnoff straight ahead of us, and only twenty-one miles away.

I turned my head toward the side window to kiss Bryan's matted curls and caught sight of a black Lincoln Navigator parked in an empty lot. It was the only shiny vehicle in sight, had darkly tinted windows, and more chrome than a plumbing supply house. But it could've been covered bumper to bumper in an inch of mud and I'd still have recognized that rig. Even in Missoula, it stood out like Doris Day perched on a skid row barstool.

I'd noticed it parked next to Jill's Lexus on Higgins Avenue in downtown Missoula once too often for it to be coincidence, but never mentioned it to Mike and still didn't. He had more than enough to contend with. He couldn't risk getting a ticket for child

endangerment, and, once there were a few miles between us and Jill, he pulled off the road to put Bryan
back in his carseat. The poor baby needed changing
too. I laid him on my lap, found an envelope tucked
under his shirt, passed it to over to Mike, and he read
the note aloud.

"Drop the divorce idea or I'll take him again. You
know you can't stop me. And next time you won't get
him back. That's a promise."

We'd been digging in for a war of attrition, but Jill
had produced a weapon of mass destruction by giving birth to Bryan.

"That sick bitch. She'd do it too. And she's right,
Mom. I can't stop her. Even if she hadn't typed the
note and I could prove she wrote it, it's not illegal just
to threa—"

"Oh my god, he's bleeding!"

"What? Let me see!"

I wiped, we looked, I wiped again. Then we
looked closer and agreed the blood was coming from
the skin on his little butt cheeks, like raw hamburger
from wearing wet, filthy diapers. The baby wipes
were useless. Every one of them in the container
had dried out because the lid had been left open the
last time someone used them, and it said something
maddening about how long ago that must've been.
Changing Bryan's diaper only worsened his pain in
the short term, as did my futile attempts to remove
the dried boogers from his red, chapped nostrils

with a Kleenex. His screams and the look on Mike's face made me cry too, and I frantically wiped away my tears.

"You don't need salt on that sore bottom, do you, kiddo? And, Daddy, don't you worry. Nothing's wrong with your little guy a bottle and a bath won't make better. Then a few days of Aunt Amy's TLC, and he'll be right as rain again."

"I know Bryan's okay, Mom. But damn it. If he hadn't been...that bitch wouldn't have lived through what I'd have done to her. This is bad enough. How could she leave him like this? Her own son, for god's sake!"

"Hard to fathom what makes that woman tick, Mike. Don't think I'd want to anyway. Too much like being inside her head."

"That really is a horrible thought. Bet she'd think twice about doing it again, though, if I took a wire brush to her bare ass till it bled."

"I'd be more than happy to hold her down for you."

He tried to smile and patted his son's tummy.

"You'll be okay now. Your ole dad's not going to let anything bad happen to you ever again."

Mike got out and dropped the dirty diaper in the truck bed then took on the heart-wrenching task of wrestling Bryan back into his carseat. Little guy fought with all his might to avoid being strapped into it again. God only knew how many hours, or days and nights, he'd spent there. Cruel not to hold him close to me again, but our voices and the familiar truck soothed him, and the time between sobs finally lengthened into fitful sleep.

The gas station at Simms had everything we needed, clean bathroom, drinking water, dish soap to clean a bottle for Bryan, milk to fill it, and a microwave to heat it. I rushed back to the truck, knowing the baby had to be starving, but, even so, there he was, standing on Mike's lap playing with the steering wheel. I waved the bottle at him, and he reached for it, fell into his dad's arms, sucked it down like he hadn't been fed for days, then promptly fell into a deep sleep.

He didn't even wake up when Mike eased him back into his carseat, and I jogged back to the store for a handful of payphone change. We still didn't have cell coverage, and Amy couldn't be left in suspense any longer. I fed all the coins in, dialed, then, still fearing a run-in with Jill, pulled the metal-wrapped cord across my neck so I could talk while facing the highway.

"Hello...Mom?"

"Hi, honey, sorry it took so long to—"

"Is Bryan okay?"

"Yeah. Little worse for wear, but okay."

"Thank god! Wait...a little worse for wear?"

It hurt to tell Amy what Bryan's mother had done to him. Her sadness soon turned to fury.

"That awful witch! We can't let this happen ever again! You should've taken photos of what she did. So Mike would have proof."

"Proof that Bryan was mistreated...not of who'd done it. Just his word against his wife's. And what if she accused *him* of doing it...or you? We know who they'd believe."

"Yeah, I guess she really could turn it against us. We have to protect Bryan from her somehow, though."

"Well, Mike can't try divorcing her again. That's dead open and shut. Never was a good idea. There's not a judge in the state who'd give him sole custody. We just have to pray she never takes Bryan again."

"There's *got* to be something else we can do. When will you be home? I can't wait to have that baby in my arms again."

"Not until tomorrow morning, I'm afraid. We decided to stay in Great Falls tonight."

"As much as I want to see Bryan...I'm glad, Mom. You guys must be exhausted. All three of you. And Paul says you're not to worry about anything here."

The phone buzzed to let us know our time had nearly run out, and I reassured Amy I'd call and tell her all about getting Bryan clean and comfy again. I returned to the truck feeling somewhat in control again. It gave me the luxury of griping about little things, and I could no longer ignore the musky assault of Jill's perfume. Bryan's hair, his clothes, and everything she'd touched had absorbed the damn stuff.

"Jesus, Mike, does she wear that shit a bottle at a time?"

"I doubt it. I gave her some when we were dating, and it lightened my wallet around eight hundred dollars."

"Good lord."

"And hate to tell you, Mom, the damn stuff never wears off. I'll go buy a new carseat and diaper bag after I get you two settled in a motel room. Whatever else we need too. Just make a list."

He handed me his notebook, and, after flipping past the pages of scribbled calculations and dimensions, I wrote down zinc oxide, and the list grew from there.

"Here you go, Mike. And, before you take off to get all that, I'll get Bryan ready for his bath then put his filthy clothes, the soured bottles, and those dried up wipes in that stinking diaper bag, and you can toss it, unused Pampers and all, in a dumpster."

"Sounds like a plan."

We relaxed for the first time in seven days and, when we got to the motel, celebrated by shelling out for a suite with a garden tub. Ecstatic at being able to crawl around in a few inches of water, Bryan wanted to stay there. Getting my hands around his slippery little body to lift him out of the tub and bundle him into a towel turned into a battle of wills.

I won in the end, though, and carried my squirming grandson out to Mike, who'd just returned with twice what I'd put on the long list. The bed nearest the door was nearly covered with shopping bags.

"He loves that tub, Mike. And he smells delicious now."

Mike held out his hands. Bryan stretched toward him, and the towel fell to the floor as the baby moved from my arms to his dad's.

"Yes. You do smell good...good enough to eat!"

Mike lifted his son in the air, nuzzled his neck, then blew raspberries on his tummy, and Bryan, small chest white and tender between his father's dark, callused hands, squealed with delight.

"What happened to you, Mom? You look like you fell in."

"Little guy wasn't thrilled about getting out."

"Did you get your grandma all wet?"

Bryan giggled and grinned.

"He's got scratches, or cuts of some kind, on his arms, Mike."

"Oh god! Where?"

"Right behind his elbows. Probably just from Jill's long fingernails or something. And they're healing. Just makes you wonder what he went through."

"Tell you what, Mom. I can't even let myself think about it. Or I'd have to go find that bitch and kill her."

Mike laid the baby on the bed and tried to look him over, but Bryan made a lightning crawl to the pillows and sat there slapping his knees like a tiny, maniacal Buddha. Mike finally cornered him long enough to perform an inspection but found no other marks or tender spots.

"You're right, Mom. There's nothing else. Just those scratches on his arms."

I let the mystery of how he'd gotten them drop and organized the results of Mike's shopping spree. By now it was nearly eight o'clock, and we hadn't eaten. The thought of leaving that room didn't appeal to either of us, so, once again damning the cost, we ordered room service. Soon the aroma of steak and baked potatoes filled the room. We devoured every morsel, and Bryan gobbled up three jars of baby food and some sliced banana.

Our late supper finished, Mike picked up the shopping bag I had ready for him then went into the bathroom and began refilling the immense tub. He came out wearing a towel around his waist, carefully extracted his banana-smeared baby from the highchair we'd requested, and carried him out of the room at arm's length.

"Want to have a bath with Dad? Check out all your new tub toys?"

Seeing the two of them together again made me so happy I had to share it with Amy even though we'd already been on the phone while Mike shopped. I didn't tell her about Bryan's arms. That could wait until we got home so she could kiss those owies all better. We were still talking about how lucky we were to have gotten our baby back when Mike carried him into the room, and I held the phone to Bryan's ear so Amy could tell him goodnight.

He went quiet, looked puzzled for a second, then clutched the phone and beamed. Mike and I were euphoric too, but a week of lost sleep shut us down then slammed us into a sleep coma. Bryan included. By morning, bottom already healing, he was all smiles and happy babbling.

"Wish I could forget what that bitch just put us through like Bryan can, Mom. Wonder what she'll try next."

Mike's voice conveyed resignation and dismay, and I tried to brighten his outlook.

"Maybe she'll back off now that she's made her point."

He looked dubious, but the optimistic possibility cheered him a little. On our way home, we found reasons to take Bryan, napping or not, out of his new but despised nevertheless carseat. Ignoring a twenty-five mile an hour wind on the eastern side of the mountains and the possibility of getting rear-ended on the western side, we stopped for historical highway markers and fishing sites we'd ignored for years. At each one, Mike lifted his son onto his shoulders and took him for a short walk. We stopped at gravel pits too. The perfect places for Bryan to throw rocks, and, of course, they were his favorite.

Subconsciously or not, we delayed our return to the frontline and didn't make Bonner till six. I phoned Amy to beg forgiveness, and, while we covered the last few miles home, she paced her front lawn. Before Mike could turn into the driveway, she ran to the truck with tears of joy streaming down her cheeks, and Bryan let out a giddy, high-pitched bleat the instant he saw her.

Jill showed up six days later. We mourned her return for a month.

Now, almost a year later, at the worst possible time, my son's wife had taken Bryan again. Why? Mike certainly hadn't instigated it. He believed she'd meant every word in that note and had done nothing in the intervening eleven months to give her a reason to carry out her threat. Divorcing her was no more than the unattainable goal dogging his days.

We should've done something about that damn woman sooner. What if we'd left it too late? The possibility poured into my mind like salt into a wound. No longer concerned about roaming minutes, I'd been clutching my cellphone the entire time and used it when Mike called back. The relief in his voice heralded good news before the words sank in.

"It's okay, Mom! Amy just got a call from Jill. She left Bryan at some drop-off daycare center. Paul and

I are only a few blocks away. Call you when we have him."

A reprieve of miraculous proportions. But what in hell was Jill up to? Had she canceled her Saturday meeting with Phil? I hadn't thought to ask Mike or Amy if they'd talked to their dad. Did he even know what had happened? I called him. His terse hello, muffled voices, and the sound of him walking away before saying another word told me I'd caught him working and he couldn't talk long.

"Have you heard from the kids, Phil?"

"No. But they couldn't have reached me before now."

He didn't have time for anything but the briefest rundown on Jill's latest incursion. And I couldn't ask if he thought her odd behavior tied into the illuminating conversation I'd overheard a couple months earlier. It had revealed Jill's incomprehensible actions were part of a cold-blooded scheme, and, if we were seeing the final stages of it, our own plan could be blown to hell before we had time to wave goodbye.

I'd overheard the conservation in Helena at the March Builder's Conference when I skipped the mid-afternoon presentation and decided to take a snooze in the large empty bar. But my nap hadn't lasted long. Two men, failing to notice me slumped into the corner of a tall-backed booth, had carried their drinks to the booth directly behind mine and shared their conversation with the one person they shouldn't have.

"Well, this time next year you'll be surveying. Hope you're prepared."

"I am. It's a big project, and I'm not one to chase nickels with dimes. I'll hire someone to guard my equipment if I have to."

"And you will. Remember that poor bastard who let those subdivisions close in on him. By the time he decided to cash out, the elk had been channeled onto his land. Neighbors liked using that open space, too, and got his land designated a game corridor before he knew what hit him."

"Yeah, Danny. I remember. Because while those nice, law-abiding citizens were making *that* happen, they were destroying my surveying equipment fast as I could set it up."

"I heard about that. And Missoula's born-again hippies aren't going take losing this open mountainside any better."

I'd thought it damn strange we hadn't heard anything about an impending development right on our doorstep, wanted to hear more, and didn't make a single sound or move a smidgen of an inch.

"What I don't understand, Danny, is this. If they want to hang on to their land so bad, why in hell not sell to a land trust? Get the big tax breaks on the money and, for all intents and purposes, still own it."

He'd asked a good question. Land trusts are a lu-crative deal. Without them the entire valley would've been subdivided, up, down, across, and sideways. The bureaucracy involved put us off the idea, though. Too much like doing business with the government. But owning bare land above a crowded valley is like dangling your bare feet over a river full of piranha; it gets tiresome after the novelty wears off. I'd sus-pected they were talking about the Michelsons and their dry foothills across from the airport.

"I can't tell you why they didn't go for a trust. Never understood it myself. Bare land price for those three sections is about eight million. Nothing com-pared to what it'd be worth subdivided, though."

The man who wasn't Danny, either huge or hugely overweight—because the entire booth jiggled when-ever he moved—had cleared his throat and rattled the ice in his empty glass until the bartender brought another round. I'd feared the kid would alert the men to my presence by asking if I wanted anything. But he either hadn't noticed or ignored me—and that was the mundane occurrence that saved us.

"But, Danny, people have been trying to get them to let go of that land for years with no luck. They've held out this long. So, what makes your gal so posi-tive she can get her hands on their land, now?"

"I really don't know. She never shares any de-tails...but always comes through for me. Don't know why she even bothers. It's not that she needs the money. Could be for the power that comes with it, I guess. Or she gets off on the sport of it. Once she has control of some poor bastard, she's got the compassion of a lone wolf ripping the guts out of a newborn calf. All I really know is that she originally planned to get the land by marrying and divorcing him. Then she found out about some ironclad prenup protecting that Crandall land and—"

My reaction to realizing they'd been talking about us, about Jill, about our mountainside, had been anything but quiet. I scooted out of the booth as fast as the vinyl material would let me and ran to the lady's room, only place I'd been able to go and still keep my back to them. They'd made a run for it too and were nowhere in sight when I peeked out the door seconds later.

I'd immediately phoned Phil, not the kids, and drove to his place while puzzling over how Jill planned to gain control of our land. Those men were right. A prenup protects the undeveloped ground they wanted. Jill wouldn't get as much as a square foot of it if she and Mike divorced. And, thank god, not if he died either, or he'd have already been six foot under. There were other ways, though, ways too harrowing to have considered on my own. I'd never been so happy to see Phil, even though he'd soon confirmed my fear that, by playing her custody card, Jill would use Bryan to appropriate our land.

That chilling deduction explained her deliberate pregnancy to force Mike into marriage, befriending Amy for family information, neglecting Bryan from infancy on, and making the type of alliances she had. It explained everything. So, what had she been waiting for? Did she think we weren't sufficiently devoted to Bryan yet to hand over the land? Or did her partners have some timeline they wanted her to follow? Phil and I had no way of answering those questions, but discovering Jill's motive uncovered a demoralizing truth. We hadn't been standing our ground for all those months—we'd been hazed into a nice tight target, and Jill could drop the bomb whenever she pleased.

Mounting an offense had led us into unexplored territory, and drawn-lines shifted under the morass of moral uncertainty we took on board there. But any misgivings had been dispelled when Phil led me into the bedroom and passion sealed our pact. Then he explained how his work had made the decision easier for him by instilling the fact soldiers are sent to war at the behest of wealthy old men who want something belonging to another country, or prosper from supplying the products needed for a conflict, or both. A fight to protect our family was far more just, and learning about Jill's intentions had left no doubt it needed protecting.

The scalding truth I'd chanced upon that afternoon, and what Phil and I had decided to do about it, remained our secret. Best to let the kids' heartache continue a little longer and increase the odds of winning. From the very beginning, it had been strictly need to know. But I'd unilaterally included Marie—because I needed her to know—and that was close enough.

In the interim, our resolve had waxed not waned, and now we had to find a way to overcome Jill's latest roadblock. If it even was a roadblock and not just a minor detour. Maybe she never intended to keep Bryan. Maybe she just took him to refresh our fear of losing him. Before my theory could spring any leaks, Amy called.

"They have Bryan, Mom!"

"Thank heavens! Is he okay?"

"He's fine. Paul said he looked like he'd been crying the whole time, though. And he was cold. Jill wouldn't even wait for me to grab his coat. What in god's name is she doing? It makes no sense whatsoever...even for her."

"She never said anything at all when she took him?"

"Not one word. Mike's all fired up, though. Says he's going to take Bryan and run off to some country without extradition laws. And stay there. And he just can't do that! If he does, I swear I'll go too. What about Paul, though?"

Amy choked on her question then washed it down with tears.

"Take it easy, honey. You're thinking way too far ahead. I'll call your brother. Try to talk some sense into him."

Not wanting to hear what I had to say, Mike took his time answering the phone. I surprised him by taking a different tack, didn't try to badger him out of the idea, just tried to keep him from acting on it right away. If our luck held, it wouldn't matter after Saturday anyway.

"Hi, Mom."

Just as I'd expected, his voice was flat and heavy with resistance.

"Mike, before you say anything, I get why you want to take Bryan and clear out. And you're right. It's the best way to keep him safe...but don't jump without a chute. Just get some things together and stay at my house tonight. Jill won't come around there."

Likely sensing what I'd do to her if I got half a chance, the woman stayed clear of me and wouldn't come near my place. But Mike had primed himself for an explosive, situation-annihilating bid for independence. Getting him to let go of that and bide his time would take some doing.

"I dunno, Mom."

"Trust me. Jill won't show up at my house. You won't have to worry about her beating on your door any minute. You'll be able to concentrate. And you can talk things over with Paul and Amy. Think what losing Bryan would do to her...she wants to go with you."

"And how would that work, Mom? Exactly what I was afraid of when she started watching Bryan for me...that it would ruin her life too. Should've never dragged her into this. Should've never dragged any of you into this."

"You couldn't have kept us at arm's length, Mike. We wouldn't have let you."

"Thanks, Mom. Just wish those social services people would've given a shit. Oh no, they're only interested in protecting mothers. Don't give a damn about their poor kids. Bet if we'd turned somebody in for starving and neglecting a puppy, though, they'd have been in a shitload of trouble. Woulda probably been on the goddamn news."

"That's a sad fact, Mike. But at least nothing disastrous has happened. You think Jill might've only been rattling your chain?"

"Hell if I know what she was doing. But I'm not playing her games anymore. I've had all I can take!"

"Okay, okay. Just promise you'll think things over for a day or two. Please."

"What if it's too late by then?"

"It won't be. I think she's accomplished what she wanted to. For now anyway. How about a compromise? Stay at my house for tonight...then decide. And Bryan would need a passport, wouldn't he?"

"Dunno. I'll check it out. You know I don't really want to leave, Mom. Just that, getting Bryan out of the country...while I can...it really is the only way to make sure that bitch can never take him from me again. And deep down, I bet you think so too."

I thought if he wanted to make things worse and cock up Phil's plan, it was a damn good way to do it. I thought Jill would find him and spirit Bryan away no matter where he went. I thought he better not rock her boat because it would be easier to sink if it held steady. But there were only two names on the need-to-know list now, and Mike's wasn't one of them. So I could only agree.

"Okay, honey. Not saying you're wrong...but will you wait?"

"Yeah. Guess going to your house for tonight isn't such a bad idea. I'll pack up and head over there."

Mike's intentions were barely recognizable as I relayed them to Amy. No need for her to agonize over something that would be a moot point after Saturday. I didn't have to conceal anything from Phil, though, and called as much to halve my burden as to fill him in. He didn't even say hello before asking the question that underlined his good-guy status.

"Did we get Bryan back? Is he okay?"

"Yes, thank god, and he's fine. Jill called Amy to let her know she'd dumped him at some daycare place, then Mike and Paul went and picked him up. No idea why she took him in the first place. But Mike's had it... sick of her BS and wants to make a clean break. Take Bryan and leave the country. Doesn't really matter, he could just come back home. But if Jill found out—"

"She wouldn't show up Saturday."

"Exactly. She'd go on a rampage and forget all about meeting you. We've got to put the skids on our son. I did talk him into staying at my house tonight, though. Jill won't come around there. No matter how bad she wants to start a fight so some cop will force Mike to hand Bryan over to her. Oh, and the little guy doesn't have a passport, so that'll slow things down."

"That's a real break. They can't get all that far without one. And even if Mike pays to expedite it, it'll take longer than we need. Then again, even if he as much as leaves town, Jill might not—"

"Yeah. Even that could screw up your plan."

"I'll call him as soon as I hang up."

"Okay, good. And you'll be in Missoula tomorrow. You can put some man-to-man pressure on him...convince him to stay put until Jill isn't a problem anymore."

"I'll try."

"And I'm betting you succeed. Mike listens to you more than you think."

Phil wrinkled his perpetual three-day beard growth and smiled at that. I could hear it in his voice when he said goodbye. Mike being ready to do a bunk diluted my jubilation over getting Bryan back, and I dreaded going to Walter and Becky's house even more than I had the night before. When I pulled into their driveway, Karl was wandering around the lawn gazing at his boots, and I jumped out of the truck before he could open the door for me.

Our drive out to the ranch might never have happened. I would've admitted to being nothing short of surly, and Karl, usually a too-talkative, charming-nevertheless caricature of himself, had morphed into an introvert. We remained silent, and I followed him through the side door into the garage, large enough to hold four vehicles in addition to the usual flotsam and jetsam of dedicated consumers.

The door into the house, tucked between an upright freezer and extra refrigerator, opened into a hallway filled with a nearly forgotten aroma—the mingled scents of coffee, fried chicken, and warm cinnamon rolls. The inside of Mom and Dad's 1955 Chevy Impala had smelled just the same during my first solo drives taking breakfast or lunch out to Dad, summer fallowing up near the Canadian border on the Hi-Line. A unique scent that brought the feel of sunshine taking over the day, the sight of strip-farmed wheat fields as far as I could see, and the excitement of watching Dad stop a gargantuan D8 Cat at the end of his round. The tracked machine had no cab, and he'd coped with the boiling dust by tying a dishtowel over his face and wearing tight goggles. When he raised them, his dirt-blackened face had a pair of white targets with blue bull's-eyes.

One childhood memory triggers more, though, and the rest weren't the comforting kind. Being there in Walter and Becky's bastion of happy families made things worse. But I kept following Karl, and he led me into the overly large family room made homey with a lowered ceiling and south-facing, paned glass windows.

"Nice room."

"Best part of the house. Make yourself at home, Lynn. I'll let them know you're here."

I had zero tolerance for a quiz session and was determined not to let my anguish show. Tricky when you have a face that's a reader board of your every emotion. Phil had alerted me to the handicap not long after we'd met, and I never forgot his words.

"Sweetie, if you had to make a living playing poker, you'd starve to death."

My craving to slip away increased tenfold with each person straggling in—Darlene, Becky and Walter, their daughter Susan, their son-in-law Steve, and two grandkids. The bubbly little girl had Marie's high cheekbones and elegantly straight nose. Her older brother, a young Walter, proclaimed he was six years old and gave me a smug smile before running to his grandpa's lap.

They were that perfect family on Mormon missionary handouts, residing on the cloud of equanimity that forms around believing hard work and decency protect you from their antitheses. Jill's machinations had dissipated our cloud—as if it were nothing more than an accumulation of unshed tears. And we'd landed hard in a hellish place where outcomes are determined by a fearsome roll of the devil's dice.

"So, Lynn...did you and Karl have a nice day?"

"We did, Becky. How'd things go here?"

"Okay, I guess. Tomorrow might seem a little soon for the funeral. But you're the only one living very far away...and you're here. Your kids wouldn't have wanted to come, would they?"

"No. Not with what they've got on their plates right now."

Nothing I'd meant to share, followed by a prolonged silence as they waited for an explanation I refused to provide. And Darlene didn't rescue me as she had the night before, but Becky's desire to feed us won out over her nosiness.

"I hope everyone's hungry. People have been dropping by with food all day."

Walter settled deeper into the leather La-Z-Boy recliner a couple sizes too big for him and dispatched his minions.

"You girls go on into the kitchen then. Let us know when it's ready."

Karl, alone on a seven-foot sofa, sat facing a formidable trio—Walter, his grandson, perched on the arm of the recliner with grandpa's arm around him, and the boy's father. No wonder he looked envious and forlorn as he watched *us girls* file out to the kitchen.

"I think buffet style. Don't you, Darlene?"

Becky only got a nod, and even that seemed more than Darlene cared to contribute. Her melancholy seemed out of proportion to the loss of a mother-in-law she wasn't particularly close to. Stark comparison to Susan and Becky, seemingly unfazed, cheerfully working as an experienced team, automatically relocating anything Darlene or I set down. For them, each meal flowed into the next. After working out what they'd serve for breakfast the next morning, they talked nonstop about the reception luncheon at the church. Becky had obviously given it great consideration.

"Everyone will bring salads, side dishes, and desserts, Susan. It never fails. So let's concentrate on the meat and some decent bread."

Her daughter agreed. Then they discussed the intricacies of braising roasts, basting ham, and punching down dough. I got the gist of it, but that's about all and came to fully understand the look on home buyers' faces at a construction site.

When food and drink covered every available horizontal surface in the kitchen and we'd set the dining room table, Susan stepped out of the kitchen and yelled, "Come and get it," down the hall. It was homemade food heaven, and my failure to join the others in seconds and thirds had created a disturbing blip on Becky's radar.

"Lynn! Ain't you gonna eat more than that? Better have some more fruit salad at least."

I followed her instructions to avoid drawing any more scrutiny and made sure my strawberry whip lasted until everyone finished eating. With so much clearing up to do, Darlene and I were allowed to help but got in the way more than anything. She smiled at me when we were instructed to take some of the leftovers out to the refrigerator in the garage, but the illusion of kinship I'd experienced the night before had evaporated.

We worked without speaking, and Darlene remained silent when we returned to an empty kitchen. I cleared my throat to get her attention, raised my phone, then practically race-walked to the great room and found it living up to its name. The ten-foot high windows presented a sweep of lawn glowing neon-green under a sky turning a thousand shades of blue, and the scene held my attention till the cancan sunset connecting them faded to a lackluster gray.

I didn't even bother to check my phone. I'd have heard it if the kids or Phil had called, and any work messages left while Karl and I were out at Marie's ranch could wait till I gave a damn. But, no matter how much I wanted to, I couldn't hang out in that room watching it get dark. The group wouldn't permit my absence for much longer. I looked hard at that front door, though, before returning to the family room. Luckily, I walked in just as Becky and Walter's grandkids were being shooed upstairs for a bath, and I was able to sit down on the long sofa without becoming the object of attention.

When the kids were brought back down in their pajamas to say goodnight, they distributed hugs and kisses all around until they got to me. But, before the little girl ducked around the corner, she brushed her blond ringlets aside and blew me a kiss. Missing Bryan, I gazed at the spot where she'd vanished too long, turned to find everyone staring at me, and had to smile before they'd start talking again.

My contributions to the conversations didn't amount to much. We had no common ground. They led pure, plain, simple lives in a world where heartbreak and hardship show up when and where expected. Their troubles could be understood and pigeonholed, but Jill had turned our lives into a stupefying drive around a perpetually dark city mined with quandaries, chaos, conundrums, and catastrophes. I wanted to stand up and shout a warning. Guard your good fortune well, or it will slip out from under you quicker than a cheap rug. Not being daffy or caring enough to manage that, I kept my mouth shut and went on grinning and frowning when expected to.

Walter had leaned back, hands behind his head, knees spread, belly and crotch exposed. This was *his* turf. He injected their harvesting business into every discussion, even when his daughter tried to talk about her new home. But his willingness to talk about custom cutting wheat only extended to bragging about how he'd outwitted difficult farmers, equipment salesmen, and seed suppliers. He sidestepped my questions about the new combines and the timing difficulties of moving equipment to coincide with ripening grain crops as if I were trying to pry out the family jewels.

Hearing stories about Marie would've been worth hanging around for, but her name wasn't uttered until Becky brought up the funeral. Then they only hashed over what she may or may not have wanted, who would or wouldn't bring what they'd promised, and when or when not to put out the food. And it couldn't be stanched. I endured it till nine o'clock, then, too loud and too enthusiastically, I cut into the women's debate over table decorations and the men's argument over the best way to delineate parking areas and announced my departure.

Unlike the previous night, I couldn't get to my motel room fast enough. And without a crumb on the carpet, fingerprint on the mirror, or clothes hanger out of place, it was just I'd first found it—except for the ringing desk phone. What the hell was Jill up to now? But Amy had reassuring news to share.

"Mike and Bryan are settled in over at your house, Mom."

"That's a relief!"

"Yup. We offered to take our crib over there. But Mike said it would be safer to have Bryan sleeping with him, and I'm sure happy about that. Parked his truck out in the equipment yard too...with two packed suitcases. He's all set to make a run for it if Jill shows up. I don't think she will, though. Do you?"

"No. But glad he's ready just in case. She made any contact?"

"Nope."

"Good. Maybe I was right when I told your brother she was only trying to shake him up."

"Paul thinks the same thing."

"Good, and you never know, Amy...maybe she had to leave town and just wanted to do Mike's head in before she left."

I thought maybe Jill had something going on in Helena and would stay there till she met with Phil on Saturday. I'd fallen into a puddle of optimism, but Amy yanked me right back out.

"If she's gone, it won't be for long. Bryan's well-baby checkup is tomorrow morning, and she hasn't missed one yet. Always wants to make it look like she cares...play the angelic Mommy role. Says things like, 'I never let anyone watch my baby but his auntie.' Makes me want to hurl every time."

"I bet it does."

"Mike wanted to go with me...won't let Bryan out of his sight now. But he can't risk running into Jill."

"Maybe she'll surprise you and not be there."

"Sure would be nice. Probably too much to hope for, though."

"I'll keep my fingers crossed, honey. Like to talk longer, but what a day it's been, and—"

"Before you go, when's the funeral?"

"Tomorrow morning at ten."

"That soon?"

"Doesn't take near as long to arrange things here. And no one's coming from any distance. Oh, almost forgot to tell you. The cemetery is half way to Miles City, and I'll be staying there tomorrow night."

"Want me to make a reservation?"

"No. You've had enough to deal with today...and work on top of it. I can make one."

"Okay. Might not be able to get flowers delivered to the church in time."

"Don't worry about that either. We'll do something later."

"Good thing you went to see her, huh, Mom? And we're all so sorry. But, from what you said...it might've been a blessing."

"Yeah, I think so. Sometimes death is the only good answer on the horizon."

I'd revealed everything with that depressing truth, but Amy had no way of discerning it. We said goodnight, and, after making the motel reservation, I spent an hour staring at the TV. It wasn't on, but the black screen insisted on displaying reasons for Jill taking Bryan then returning him right away, and they were all horrifying. The slightest buffeting of Jill's life could become the hurricane that disintegrated ours.

My trepidation slipped away in the bathroom, once again gleaming like the fifties, but came back stronger than ever as soon as I fell into bed. Calling on my repertoire of ways Jill could die, I fell asleep as the quicksand sucked her under and her long red hair floated across the bubbling surface in a pretty sunburst pattern.

THURSDAY

I woke up afraid—fist-clenching, lip-biting, stomach-churning afraid—and the predawn light merely disclosed unrealistic suppositions and operational flaws. What if Phil got caught? What if that guy on Wedding Drive came home unexpectedly? We still didn't have a backup plan. And how could we do such a thing, anyway? But how could we not?

Jill had infected our lives like black mold, only responsive to expert mitigation, and Phil had only one way to save us. And what would Marie think if I went soft? I had to buck up. I'd known setting things right wouldn't be easy since overhearing those men talking in Helena. Should've known it when Jill took Bryan to Remount. But, just as Marie had said, we wanted a safe, easy way out, and, instead of counterattacking, we'd wasted time turning to a social worker for help. Heartened by the sympathetic receptionist who'd made the appointment, we went there feeling encouraged and walked out feeling sucker punched.

After filling out forms for thirty minutes, we'd waited another thirty before being shown into the office of a gaunt, middle-aged man who'd acquired the sociology degree hanging on the wall above his head eight months earlier. His hair, bleached color-crayon yellow, intensified the sallowness of his face and the dark circles beneath his bleary eyes. He'd listened to our story without asking a single question or making a single comment. Then, staring at the tattoos on the back of his hands while sliding our stack of forms from one side of his desk to the other and talking without pause in the singsong manner of ex-cons, he'd enlightened us on the laws protecting the rights of mothers.

We couldn't have been barking up a more incorrect tree. Proving a woman to be an unfit mother is next to impossible, lowering Mike's chance of gaining full custody of Bryan to nil. The government doesn't correct biases; it shuffles them around. And Jill had disciplined herself not to say or do anything around witnesses that didn't make her look like the victim. Even if an attorney could've convinced a judge to question her parenting skills, they'd only have ordered her to undergo psychological examination— just expensive entertainment for someone like her.

She would've thoroughly enjoyed hoodwinking a psychologist into believing she was a devoted mother with an insensitive, abusive husband and meddlesome in-laws. She'd have been declared a sane, intelligent, well-educated woman because, contrary to what we'd first assumed, Jill wasn't psychotic, bipolar, depressed, or any other trendy kind of screwed up, just bad to the bone—and they don't test for evil.

We were left with only one way out, and I prayed Jill would still meet Phil on Saturday. One thing made me believe she would. She'd smelled a scandal when Phil said he wanted to discuss what he'd heard about me, and she wouldn't willingly give up adding something like that to her weapons pile. I recited that fact to myself until the sun escaped the horizon then opened my pocketknife and cut the tags off my new gray sweater. The black slacks had to go into the shower above a few inches of hot water. Not enough time for the wrinkles to hang out after all.

Dreading the funeral and needing something to do for the next two hours, I slipped into the dirty clothes I'd worn during the trip and, thinking we should build a carwash in Red Bend, went outside and had a go at the truck. It took an entire roll of paper towels and a full bottle of glass cleaner just to scrub the bugs off the windshield and headlights. And Mike still hadn't called. Was he waiting until the last moment to tell me he'd decided to break his promise and leave town immediately? Or had he slept in after a restless night?

I topped off the washer fluid, checked the oil, spiffed up the cab, then couldn't take the suspense any longer and went in to phone him.

"Hi, Mom. Was just about to call you. How're you doing? The funeral's this morning, right?"

"Yeah, at ten. And I'm okay. Hanging in there anyway."

"Amy told you I got settled in at your place, didn't she?"

"Yes she did. And I loved hearing it. Get any sleep? Find everything you needed?"

"No problem with that. You're a creature of habit, Mom...everything's right where it used to be. And, yeah, I actually slept pretty well. Bryan too."

"Well that's good. And, believe me, you're way better off not leaving till you have a solid plan."

"Hope so, Mom. Looks like I'll have to wait awhile anyway. Bryan did need a passport. And, even paying extra to speed it up, it's still going to take a few days."

"You already went to the post office and got that going?"

"Yup. Oh, and Dad called last night. Said it wouldn't be right for me to take Bryan and leave before you got to say goodbye to us. And I had to agree with him. But it turns out I'll be here waiting for that passport anyway."

"Thanks, Mike. Thanks so much. And you won't regret it. I promise."

"Don't know how you can say that. But I sure as hell hope you're right."

I'd be hearing that a lot before I got home, and it was already making me nervous.

"You can count on it. Anything from Jill?"

"Nada. She might've taken off yesterday. I had Paul check on the house early this morning, and she wasn't around. With any luck, she's found a bigger fool than me to latch onto."

"You weren't a fool, Mike. Just in the wrong place at the wrong time."

"Yeah...happy and clueless as a Thanksgiving turkey. Can't figure out what that bitch is up to. Hope she drove off a cliff somewhere."

Couldn't tell him how close he'd come to foretelling Jill's future, so I asked about the jobs we had going, and we talked about work until the conversation ended. My son sounded older than his years, sick and tired of grappling with his devilish wife and worn out from packing around all that guilt—heaviest substance in the universe.

He just couldn't forgive himself for succumbing to Jill's advances. Oddly enough, I'd overheard the conversation that gave her game away in the same place he'd met her. We all knew the story, his lamentation whenever he was downhearted, as though reciting it might change the ending.

———

Mike was in Helena for the January Builder's Conference, standing with a group of Missoula contractors in the lobby of the Colonial Inn, when Jill descended the grandiose staircase like she owned the place and half the town too. Each dainty bounce drew attention to her ample breasts, and her long, curly, red hair seemed to flow over her shoulders down to her waist. All eyes were on the petite, porcelain-skinned, green-eyed beauty, the type men want to put on a pedestal and women want to shove in front of a speeding semi.

Jill had room to walk around the men gawking up at her, but chose to cut through and bumped into Mike hard enough to knock the speaker schedule from his hand. She pretended not to notice then sought him out that evening. He was sitting at the bar with the rest of the guys when she pressed her chest tight against his back and whispered a tantalizing apology in his ear. He'd never encountered a woman as bold and exciting, but the strings attached to what she had on offer quickly turned to ropes—all in the shape of a noose.

Mike's alluring new girlfriend quickly contrived to become pregnant even though he was a cautious guy. AIDS aside, two of his friends had children with women they didn't love or trust, and he didn't care to make it a trio. But, barring a vasectomy, a man can only do so much. Jill hid the pregnancy as long as possible then took a six-week vacation with friends— a Caribbean cruise planned months earlier, she said.

On the Fourth of July, she called Mike to say she was back home and wanted him to come to Helena the next night because they needed to talk right away but not over the phone or at her place. He was half hoping she'd decided to break it off. It didn't seem likely, though, because she'd set the meeting at Martini's, the bar in the Colonial Inn where they'd met six months earlier.

Mike got there early, planning to have a beer or two before she showed up, but, glowing and more tempting than ever, she was already sitting at a table. In front of her she'd spread out what he assumed to be vacation mementos and photos. When he saw they were actually ultrasound images, a gynecology report, and pamphlets explaining prenatal DNA testing, he went back to the bar and changed his order from a beer to a large whiskey.

Jill announced she was four months pregnant and informed Mike he had an appointment for DNA testing the next day. She said he needed to be as certain as she was that he'd fathered this healthy baby boy and offered a profusion of excuses for not informing him earlier. He didn't buy any of them. He believed she'd done it on purpose to increase the odds of getting him to marry her. She insisted their wedding be in Hawaii, only the two of them, followed by a one-week honeymoon. Even though Mike detested the idea of not having friends and family at his wedding, he gave in, and they were married two weeks later by a justice of the peace in Oahu—fait accompli.

Why Jill trapped him into marriage had puzzled Mike, and still puzzled him. Not for his money. She had her own and never asked him for a dime or used the credit card he'd given her. He hadn't understood. None of us had. She wasn't a leech but a predator—and as vicious as they come.

The five months preceding Bryan's birth had passed without incident, making Jill's behavior afterward all the more bizarre. She shunned her baby from the time he opened his lake-blue eyes on the eighteenth of December, and our need to protect him grew in direct proportion to her abusive neglect. We hadn't seen she was neglecting her son to tyrannize us, a lack of vision that came close to bringing about our downfall because Jill had no such handicap.

The enlightening, frightening conversation I'd overheard in Helena proved she had no trouble seeing well into the future. When I'd broken our need-to-know policy and told Marie what I'd learned, she hadn't been surprised about Jill's farsighted aspirations. Marie seemed to have viewed her tiny portion of humanity through a microscope and possessed an unsentimental, comprehensive understanding of how the world worked. I couldn't imagine how I'd navigate it without her and figured I'd hold up about as long as a sailplane cut loose in the path of a tornado.

Unable to put off going to her funeral any longer, I topped the black slacks with the gray sweater, pulled on riding boots, then brushed my hair, dabbed on a little lipstick, and took a last look at the bathroom of my childhood dreams before walking out the door. I felt naked out there. The cool air blew right through the thin fabric of my dress clothes. Shivering, I threw my duffel bag on the back seat then quick-timed it to the office and found a note on the door; *Sorry, closed for funeral, please leave key in box.*

Each block closer to the church peeled away a little more confidence, and, experiencing all the grief absent when my parents died, I wanted to hide in a dark room not share it with people I hardly knew or didn't know at all. But I parked in the roped off area of the churchyard, got out of the truck, and fell in behind two Bethel Lutheran regulars.

"After this load, you get Bertha's casserole for her. I can handle the rest of what I brought. Wonder what time we should start putting out food?"

"Hard to say. Pastor's so damn long-winded."

"That's for sure. Won't mind when this one hands in his notice. Wouldn't ya know he'd be the one to last so darn long."

"That's the way it goes, doesn't it? Ain't fair, him being the one to hold out. None of the others did... one winter and they were gone."

"We might be stuck with him. Sure do miss Reverend Corey. Course he'd be about a hundred years old now. Bet he'd do a better job, though."

Propriety hobbled the women's laughter, reducing it to a quick giggle.

"We can't ask him to leave. Might hurt his feelings. And how would that make us look?"

"No, don't want to give the church a bad name. Just have to wait it out."

This mist of politeness above a swamp of selfish concerns is what's mistaken for kindness and acceptance by outsiders, and their awakenings are rude indeed. I followed the women up the stone steps and into the church, blazed a trail through the murmuring groups, then stationed myself beside Marie.

She looked more alive than she had when I'd first caught sight of her in the hospital, except for the unlikelihood of her hands being crossed above her breasts. Those lifeless hands had once been so nimble. All in one swift motion, she'd been able to center a triangle of paisley scarf against the nape of her neck, draw it around her hair, tie it into a knot on her forehead, and tuck in the ends so they never came loose. Not even when she'd rested her head against a cow's hollow flank to stay balanced on the three-legged milking stool.

Marie could reach under broody hens and retrieve the eggs safe from my bloodied fingers and evade the assailing hooves of rangy Herefords conscripted into milk cow service long enough to fasten kickers above their hocks. Her hands were strong too, and she'd carried full buckets of milk—four, sometimes six trips—from the barn to the house twice a day.

And, her stride in perfect counterpoint to the sloshing liquid, no more than a few drops cratered the dust around her feet. Nine months out of the year she'd hauled those buckets to the porch and poured the contents into the separator. Warm, foamy milk surging around a cold steel bowl echoed in the white satin rippling against the gray metal rim of her coffin.

"Lynn! You came all this way!"

The woman's jarring voice made me jump and hit my hip against the casket. I automatically looked at Marie's face to see if it made her smile then felt a little foolish and a lot sadder.

"Didn't mean to startle you."

Unable to recognize the woman, I mumbled a greeting and got away while she jiggled yet another flower arrangement in among the rest. Following the rug parting the pews, I wound up back in the vestibule among the kindred spirits, casual friends, shirttail relatives, neighbors, and harmless enemies Marie had collected during her seventy-seven years. She'd never lived anywhere else and didn't apologize for it.

"I didn't need to do much traveling to figure out there's a heap a places worse...but not one better."

I'd have said it was the perfect epitaph if anyone had asked, but they didn't, and I soon had a bellyful of inane conversations with strangers who knew too much about me. Edging into the hall, I slipped past the sanctuary where the family had gathered and circled back to Marie.

During my short absence, the crowded flower arrangements, ribbons flattened and cards dislodged, had been smushed together to make room for even more. Bold irises intruded on pink rosebuds, disheveled fronds of baby's breath resembled the weeds they are, and formal arrangements of lilies had been robbed of artistry. Marie's casket seemed to float in a riotous garden, and the plethora of floral tributes could be seen as belated apologies for chiding Marie about being a slave to her flowers.

It took a great deal of time and effort to grow anything less adaptable than Russian lilacs, hollyhocks, and pinks in eastern Montana. One summer, I'd heard a friend ask Marie why she wasted so much time growing things you couldn't eat and was impressed with her backhanded agreement. She'd said, yes, it could get to be a little work, but her voice and expression made it clear she pitied the woman for being so lazy.

Marie had believed hard work never hurt anybody and put her money where her mouth was. She'd never been afraid to get her hands dirty and, unless planning to go into town, dressed accordingly. It seemed wrong for her to spend eternity in the "Sunday go to meeting" clothes she couldn't wait to change out of as soon she'd donned them. I'd have rather she'd been laid out in her normal attire of men's western shirt, blue jeans, and beat-up cowboy boots. Even though, lying in that silky coffin, they'd have made her look like a tumbleweed on wedding cake.

I'd still been smiling at that image and imagining Marie grinning too when a sober-faced young man came over and ushered me to the third row of pews—behind her children, in-laws, grandchildren, nieces, and nephews. Her brother, a professional bronc rider I met only once, had passed on years earlier. I imagined them playing together as children and slid to the end of the pew under a stained glass angel rendering the sunlight into something less indifferent.

People continued to trickle in until even the space next to me was taken. Then the organist struck the first chord, and we fumbled through LBW hymnals to find the correct page. After our singing trailed off, the pastor began a lengthy Bible reading, followed by an even longer sermon. When he came up for air, our enthusiastic rendition of "Jesus, Lead Thou On" had a beseeching tone. Oblivious, he waited for dead silence and everyone's attention to rest on him then just cleared his throat, adjusted his glasses, and perused his notes. It seemed he'd been struck mute, but he opened his mouth and destroyed that happy notion.

The two church ladies I'd followed into the building were right about this guy being long-winded. He commenced the eulogy by saying he'd only been ac-quainted with Marie Leister Taylor for a short time and demonstrated his unfamiliarity with her and the rest of the community by anglicizing her German maiden name to Lester. On and on he droned, recit-ing what he'd been told or surmised about her—one or two items coincidently true, none interesting.

Or, as he would surely have phrased it, the man had articulated for forty-five minutes, perhaps more, perhaps less, without imparting anything of note, and the far, far too time-consuming, uninformed, uninspiring service he'd delivered didn't do the slightest justice to a wonderful, caring woman, but gave ample testament to the verbosity I'd overheard two women, members of his own congregation, ex-pressing unhappiness and regret over earlier that very same day.

Dear god that man could talk. My gaze drifted toward my nose, and his dull, tentative voice did nothing to keep me from worrying about the recent events at home. But it was the perfect time and place to beg for divine assistance, so I prayed Jill would keep her appointment with Phil on Saturday. By now, the obtuse reverend had encroached on the noon hour, and one brave soul in the restless congregation signaled him to wind things up.

He didn't understand or ignored the gesture and didn't stop talking till the coughing and clear-ing of throats overpowered his words. If it caused him to bring his vacuous sermon to an awkward, abrupt end, no one heard it. We'd stopped listening long before he stopped talking, and, whether by co-incidence or spirited intent, the final hymn, "Jesus Lives! The Victory's Won," once more articulated our sentiment. I thought about what Marie's reaction would've been, and we shared a silent laugh as the pews that had trickled full emptied like a breached dam.

We mourners, joyful and chatty as kids at recess, pressed into the wide hall then spilled into a large room filled with tables of food. At long last, we'd made it to the Promised Land. But there was a line, and I spent the time admiring the reception build-ing. Built in the twenties, it sported the eye-pleasing combination of white stucco walls, dark, heavily var-nished pine moldings, and bead-board wainscoting. Authenticating the room, a box of dusty kindling leaned against an old coal-fired kitchen stove, its curved, nickel-plated trim reflecting our faces like a funhouse mirror.

A wood-burning version of that same stove held center stage in the kitchen at our cabin. It reminded me we had to make damn certain the kids would be there this coming weekend regardless of Jill's shit-stirring. Otherwise, persuading Mike not to do a run-ner would only land him right in it. My angst soon ratcheted into dejection—too many strident voices and unfamiliar faces. It hadn't been easy to spot Karl and Darlene with him in a suit and her in a black dress, and, trapped by a circle of folks expressing sympathy, they could only smile and shrug anyway. So I found an empty chair, sat down, and relaxed a little when the elderly woman next to me asked a question.

"There wasn't even this many came for Mable Hanley's funeral, was there?"

But, before I could respond, she realized she'd asked a stranger, informed me I didn't even know Mable, as though the fact made me mentally deficient, then turned away and forked a little more food into her mouth. Sitting at that table felt doubly awkward after everyone finished eating, and I nearly cheered when Karl stood up and raised his country-singer voice to gain everyone's attention. Walter, sitting next to him, grimaced and scrutinized the gingham table cloth.

"As you all know, Mom won more than her share of blue ribbons every year. Especially for baked goods. And she put in some mighty long nightshifts in the kitchen getting ready for the fair. But I'll always remember her best being outdoors. Specially that day I saw her hell bent for leather on ole Rocket. I was only seven. But it's clear as yesterday.

"Her and Dad were riding out to check on the heifers...in a hurry...and told me and Walter to stay home. I had a real hankering to see them new calves, though, and got the bright idea of sneaking out of the house and following on foot. I didn't make it past the creek before I heard a horse coming at a hard gallop. It was Mom. And she never ran a horse like that for no reason, so I got to wondering if something happened to Dad. Then I realized she was reining straight at me and figured out too late I'd been pretty easy to spot in my red coat.

"I made a beeline for the house...but them hoof-beats just kept getting louder and louder. Mom never even hollered at me. She just snaked out a loop. And when it settled over my shoulders and that horse set up, I hit the ground so hard what little wind I had left got knocked plumb out of me.

"She kept me at the end of that rope, too, more down than up, all the way home. When we finally got to the house, she cut me some slack...but started re-coiling while I was still trying to get out of the damn loop! Didn't say a word the whole time. Just put that horse in a long trot and headed back out. And I tell you what. She sure as hell didn't have to look back to know I wasn't following her!"

Karl laughed harder than anyone then grabbed his hat and ducked out the side door. I turned in my chair and watched him through the window behind me. After strolling across the lawn, he stopped at the flower bed, pushed back his hat, and lifted his face to the sun. Moments later, Darlene joined him. He took her hand in his without shifting his skyward gaze, and I looked down at the box propping the door open. It was full of old Sunday school books, and the Jesus adorning the covers had a decidedly seventies look about him.

Pondering the ineffable lack of information about Christ's appearance, I didn't hear Becky approaching. When she tapped my arm and loudly offered a penny for my thoughts, I whipped around to face my accoster, caught my foot on the corner of the box, bent over to pick up the spilled books, and the door swung shut against my head. Becky tried not to laugh but failed spectacularly. Then Walter and his entourage came over to see what had caused all the ruckus.

This being klutzy thing hadn't happened since the eighth grade right after we'd moved to Missoula. Back then, the colliding with doorways, getting tangled in my own feet, and dropping school books in hallways came from being an outsider in yet another new school. My current edginess stemmed from valid fear and worry but still made me feel like an oaf. I tried hard not to show it, waited for Becky to control her laughter, then answered her question with something of a lie because, while true, it wasn't what I'd been thinking about.

"I was just mulling over how many friends Marie had here, and how we'd always agreed there isn't a better place to live."

Becky felt compelled to verify my statement, and I understood why. Compliments offered about this part of the state are about ninety percent hogwash, about ninety percent of the time.

"Lynn really does like it around here. Might even move here someday."

That's when her "I'm six years old now" grandson looked me straight in the eye and let me know in no uncertain terms where I stood on that score.

"My dad says, even if you move here...you'll still never be one of us."

Open-mouthed silence rolled in like a tidal wave. I gritted my teeth, produced a kids-will-be-kids smile, and walked outside before anyone could catch their breath to say anything.

The brat had exposed an insufferable truth, and to hell with Rimrock County. I liked the idea of moving to northeastern Montana better anyhow—less people and more space. I turned to glare at the church and saw Karl smiling and waving his hat as he walked toward me. Then, as had happened too often since coming back to Red Bend, I wanted to run into his arms and stay there until he made the pain from the insult and everything else happening in my life go away.

"There you are, Lynn. Anything wrong?"

"No. Just needed a little fresh air."

"Say, folks are trying to carpool out to the cemetery. I told Walter I'd hitch a ride with you...if that's okay."

Okay? It was a lot more than okay. He'd just saved me from a long, lonely, miserable drive.

"Of course it is. Love the company. But I've decided not to come all the way back here. I'll take off right after the funeral and spend the night in Miles. You can easily get a ride home, though, right?"

"Oh yeah, no problem. But dang, Lynn. Woulda been nice having you around a little longer. What's the rush?"

"Want a list?"

"That bad, huh?"

"Yeah. Things started unraveling soon as I left."

"Works like that, doesn't it?"

"Sure does."

"Well, Lynn, can't thank you enough...for coming all this way and everything. Seeing you meant the world to Mom."

"And seeing *her* meant the world to me, Karl."

We'd reached my truck, and he held my hand for so brief a time I could've imagined it.

"Hey, Karl, before you open that door, let me clear the front seat off. My usual passenger rides in back in his carseat."

I opened the passenger door, pulled the sticky notes off the dash, grabbed my jacket, gloves, tape measure, and a box full of job folders, then dumped the whole works in the back seat next to my duffle bag.

"Didn't mean for you to have to move your office."

"That's about right, too."

I laughed, happy to catch even a glimpse of Karl's grinning, joking self again. When we got in, he moved his seat back about a foot, and I couldn't deny the man looked good there.

"Nice truck, Lynn. You like it?"

"Yeah, I do. Ordered the 325 horse. Does great towing on the highway. And...way too much of the time...that's what I'm doing now days."

"Say, Lynn, why doncha take that first road off to your right, and we won't have to eat dust all the way to the cemetery. Sure get tongues wagging, though."

He was right. I checked the mirror in time to see a bald man stare at my truck so intently he nearly ran his old Dodge station wagon into the back of Walter and Becky's brand spanking new Ford Expedition. I wouldn't have wished that heap on anyone—served them right, though, for having such a mouthy grandson. I hoped to god Karl hadn't heard about me being wounded by a child. I didn't want to think, much less talk, about it. And we had forty miles, most of them over dirt roads, between us and the old cemetery northwest of Marie's ranch. But even if he knew, Karl had other things on his mind, and at some point during the long, dusty ride he decided to confide in me.

"Darlene got some bad news yesterday."

His voice broke with anguish, and he turned his face toward the side window before continuing.

"She found a lump in her breast last week...went in for an X-ray. Now they want to do a biopsy."

That explained how he'd acted at Becky and

Walter's house the previous evening and why Darlene had been so torn up.

"Oh god, Karl!"

Damn. Was that the best I could do? He'd just told me his wife might have cancer. What could anyone have said, though?

"Bad enough, Karl. But a helluva thing to find out the same day your mother died."

"Yeah...Darlene's doctor called while you and I were out at the ranch. I knew she had something on her mind when she phoned about supper. But I never expected to come home to a shock like that. We can't understand it. She had some kind of supposedly better digital mammogram just last November. And it came out okay."

"They'll have caught it early then...if that's even what she has."

"That's just it. The lump isn't all that small. But it's only been six months since they said she was fine... so what the hell?"

"Makes you wonder, doesn't it. Is there really any early detection of cancer? I mean when it's only a few cells...no need for chemo or radiation after surgery. Not a comforting thought. Sorry."

I hadn't needed to add the apology. He looked grateful, like a kid whose best friend just admitted they were afraid of monsters under the bed too.

"It sure as hell does make you wonder, Lynn. And they should've been looking harder. And been more careful too...especially where Darlene's concerned."

"How so?"

"She's from Nevada. What they call a down-winder. Grew up in the heaviest radioactive fallout from A-bomb testing. A big risk factor. Most of them women end up with breast cancer. Even the ones like her that ain't smokers or drinkers...and don't have it running in their family or nothing like that."

"My god! Are they owning up to what they did?"

"Hell no! This is the government we're talking about."

"Yeah...forgot about that."

"Oh, and mum's the word out at the cemetery, Lynn. We haven't told anyone yet."

"They won't hear about it from me."

"Appreciate that. They're doing the biopsy this afternoon in Miles. Wanted to go along but Darlene had a fit...not about to let me miss Mom's burial. Said it's a really simple procedure. Be over before she knows it. Then she'll head home."

"Darlene's a strong woman."

"Yes, she is. They'll all be wondering why she's not with us. I'm just gonna say she ate something that didn't agree with her. Everyone will find out soon enough if it's...oh god, Lynn. I can't stand the thought of her going through what Mom did."

We tossed around the usual optimistic statements—might be benign, newer treatments, her otherwise good health, her being a fighter who'd make it if anyone could—until they'd worn thin, thin enough to see through. Then, after a long silence, Karl told me the story of Lame Johnny Cemetery.

A man, known only as Lame Johnny, lived all alone in a dugout where the cemetery came to be. He couldn't ride and didn't even own a packhorse but managed to eke out a living as a trapper. His nearest neighbors were the Greenlee brothers, homesteading seven miles to the south. Whenever they went to Red Bend, they picked up Lame Johnny's latest bundle of hides, sold them, then used the money to buy his supplies and delivered them on the way home.

On one such trip, the brothers discovered Lame Johnny halfway up the snowy creek bank, less than a quarter mile from his dwelling, with his water buckets still hooked to the neck yoke. The debilitated man had died when he fell on a rock jutting from the clay and it embedded itself in his forehead. The two men were pretty sure he'd been caught outside the previous day when a storm dumped two feet of heavy wet snow over the area in as many hours.

They loaded his body in their wagon, took it to his dugout, then rummaged through the place for a Bible, letter, anything inscribed with his last name. When nothing turned up, they buried him beside his home, carved *Lame Johnny, Victim of a low snow in May, 1923* on a board taken from his bed, and it marks his grave to this day.

The wretched man must've led a lonely, pain-filled life, and maybe death had been as welcome as his bed every night. He had nothing worth hauling away except his latest cache of hides, and the Greenlee brothers went ahead and sold them. But they didn't keep the money; they placed it in the collection plate of the new Red Bend Bethel Lutheran Church one Sunday, along with a map of where they'd buried the poor fellow and a letter explaining how he died. Lame Johnny's dugout home soon fell back into the prairie, but the Greenlee brothers' kindness and honesty had memorialized him. Not a day goes by in Rimrock County that someone doesn't mention Lame Johnny Creek, Lame Johnny Cemetery, or the old Lame Johnny School.

Karl had timed the story perfectly, and it ended at the cemetery. The small graveyard, differing little from the rest of the landscape, is protected from livestock by barbed wire and from everything else by endless acres of unbroken prairie. A black Ford Econoline van, marked *Krieg & Olsen Funeral Home*, waited at a freshly dug, rectangular hole framed in bright green outdoor carpeting, and Karl reached for the door handle.

"Well, guess I better get over there."

I watched him walk away then restored my passenger-seat office and reinforced my flimsy dress clothes with a jacket before visiting Lame Johnny's grave. It was near the gate, and a distinct humming came from the entrance sign over the road. Tallest thing for miles around, it consisted of a sheet of metal with LAME JOHNNY CEMETERY written large by a cutting torch, and the breeze blowing through the letters created complex, voice-like sounds. I had no idea how many minutes passed, five or thirty, before I heard Karl softly saying my name. He didn't walk right up to me either, but reached out and gently laid a hand on my shoulder first, treating me like a skittish horse. It made me laugh.

"Hey, Lynn...what's so funny? Just didn't want to spook you like I did at Mom's house."

"And I appreciate it. Thank you."

"You're welcome."

I reached for his hand then noticed people looking our way and settled for brushing it with my fingertips. Karl stared at the ground and used the sides of his polished dress boots to push a mound of loose dirt and rocks back down a gopher hole.

"Damn...gotta get some kid out here with a rifle."

Then he looked up and trained his brown eyes on his mother's gravesite.

"Ya know, Lynn, it seems kinda odd...Mom and Dad being side by side again after all these years. What about your folks? Where are they buried?"

"Bought two plots in a cemetery along Mullan Road west of Missoula. Only time I ever knew them to plan ahead. Loved the view. Place is surrounded by subdivisions now, but they're graveyards too, in a way. With street signs for headstones...like Elk Lane, Pheasant Way, Bluebell Road, Juneberry Court."

"You sound just plain fed up with Missoula."

"Yeah. Think I am."

"Oh, and by the way, Lynn. If you do find a place up in those northern hinterlands...try your damnedest to get the mineral rights. Doubt they'll even have 'em. But you never know."

Walter had limped over to the open grave and stood on the carpet, waving Karl over then shouting through cupped hands.

"Hey! Get over here! The pastor wants to talk to us."

Parting with Karl brought more pain than expected. And our embrace lasted a moment longer than made it easy to let go.

"Bye, Karl. Thanks for yesterday. Say goodbye to Darlene for me. Tell her I'll be thinking of her. And please call to let me know how things are going...or if you just want to talk. And tell Becky and Walter goodbye for me too, if you would. I'm taking off soon as the service is over. There's a storm headed our way."

Clouds, like mounds of purple bread dough, dwarfed the western edge of the world, and the wind carried the smell of rain falling miles away. I picked my way through the tombstones and stopped behind the people gathered ten deep around Marie's grave. But, as the service began, couples, families, and friends drew together, giving me a clear line of sight to the casket, its shiny dome mirroring the last trace of clear blue sky.

Shouting over a boom of thunder, the pastor announced he'd be keeping the service short and astounded everyone by sticking to his word. As I walked away, the rising wind lifted whispers of Karl's cologne from my hair, and it lingered in the cab too. A small pleasure sullied by recalling how Jill's rank perfume had permeated everything in Mike's truck the day we rescued Bryan in Remount. And I swore— on Marie's memory—that, come hell or high water, Jill would be eradicated from our lives.

In my rearview mirror, people were exchanging hugs and handshakes, and I was glad to miss out on all that. Revisiting Marie's home, her people, her way of life, always just out of reach, had dredged up every distress and desire connected to them, and it hurt like hell. Even driving into a storm sounded better than staying, but the rain had been and gone before I reached the scoria road. Washed clean, it was a river of embers flowing into a periwinkle blue heaven and Marie.

She might not have liked seeing that road there, though. Like everyone else in the area, she had a love-hate relationship with the material keeping the gumbo roads passable year-round. Scoria, ancient clay fired in perpetually burning coal seams, makes inexpensive road surfacing material. But, much like shards of terra cotta when first laid down, it can lame a shod horse or puncture a new truck tire before the rubber hair has worn off. Another drawback is how soon scoria degrades into a powder that reverts to sticky, slippery clay as soon as it gets wet, an annoying and sometimes dangerous cycle.

There's no way to travel these roads without orange dust or orange mud covering every inch of your vehicle, and it works its way into the tiniest orifice. I'd be discovering the stuff in unexpected places for as long as I owned the truck. There were thirty miles of scoria ahead of me, no matter which route I decided to take. The prairie's a land of options, and there's always more than one way to get where you want to go.

I chose the gravel road leading to Highway 59, lush irrigated fields on my left and arid, sheep-shorn prairie on my right all the way to Miles City. When five-acre minifarms crept into the landscape, my cellphone beeped to let me know it had a connection to the world again, and I dutifully checked for messages or missed calls. There weren't any. A good sign Jill wasn't raising more hell. I called the motel to confirm my reservation, and prospects of enjoying a quiet evening in a nice place were increasing.

Miles is a bona fide cow-town, with nothing you don't want, everything you do, and no waiting in line to get it. The Yellowstone River drains twenty-two million acres and flows seven hundred miles to get there then makes itself right at home and even hosts the city park. Yet it's the bluff overlooking the wide, muddy river that defines Miles City. And atop that magnificent sandstone cliff sprawls an incredible two-story apartment complex of flamingo-pink concrete—Art Moderne gone native.

Phil is acquainted with the owner, something to do with his work. He'd stopped to see her once when I was with him, and she gave me a tour of the voluptuous structure, inside and out. I'd adored every square foot and would never stop envying the woman, and not because Phil admired her and hadn't minded telling me how much.

"You'll like her, Lynn. She's stunning, but also one of the most interesting and intelligent people you'll ever meet."

No, I wasn't green-eyed over the praise Phil had showered on her. I coveted her ownership and habitation of such an awe-inspiring building. But I didn't know her well enough to be sheltered there and had to make do with a motel that, of course, wasn't any such thing. It came with the freeway and consisted of three floors of rooms intersected by a hallway. A hotel in everything but name, and I wouldn't be parking anywhere near my door. The dusty, black lava rock entrance did offer two spectacular hanging baskets of pink and white, striped petunias, though.

I pressed my nose into the cool blossoms and drew in the scent of spice and velvety horse nostrils. If I'd stayed outside, the place wouldn't have disappointed me. The young woman behind the desk, elbows resting on the counter, cheekbones resting in her palms, continued waving her freshly painted fingernails in the air and gazing at the cowboy clock on the wall like it was Billy Ray Cyrus. I cleared my throat.

"Oh, hi. You must be Lynn? Right? Talked to you on the phone? Right?"

I nodded. She looked at the registration pad and pen in front of her then contemplated her wet nails. Rather than waiting for the green polish to dry, I helped myself to the form, filled it in, and earned her enthusiastic, albeit short-lived, gratitude. I don't like elevators, anyway, and this one made noises that don't inspire confidence. But schlepping my duffel bag up the stairs held no appeal. I'd asked for the top floor so footsteps overhead wouldn't wake me in case I managed to get to sleep despite bad plumbing, thin walls, and blaring TVs.

My room, as generic as the lobby, had a view of the parking lot and a Chinese restaurant. Why couldn't I be standing in one of those heavenly apartments up on the cliff, with nothing on my mind and nothing to do but watch the town light up as the night came down? I'd imagined myself there so successfully that I almost flung the phone across the room when it vibrated in my hand.

"Guess what, Mom...Dad's here. He's staying with Mike at your place. You must have known he was coming. Why didn't you tell us?"

"He wanted to surprise you."

"Well he definitely did. And took us all out to dinner. I asked him to stay and spend the weekend at the cabin with us. He said he couldn't, though. Has to be in Helena on Saturday to pick up a client at the airport. Said he should be able to join us on Monday, though."

Phil didn't like lying to our children any more than I did, but some truths were off limits and always would be.

"Oh, and how was the funeral, Mom?"

"Okay. Enormous turnout of people at the church. And the flowers! You've never seen so many in one place. Wish you could've seen the cemetery, too. Just perfect, out in the middle of the prairie with nothing around for miles."

"Sounds nice."

"It was."

"Say, Mom. Not to change the subject...but did Dad tell you he's taking the enclosed trailer back to Helena with him?"

"Yeah, honey. I think he did mention it."

"He said to tell you he'll bring it back with him next time he comes over. Just needs to get rid of some trash."

Phil's little joke made me smile, and the call ended on an upbeat note. My good mood survived a dirty shower curtain but disappeared with the hot water. It ran out before I'd rinsed the shampoo from my hair, and being forced to take a cold shower left me ticked off and ravenous.

So, barefoot, shivering, and wearing only a tee shirt over a ratty pair of sweat pants, I snuck down the hall to the vending machine. I made it back to the room with an armload of chips, candy bars, juice, and water without anyone seeing me—only to end up standing outside the door searching my pockets for the keycard I'd left lying on the desk. Damn it, what happened to my peaceful evening? Stacking my make-do meal against the door, I sprinted for the elevator, and, hallelujah, it was empty.

The lobby wasn't, however, and everyone stared—everyone except the ungrateful girl behind the desk. I'd saved her newly painted nails from ruination. How could she leave me standing in line barefoot and bedraggled? Unwilling to draw more curiosity by cutting in front of everyone to plead my case, I waited, fumed, and worked out exactly what I'd say to her. But, by the time she handed me a new keycard, fifteen extremely uncomfortable minutes later, getting back to my room mattered more than pointing out her abysmal front desk skills.

I scurried to the elevator, filled with other passengers this time, and an overdressed saleswoman backed into a corner as if I were a rabid dog. God knows what she thought when the doors slid open and I took off full speed down the hall because I could hear my cellphone blaring The Beatles' tune *Help!*

Amy had talked me into buying that ringtone—absolutely perfect, she said—and I kept it loud enough to hear over saws, drills, and hammering so I wouldn't forget to turn it up again. The phone stopped blaring just as I unlocked the door, but restarted while I stumbled over the drinks and snacks, and I got to it before it quit again. Mike sounded excited, but not in a happy way.

"Mom, you will not believe this."

I thought, yes, with the way things were going, I probably would. After kicking my hard-won supper into the room and closing the door, I flopped down on the bed and ingested the latest news.

"Dad watched Bryan so I could come home and pack a few more things. And guess what I—"

"Wait. You're at home!? Jesus, Mike! What if Jill shows up?"

"No worries, Mom. I parked out by the river where she can't see my truck. And I'd be able to sneak out the back door before she even got in the house. Anyway, decided to have a snoop around her room while I had the chance. Guess what I found?"

"What?"

"Money. Thirty thousand!"

"No way!"

"Yup. Right here in my hand...nice neat stack of hundred dollar bills."

"Wonder where she got it? Why didn't she put it in the bank?"

"Dunno. It wasn't even hidden. Just in the drawer with a bunch of scarves."

"What the hell?"

"Blows your mind, doesn't it?"

Not as much as I pretended it did. Probably pay-off money, Phil and I figured Jill had a small army of henchmen working for her ever since I'd overheard that conversation in Helena. And the man named Danny had said Jill always came through for him, so the money could've been a recent payment from him too.

"Wonder if that money is coming...or going?"

"No idea, Mom. But it might mean there's something I could get over on that bitch. Then I wouldn't need to skip the country."

Before I could open my mouth to encourage that idea, Mike began working through the flaws in his reasoning.

"Naw, probably not. It's just money. Doesn't prove anything. She's too damn careful to do something that would let me get custody of Bryan."

"But it could be worth a shot, Mike. You never know. She might've slipped up somewhere."

I didn't really believe it but wanted to give him another reason not to leave town.

"Yeah. Maybe so. Might be time to try and find out *everything* that's going on with that bitch. Hire a detective. Get some independent proof."

Oh dear god, what had I done? That's all Phil and I needed, some private dick following Jill to her meeting with Phil in Helena. Mike's idea had to be expunged immediately.

"No, Mike. That'd be way, way too risky. You could hire a friend-of-a-friend of hers without even knowing it. Why not talk to your dad? He can find someone you can trust. Otherwise, hiring a detective is a weapon that could blow up in your face."

"Yeah...about be my luck, too. I'll wait and check with Dad."

Another fire put out, for as long as it mattered anyway. But I wanted a recommitment to the promise Mike gave me that morning.

"You're still not going anywhere just yet...right, honey?"

"Yeah...talked it over with Dad again tonight. And it does make more sense to wait awhile. It's just... standing here holding this pile of cash makes me think now's the time. Be sweet to make that bitch foot the bill."

"Yes it would. But put it back. And don't make yourself crazy wondering what Jill's up to. Like I said before, not likely she'll take Bryan again. Or why didn't she just keep him? Apparently she's got bigger fish to fry. Go home, though, would ya...before she shows up. And try not to worry."

Whether he bought my theory or not, being worried didn't begin to describe his emotional state. He left the carpeted bedroom but, instead of getting out of the house, began pacing the dining room. His footsteps echoed on the hickory floor, and I could hear him repeatedly picking things up then setting them down—searching for answers he'd never find.

"Why did I ever get involved with her, Mom? Now everyone's life is ruined because of my stupidity."

I had the power to strip away my son's guilt, tell him it hadn't been bad judgment, rotten luck, or carelessness that got him into this, let him know he'd been targeted—a perilous, self-serving revelation that couldn't happen. We both had to endure his misconceptions until, maybe one day, I could tell him at least that part of the story. In the meantime, I could only try to reason away his self-recriminations.

"You weren't stupid, Mike. Nice guys don't stand a chance against women like Jill. For now at least, just be glad she doesn't have Bryan."

"I am, Mom. Every time I look at him."

We said goodnight, then I fretted about Jill's reason for having that money. Her problems became ours if they stopped her from being in Helena on Saturday. That worry and the shock of Mike going back to his house had ruined my appetite. I was stowing my vending machine meal, bags of chips getting flatter and flatter, in my duffle bag when Amy phoned.

"Did Mike tell you about finding that money, Mom?"

"Yeah, he did. Pretty damn strange. Even for Jill."

"It really is. Do you think it has something to do with why she's not home? And why she didn't keep Bryan?"

"It could, Amy. And we can be damn thankful if it did. But it's still worrying."

"Jeez, I know. That's what Paul and I were thinking. That there's something shady going on, and it could come down on Mike...guilty by association. The people Jill hangs around with are sleazeballs. Don't care how important they think they are."

Sleazeballs? A generous assessment of Jill's friends. She'd ingratiated herself with a clique of cocaine-sniffing ex-jocks and their cheerleaders whose values and morals had pinnacled in college. We managed to run a successful business without pandering to these two-bit power brokers, and it had gotten much easier when the demand for housing swamped their old boy network. Then they could no longer manipulate every single planning board decision in their favor, and the playing field sloped considerably less.

When Jill finally accepted the fact Mike, Amy, and Paul wanted nothing to do with her new friends because they didn't like or respect them and sure as hell didn't trust them, she'd turned the situation to her advantage. Hosting dinner parties, playing golf, and attending events without involving Mike, or anyone else in the family, gave her more opportunity to vilify him.

The reason she'd gone to all the trouble to collect and mislead these enamored officials, businessmen, and professionals had only become apparent after

I'd tumbled to her plans to appropriate our land. They were there to grease her battlewagon. And Amy, without even knowing about Jill's Machiavellian plan, had come to understand her malevolent nature.

"Remember that argument we got into, Mom? Happened my first year in college. The psych professor told us evil didn't exist. That it's just a point of view. When I mentioned what he'd said, you called it BS. Just another way of saying if you don't mind, it don't matter. And you told me if everyone thought like that...we'd be on a fast track to devolution."

A vague memory, but I listened and knew she would be combing her fingers through her hair, lifting the straight, smooth strands then letting them fall to her shoulders again and again. My daughter had been using used her blond locks to sift through her troubles since she was three years old.

"Well, Mom, you were right. Good and evil are real. They're not just adjectives. And Jill isn't crazy. Never lived through some horrific childhood. Isn't a raging alcoholic or a drug addict. She's just plain evil."

"Yes she is, Amy. Through and through. And not the find-it-in-your-own-backyard garden variety either."

"I know. And I shouldn't say this, Mom. And I wouldn't say it to anyone else...not even Paul...but I hope she's not home because she's laying dead somewhere. Not optimistic about that, though. Not unless she misses Bryan's doctor appointment tomorrow."

"You still think she'll show up just to playact the good mommy?"

"Afraid so. And act is the right word, too. She doesn't even want to hold Bryan until the doctor walks in. Then she stretches out her hands with those long fake nails and makes some comment like 'Come back to your Mommy now.' I'm surprised Bryan even goes to her. And he wouldn't...if he didn't like getting his hands on her hair so much. You should see her trying to untangle his fingers without revealing her true colors. It's all I can do not to burst out laughing."

"I bet."

"And whenever the doctor asks Jill a question, I have to answer it for her. And after Bryan gets his shots, it's *me* he wants. Not her. But the doctor is always too busy trying to impress her to notice any of that. And he shouldn't even be the one giving vaccinations...his nurse normally does that. Guess he can't tear himself away. What is it about women like Jill anyway?"

"Amy, I've been wondering that since seventh grade. And, later on, even asked men. If they know, they're not telling."

"Well, I don't understand it at all."

And she wasn't likely to. Why men are drawn to women like Jill is an everlasting, antagonizing mystery. I told my daughter not to feel bad for wanting that woman dead, we all did, then said goodnight. Fatigue had smothered my burning curiosity about the money Mike found. I flopped into bed just as my cellphone gave a pre-ring vibration and clattered against the nightstand. Mike again, sounding spent, but not angry or at his wits' end. I sat up, stacked all the pillows against the wall, then fell against them.

"Dad thought I'd better call and let you know I'm safely back at your house."

"Thanks, I'll sleep better now. You got out of there without Jill showing up, then?"

"Yep. She musta taken off somewhere."

"Must have. So relax. Get some rest. Talk to your dad while you can. And thanks for calling...even if it wasn't your idea."

Mike's sad laugh made me feel bad for teasing him. I took it out on the pillows then slipped under the covers. But the cheap sheets came untucked the first time I rolled over, then, just as the sandman made a tentative move in my direction, a man banged into the room next door.

He went directly to bed, but only quit snoring when he coughed, and I was miserably aware there were only inches of un-insulated wall between his head and mine. Retreating to my pickup for a few hours sleep seemed like a good idea. Then I remembered the freeway exit ramp and the open-twenty-four-hours truck stop across the street and stayed where I was.

There'd be another miserable night in a motel, too, before I could go home, be in my own bed, and support the kids in person instead of by phone. I couldn't imagine Phil needing my help to get the enclosed trailer ready or needing any help the next day, on Saturday, either. But not being able to imagine it didn't mean it wouldn't happen. Life had often gone out of its way to teach me that lesson.

In the end, exhaustion won out, and sleep carried me off to a nightmare. I was with Marie. We were horseback on her government land, just the two of us, on a hot, blustery summer afternoon. A terrible day to be working cattle made worse because she'd worn her square dancing outfit. No matter how well she tied the wide flared skirt and crinoline petticoats with the saddle strings, or wound them around her thighs, or tucked them between the stirrup leathers and her knees, the slick material worked loose, flapping in the strong wind, spooking the herd again and again.

When Marie accepted defeat and left me in charge, I cried and begged her not to go, told her the wind would go down and everything would be okay, told her I couldn't keep the herd together without her help. But my tears, promises, and supplications didn't stop her. She gathered the reins and rode for home at a high lope, turquoise ruffles undulating around her as though she were being consumed by an oceanic predator.

Then a thunderous bang—in the dream or in the real world—woke me, and panic faded in the light of consciousness. Skin clammy, heart racing, I sat up, saw it was only three o'clock, turned the pillows over, and, this time, drifted into oblivion.

FRIDAY

Wishing pestilence and poverty on the loudmouths letting doors bang shut out in the hallway, I got out of bed and opened the curtains. The few thin clouds blemishing the sky were vaporizing like contrail. Cheered by that snip of good fortune, I dressed, grabbed a banana from the breakfast room on the way out, and let the breeze draw me to a nearby espresso stand. My double, almond latte, being the first to scald my lips since leaving home Tuesday, tasted like the best ever handed to me.

I'd missed the energizing, creamy comfort in a cup, took sip after sip as the truck powered up to freeway speed, and, despite fresh air and a high, blue ceiling, reverted to my Missoula life. Cellphone coverage disappeared ten minutes out of Miles City, but my phone rang anyway. I stopped on the shoulder of the interstate to hang on to that aberrant band of coverage and flipped open the phone. Amy sobbed out two words.

"Oh, Mom!"

"What happened?"

"It was awful!"

"What was awful?"

"Bryan's doctor appointment!"

"Oh no! Is he okay?"

"Yeah. He's fine. It isn't that."

She blew her nose, sniffed twice, then the sound of her new bentwood rocker swishing over the carpet resumed.

"What is it, honey? Tell me."

"It's Jill! She...she almost took Bryan!"

Now what? Just two more days, that's all we needed. I turned on the hazard lights and helped my daughter pull herself together long enough to tell me what happened.

"Amy, take a deep breath, and start at the beginning."

"Okay. Well...uh...Jill missed Bryan's appointment. And I was so happy. But after...when we were leaving...she was out there in the hall. So I figured, good, she got the time wrong. I never thought—"

"Just take another deep breath, Amy. And don't hurry."

I'd said those last three words while praying the cell coverage held. But finally, rocking a little faster with each word, Amy spit out what happened.

"Oh, Mom! Jill tried to pull Bryan out of my arms! Said something came up yesterday. But now she could take him. Said maybe for quite a while! He wouldn't go to her, though, bless his heart...he hung on to my neck and screamed. And I don't mean he cried. I mean he really screamed. I couldn't let her take him, Mom. I just couldn't. But I couldn't stop her either. So I exaggerated everything and said Bryan would be really, really sick after his shots. Be feverish and cry constantly and not sleep. Told her she'd be a whole lot better off waiting till morning."

"That was quick thinking."

"I thought it must've worked too. But I'm not sure she heard a word I said. She had this creepy smile on her face and said, 'Never mind, I have a better idea.' Then she just walked off."

"My god, Amy. What the devil is—"

"I couldn't stop shaking, Mom. And I ran down the hallway to that little waiting room by the lab. You know...the one you can't find even when you know where it is. I was afraid to go back to the parking lot by myself. So I called Paul and had him come get us. Not Mike...in case Jill was still hanging around."

Amy's breathing sounded closer to normal, and the furious rocking slowed.

"Coverage is bad here, honey. Might lose you. So don't worry if we get disconnected."

"Okay. But before we do...you think Bryan remembered Jill nabbing him on Wednesday? And that's why he wanted absolutely nothing to do with her this time."

"Could be."

"Oh, Jeez, Mom. Thank god she didn't take him today. What made her change her mind so quick, though? And that 'Never mind, I have a better idea' makes my blood run cold. We cannot let that horrid woman take Bryan. Not ever again. Not that Mike would let it happen. Not now that he's forewarned."

If Amy believed her brother could prevent the worst from happening, I wasn't going to point out why he couldn't. Knowing the exact temperature of the hot water we were in wouldn't help her cope. She took a big gamble caring for Bryan, and anted up another piece of her heart every day.

"How's your brother taking it? Is he still going to wait for me to get home?"

"I think so. Paul and I—"

A pack of semis blew past, the truck shivered, and Amy was gone. I tried calling her, but the ring croaked and reverberated as if I'd phoned from another dimension. Then it stopped, and the line went dead. Cussing Jill, cellphone companies, and the world in general, I checked my mirrors and accelerated into the traffic.

Amy's news incubated virulent possibilities. I loaded my Ravel CD, let *Bolero* beat down the chaos of the miserable present and murky future, and withdrew to the distant past, where time had taken the edge off reality. Scrutinizing that impotent landscape like a spy in enemy territory, I settled on early autumn 1961, a time when Dad grabbed his rifle a few nights a week and the two of us went hunting.

Mom stayed home on those freezer-filling outings. There were no fights to put up with, and, because hitting a bird's head with a .22 isn't easy, Dad didn't get too drunk—good as it got. I was a gangly ten-year-old that year, honing my driving skills on gravel roads while Dad, squinting into fields painted gold by the setting sun, looked for sage hen, grouse, or pheasant. Hunting speed meant staying in second gear, but it hadn't been boring.

I'd divided my attention between spotting a bird's oval head breaking the geometry of stubble-wheat, avoiding chuckholes, and noticing when Dad drained another beer. If he had, I would veer toward the shoulder of the road while he wrapped his fingers around the neck of the bottle and sent another empty spinning and sparkling through the twilight. If, on some rare occasion, it didn't land in the center of the barrow pit, I'd be sent out to retrieve it.

Even my alcoholic father had ethics. So what dark strand of genetics produced a woman like Jill? A person who ruins lives, even her own son's, and probably only for the thrill of it. At least Phil and I knew why she'd pounced on us. I pitied Mike and Amy, and Paul too, still as bewildered and as frustrated about the caustic events dissolving our lives as they'd been one particularly humiliating night the previous summer.

———

Mike usually took his son along when he worked weekends, but a rush job halfway up Rock Creek isn't a good time or place to have a baby along for the ride. He and Paul were leaving at four in the morning, Amy would be watching Bryan, and it made things easier on her and quicker for Mike if they just stayed the night. We'd be slowed down enough as it was.

The narrow road beside Rock Creek had held its ground between mountainsides and the boulder-strewn water for over a hundred years, but tourists and fisherman inch along as though it might crumble beneath them any second. A grievous annoyance when time is money. The job to deconstruct a century-old barn needed to get done over the weekend so it didn't slow down our regular work. We'd only bid it for the salvage rights.

For the roof beams, sure, but mostly for the walls—wide quarter-sawn boards you can't beg, buy, borrow, or steal anymore. The timber required to mill such lumber is a thing of the past, and the surface of those boards could never be reproduced anyhow. The sides weathered by sun, wind, snow, and rain were soft and gray as eiderdown, and the sides rubbed smooth by hides, horns, hay, and gloved knuckles resembled the yellowed keys of an old piano.

That irreplaceable lumber ended up costing more than overtime pay, though. Forgetting what could happen, Mike told Jill he and Bryan were spending the night at Paul and Amy's house. She showed up around midnight, loud and welcome as

The Blitz. They awoke to the roar of an engine at full throttle, squealing tires, screeching brakes, and what sounded like someone trying to beat a horn to death.

Mike and Paul tore outside, with Amy on their heels, and witnessed Jill's fancy Lexus SUV coming to a stop with its bumper one coat of paint past the garage door. She got out and stood beside it, her diamond tennis bracelets flashing in the motion detector light as she waved away the acrid smoke from burning rubber. The foul air did nothing to hinder her megaphone voice, however, and it carried into the returning stillness like a tardy warning siren.

"You bring my son out here right now. Or I'll come in there and get him. He's only nine months old. He needs to be at home. Not packed around in a truck every weekend like a dog. And to god knows where at night."

Jill spewed these imaginative denigrations in hopes someone would repeat her words to the police if they showed up, and she had no shortage of listeners. People congregated in the cul-de-sac like it was a warm day in January. Amy went into the house to check on Bryan, but the drag strip noises hadn't interrupted his baby sleep. When she returned to find even more gawking neighbors on her front lawn, she told them they could help most by going home; everything was okay—nothing for them to be concerned about.

They lingered anyway. Her nosy neighbor, Greg, wearing a robe, compression stockings, slippers, and a Griz baseball cap, leaned against the split rail fence separating their lawns, took another sip of beer, and said he'd decide for himself whether things were okay or not. The meddlesome man, aching to be a hero and call the cops, wouldn't be saving anyone. He'd just be putting a baby in harm's way.

The police automatically hand kids over to their mother in these situations, and Mike had learned trying to stop that from happening would only land you in a squad car. Worst of all, cops show up in pairs, and at least one of them would be male. Jill would look into his eyes, as hers filled with tears, and deliver her lies up close and personal. She could cut a man's IQ in half whenever she needed to. And it wasn't going to be long before someone called 911 and let her prove it.

Thinking on his feet is not Mike's forte, but his wife's little black dress and makeup told him she didn't plan to spend the night with a baby. She'd created the outrageous spectacle to drive home the fact she could take his son away from him whenever she liked—and to pinch back any new growth on the stump of self-respect she'd left him. He called her bluff.

"Okay, Jill. You win. I'm damn sure not going home, though. So, if you want Bryan, you'll have to take him with you."

Mike tossed his keys to Paul, asked him to get the carseat out of the truck, then turned to his sister and told her to go in the house and get Bryan. She was horrified until her brother rubbed his right temple with his left hand, their childhood signal to play along. Amy nodded but didn't budge. Jill glared. Paul clenched his fist tighter around the keys he'd caught and waited. Mike held his ground, terrified *his* bluff would be called. It got real quiet.

Then Jill looked at her watch, gave Mike a smile that promised a holocaust of revenge, and departed as violently as she'd arrived. Amy ran into the house and the neighbors dispersed, but Mike and Paul stayed outside to witness Jill's retreat, watching until, brake lights flaring, she'd bullied the Lexus around the sharp turn at the end of Saint Michael's Way. Paul contemplated the empty street then spoke in a voice so cold and unfamiliar it startled Mike.

"I'd give an awful lot to hear that woman take her last breath."

I'd been told the details of what happened that night many times. Mike took refuge in the battle he'd won whenever expectation of winning the war against his wife receded to a bright spot on a past horizon. But that sweet, single victory couldn't keep the hope drum beating forever, and his sister's encounter with Jill outside the doctor's office would have Mike ready to up stakes and run again.

Amy had her own reasons for preventing her brother from fleeing, though, and with Paul's help might've succeeded. It took forty-five minutes to get within range of a cell tower. But, when I did, Amy had the news I'd been hoping for, and I phoned Mike to hear it again from him.

"No, Mom, I'm not going to break my promise. But it's a hundred times harder to stay after what that bitch said to Amy outside the doctor's office this morning. I can't make any sense of it. Starting to wonder if she's doing drugs like the people she hangs around with. Jesus! Maybe that's what the money—"

"Don't even think it! Anyway, whatever else she is...she's no addict. I don't think she'd give up that much control."

"No...she probably wouldn't."

"Your dad went home, huh?"

"Yeah. Hitched up the trailer and left bright and early. We had a good talk last night, though. He's going to get Bryan and me and take us to his place when he comes up to the cabin on Monday. And he said he'd ask around and find the right person to dig up something on that bitch I'm married to. And he made me promise not to do anything to raise her hackles in the meantime. I won't. But...after what she told Amy...I hope sticking around and cooling my heels isn't just plain nuts."

He'd have delivered that comment with a slight shake of the head as he raised his arm to let it fall dramatically at his side, and I heard the palm of his hand slap against his thigh. A hug might not have helped, but it hurt not to be able to give him one.

"It's okay, Mike. Believe me...waiting is better. You'll have time to come up with a plan that'll work, not one that might be your undoing. Please—"

"Don't worry, Mom. I'll sit tight till you get home."

"And you'll stay at my house?"

"Oh yeah. Not going near my place now. God knows what that bitch meant when she told Amy she had a better idea. But it can't be good."

At least Mike wouldn't be the cause if Jill didn't meet with Phil on Saturday. Hoping everything else in my daughter-in-law's life went well for her left a bad taste in my mouth. Literally too, because I'd just driven past the oil refinery outside Billings, and I waited for an exit on the other end of town to stop at a box store. Bryan and I needed more equipment to build networks of roads in the five yards of good dirt I'd dumped in the equipment yard behind my house. As I perused the toys, a man in the next aisle began shouting, slurring his words and sounding so like my dead father it made me flinch.

"Where'n hell they hide the shittin' hair brushes 'round here? Old lady's in the son-of-a-bitchin' hospital. An' how'm I s'posed to find all this crap on her list?"

His drunken tirade continued, and, without looking, I could see his bloodshot eyes, cap canted to one side, hands in the front pockets of his jeans to anchor his wayward arms—could almost smell his unbearable breath and the alcohol oozing from his pores. The inebriated fool had spoiled my anticipation of good times like a brown leaf floating through a summer day.

I grabbed two graders off the shelf, hurried to the checkout counter, then ran to the truck. I'd planned on making a picnic of the vending machine meal from the previous evening and eating right there in the parking lot but wasn't about to do it now. Not far enough away from that man, and a hot lunch sounded better anyway. I couldn't face being in Marie's favorite restaurant without her, though, and stopped at the next one.

A full ten minutes after I'd slid into the booth, a professionally pissed off waitress sauntered over and took my order as though she'd done me a favor by being there at all. She was thin but too thin, her long red hair had been home-dyed once too often, her large boobs were created by a padded pushup bra, and her green eyes were distorted by thick glasses—Jill without money. I didn't leave a tip.

Stretched thin between an old dream and home, sixty miles later, I left the freeway to drive down a short run of blacktop more potholes than paving. But location is everything, and the disintegrating road travels through a Charlie Russell landscape of the Yellowstone River running wide and fast below soaring sandstone cliffs that miniaturize the Herefords grazing at their base.

I stopped the truck, turned off the engine, and rolled down the windows. Soon, the scents and sounds of cattle, sage, flowing water, and willows overpowered every worry. An hour later, I awoke with Karl on my mind, and he was still there when I returned to the interstate. Our lives ran distant and parallel since our first and only kiss, but something told me my visit to Red Bend had tweaked that trajectory. I switched out the Ravel CD for Leonard Cohen. He understood such things.

The menacing, old-world chords of "Waiting for the Miracle" began just as mountains scooped me off the curvaceous hills, and jutting peaks reduced an all-encompassing heaven to shards of blue. No more big sky. I'd returned to little sky country— skewed, shady, and duplicitous as Jill. The long, curving climb, cumbersome and oppressive after flying along on a straight highway, increased the pain of leaving the prairie behind. And, at the top of the pass, my feelings were succinctly expressed by a fatally undermined fir tree lying on the steep bank with its roots pointing obscenely skyward.

Bozeman valley, with scenery farther than thirty feet away, couldn't have appeared too soon. Good place to stop at a convenience store too, but they're as misnamed as motels. I waited in line for the bathroom and waited in line to buy a couple bottles of water. Then I waited for a gas pump. But things could've been worse.

The guy fueling ahead of me drove a filthy, battered, overloaded Honda Accord and looked like he'd lived life on a path to nowhere and got there sooner than expected. He unscrewed the gas cap, laid it carefully on the roof, put a cigarette in his mouth, then just stood there staring at the match he'd lit as if wondering whether to drop it into the tank or light the cigarette. In the end, he swore, blew out the match, put the cigarette back in his pocket, then grabbed the pump handle and jammed the nozzle home with enough violence to make heads turn.

Finally on the road with a full tank, I now had to endure driving ten miles of prime farmland ruined by businesses, offices, restaurants, motels, car dealerships, and subdivisions. Bozeman hadn't fared any better than Missoula, but reaching empty acreage on the other side of Belgrade absorbed my tension like a poultice. Then Mike called, and the fear and heartbreak in his sputtered words triggered a slide show of catastrophes.

"Mom...can't take this! I won't! That bitch. That heartless, evil bitch!"

"Mike, what on earth is—"

"Jill wants our land. It's not that, though. It's... it's what she's threatening to do to Bryan! Break his arm...or maybe something worse. And say I did it."

"Oh my god. She wouldn't go—"

"Told me her friends will back her up! Because she's been lying to them. Telling them she's worried about how often I lose my temper with him!"

I shuddered then felt nauseous and sweaty. She'd started her endgame—with a devil's gambit. And it was too soon, way too soon. I had a tough time believing she'd stoop low enough to hurt her child that bad, but couldn't rule it out, and the thought of poor Bryan screaming in agony as a little bone snapped had me pounding my fists on the dash and wishing to god it was Jill. She'd removed any compassion lurking in my conscience and given us every good reason to do whatever it took to save Bryan.

"Didn't believe her at first, Mom. Told her even she couldn't hurt her own son. Not do something like that, anyway. Know what she said? She said, 'Oh yes I could. Broken bone would only be like him getting his shots. Hurt a little while, then he'd get over it.' What an idiotic thing to say! And I think she'd do it, Mom. I really do."

Now, more than ever, that woman had to die. But the likelihood of Mike doing something to make her forgo meeting Phil had grown exponentially. Missing the big picture, our son could only see he had to run far and fast to protect Bryan, and, without disclosing why, what words would be powerful enough to stop him from doing the logical, safe thing?

"Hang on, Mike. Remember, Jill can't hurt Bryan if she doesn't have him and—"

"I told the bitch she'd hafta find him first. But she was ready for that. Said my chances of hiding from her this day and age were zilch. Said she'd find him no matter where we went. And make me damn sorry when she did. I gotta try, though! I gotta get the hell outta Dodge and keep Bryan away from her."

Mike was seeing red and had to be stopped from sabotaging his dad's plan to rescue him. I exited onto Highway 287, wheeled into a truck stop, parked out in the north forty, and tried to clear his vision.

"Swear to god, Mom, if it wasn't for being away from Bryan till I got out of prison, I'd find Jill and—"

"I know honey. Believe me, I know."

"I'm so sorry, Mom."

"For what? None of this is your fault."

"Yeah...it is. I should've throttled that bitch in her sleep a long time ago. Not like there wasn't a back-hoe and loads of places to bury the body. Didn't do it, though. And now I'm paying for it. We're all paying for it. And I'm gonna find a way to fix that."

In spite of what he'd just said, Mike sounded calmer, but I'd have needed to observe his stance and look into his hazel eyes to be sure.

"What else did she say, Mike? Anything?"

"Promised to give me a divorce and sole custody of Bryan if we turned the land over to her."

"You know we'd all gladly give it up...if it meant you and Bryan would be free of her."

"Yeah. I do. But we both know damn well that bitch would renege on the deal."

He'd gauged our plight correctly. Jill had no intention of giving up custody of Bryan and her power over us. I'd have staked my life on it. She'd wait awhile then go after the business and wouldn't stop till we had nothing left. But I needed to dampen Mike's rage not fuel it, and it would take more than the comforting words I wrapped in shiny hope and handed out like Halloween candy when he and Amy came knocking at my heart. My incensed son needed a solid strategy. I dried my tears, cleared my throat, took a deep breath, and offered one.

"Yeah, Mike. That's the problem. She'll never willingly release her hold on us. But let's cross that bridge when we come to it. Right now we have to concentrate on making sure she can't take Bryan."

"I know, Mom. I have to get him the hell away from here. Far as we can go without a passport. I'm not gonna wait for that damn thing now."

"No, Mike. Please. You can keep him safe without doing that."

"No. I have to—"

"Listen to me! I'm your mother. You think I'd steer you wrong?"

"Course not. Not on purpose. But—"

"Trust me. You don't have to leave. You can outsmart Jill. Just go ahead and agree to the deal then stonewall her. Transferring that land will take time. And she knows it. All you have to do is—"

"But what if she decides to take Bryan anyway? So she can hang on to him till the deed's filed?"

"You can prevent that, Mike. For a few days anyway. Think about it. You have as much legal right to Bryan as she does. Only the cops can force you to give him to her. And, if she can't get to where you are, she can't drag them into it. And if she can't drag the cops into it...it's a civil matter."

"Yeah! That's right. She'd need some kind of court order or something before it wasn't okay to have him with me."

"Exactly. And that wouldn't happen overnight."

"Okay then. I'll take Bryan and lay low someplace. Don't care where we have to go."

Mike had accepted the solution I'd dangled in front of him. But could I set the hook?

"You already have the perfect place...the cabin. She can't get to you there."

"The cabin! It's too damn close. I can't just go there and do nothing for god knows how long."

"Hey, Mike. After what Jill said, I wouldn't call keeping Bryan safe...*nothing*."

"After what that bitch said...I should be wringing her goddamn neck. It's the only way Bryan's ever really going to be safe. And that's what I should be doing. Or getting him away from here. Not just hiding out someplace with no phone line and no cell coverage."

"But that's exactly what makes the cabin so perfect. She won't even try to get up there, because she couldn't call the cops when she did. And they won't do anything to locate you for at least twenty-four hours. We found that out last summer. Wouldn't it be nice to give her a taste of her own medicine?"

"Damn straight, it would."

Silence—Mike staring into the distance, shifting his weight from one foot to the other, looking for a way out. I tried to convince him Phil would produce it.

"And you know, Mike, give your Dad half a chance and he'll come up with someplace you can go where Jill will never find you. Or maybe, with the ways and means he has, he'll find a way to put a stop to all this and you won't even have to leave."

"Gotta nail her ass to the wall, Mom! Get something on that bitch. Something so bad there'll be no doubt at all about me getting full custody of Bryan."

"There's a good chance your dad can make that happen, Mike. Haven't lost yet."

"Okay...so maybe I should go to the cabin till Monday and wait to see what Dad can do. Gonna be hell not knowing what's going on while I'm up there, though. Jesus Christ! Why isn't there any cell coverage that close to town? And why didn't we cough up the money and get a phone line brought in?"

"It wasn't the cost, Mike. Remember? We didn't *want* anyone to be able to reach us there. And, like I said, that's exactly what will keep you safe. Even if Jill shows up, she can't call the cops."

"I know. It's just being stuck—"

"Amy and Paul will be with you."

"True. But—"

"Mike, I've never asked you to do anything on blind faith before. But I'm begging you...go up to the cabin and stay there."

"You want me to just sit around waiting. And worrying about that bitch batting her eyelashes at some cop till they take her up there. You realize if that happens, they'll force me to give Bryan to her."

"Yes, I do. But I'm positive she won't do it. Not on Memorial Day weekend. They'll be busy. She'd have to cash in some pretty big favors. And why do that if she thinks she's won? So...make her believe she has... and she'll wait to take Bryan until next week. And she won't be able to. Because by then you'll be at your dad's, if not on your way to someplace even safer."

"Okay, Mom. I just hope to god you're right."

"I am. You'll see. So, you promise you'll go on up to the cabin?"

"Okay, okay! I promise. But I made a promise to Bryan too...first time I held him in my arms. I promised to do everything and anything I could to keep him safe. Already failed him once. Twice, if you count when that bitch took him from Amy's house on Wednesday. Couldn't live with myself it happened again."

"I understand. Really, I do. Dad and I made the same promise to you and Amy. And we try to keep ours too."

This had me flying way too close to the sun. I changed the subject then cut him loose.

"Have you told your sister?"

"Nope...couldn't do it. Called Paul, and he went home to tell her. It'll be better coming from him anyway."

"Yup, probably will. I'll let your dad know what's happened. You grit your teeth and call Jill. Make sure she believes we've agreed to sign over the land. Say her lawyer can start drawing up the papers."

"Even if I do con that bitch into believing we've given in, she won't take any chances, Mom. If she's around, she'll still try getting her hands on Bryan. So I better not waste any time getting up to the cabin."

"Nope, better not. Call me when you're at the gate."

"I will."

We hung up and I called Phil, but, like our son, I had a hard time putting Jill's incomprehensible threat into comprehensible words. Phil's work must've inured him to far worse, but it's different when it's one of your own. His fury matched Mike's, but my son hadn't subjected me to the string of expletives that came out of his dad's mouth.

"Sorry, Lynn. But why did that degenerate bitch have to kick things into gear today? Twenty-four more hours. That's all I needed, and I'd have dealt with her. And if I ever regretted the need for it...I don't anymore. Looking forward to it in fact."

"I feel exactly the same way. And why couldn't she have waited...waited till it was too late."

"I suppose Mike's half out of his mind. More determined than ever to find a bolt hole. We have to stop him, Lynn. Before he puts the kibosh on his own damn rescue."

"I know. And that's where there's some good news. I talked him into only running as far as the cabin for now. And he's going to call Jill and tell her we've capitulated. She'll want Bryan as collateral anyway until the paperwork's signed and figure everyone's at the cabin. But it's hard to get to. And it'll be too much hassle for her to involve the police over Memorial Day weekend. So I'm betting she won't try to take Bryan before Tuesday and...most important... will still meet up with you tomorrow."

"I agree, Lynn. As long as Mike's reined in and not giving Jill something more important to deal with, she'll be there. She's as anxious to get something on you as Mike is to get something on her.

"Glad you think so too, Phil. Thought I might've been snowing myself right along with our son."

"How'd you ever talk him into staying at the cabin, anyhow? He's not one to sit on his hands."

"I told him, if he waited there for you to get him on Monday, you'd find somewhere he could go where Jill would never locate him. Or you'd figure out, or find out, something to stop her from ever getting custody of Bryan, and he wouldn't even have to leave the country."

"Damn tall order. Hope to hell I won't have to fill it."

"Yeah. Heads up though. If I know our son, he'll call you before he leaves for the cabin to make sure I know what I'm talking about and ask if you've got the ball rolling yet."

"Don't worry. I'll be ready with what he wants to hear."

"Bad thing now is…he's come to the same conclusion we did. As long as Jill's alive, Bryan's never really going to be safe from her."

"Oh sweet Jesus. Saturday had better happen."

Hearing exasperation in Phil's voice unnerved me right down to my boots, and I tried to persuade us both that our son would hold off long enough for the plan to save him.

"Mike won't do anything this soon. I'm sure of it."

"Damn, Lynn. How can you be so positive he'll stick it out at the cabin?"

"I think Amy can keep him there. He feels guilty about putting her through all this. And he believes you can do absolutely anything."

"Well, we both know that's not true."

"Speak for yourself. You're going to save us from Jill aren't you? And I'm just aching to tell the kids this nightmare will be over after Saturday. It feels like I'm feasting while they starve."

"I feel it too, Lynn. But keeping them in the dark is the only way to protect them."

"Don't question that for a second. Doesn't make it any easier, though."

"No it doesn't. But it'll all be over soon."

"That's what I'm hanging on to, Phil."

He went back to welding a hidden compartment into the front of the enclosed trailer he'd taken home, and I studied the rich loam in the empty field not ten feet away. How could something as innocent as bare ground cause so much grief?

When Phil's father inherited the land Jill would later birth a child to possess, he'd done the smart thing. He'd subdivided closest to the university, built spec houses on those one hundred acres, and left the rest of the parcel intact. Preserving all that land brought Jill down on his progeny, but he'd protected them from her too by being generous to his neighbor.

For years, Phil's dad had leased out over a thousand acres of grassland to the adjacent SWR Cattle Company for a pittance. And, when he inherited the land, Phil agreed to continue leasing it to them for the same token amount in return for a permanent easement through their ranch. It had allowed us to eliminate the road up the mountain, guarding the pastureland from dirt bikes and the cabin from vandalism.

Now the only access to our log cottage is the narrow dirt road to the SWR ranch house, through their barnyard, on to the locked gate a quarter mile away, then hiking, four wheeling, or snowmobiling the rest of the way. I didn't doubt Bryan would be safe from Jill at the cabin. She'd never even visited the place, using her pregnancy as an excuse to stay home, and Mike quit inviting her afterward.

It was Phil's grandfather, way back in 1905, who'd felled the trees and built the hand-hewn log cabin providing sanctuary for his great grandkids and great-great-grandson ninety-four years later. Half in and half out of the timberline, the rear of the building juts into dense woods, while the front porch overlooks a wide expanse of pasture rolling down to the city-filled valley. And, since 1920, a snapshot has been taken from the cabin's front steps every summer. We continued taking the yearly photos, and Amy created our Fourth of July barbecue tradition of adding the latest one to the special, embossed leather album that holds only one photo per page. Then we all take turns zipping our thumbnails across the edge of the pages to see the, once distant, town march up the foothills to our southern fence line.

Land is always worth fighting for—a maxim spelled out in the disking patterns in the fields surrounding the truck stop. After Saturday, we could celebrate saving ours, and I would even blubber happy tears with Amy. Be a while before that happened, though. I got back on the road and hadn't gone a mile when Amy called, infuriated, incredulous, but holding it together better than I'd expected. No doubt thanks to Paul.

"Mom! Cannot, just cannot, get my mind around this! I mean...we know Jill's evil. Still, how could she...it's so horrible."

"Don't worry. Bryan's going to be—"

"How could someone even talk about brutalizing their own child like that?"

"Don't understand it either, Amy. Just clinging to the fact she doesn't have him. And believe me...is damn sure not going to get him."

"I hope you're right, Mom!"

"I am. He'll be safe up at the cabin."

"But then what? We can't stay there forever."

"I know. But it won't be for long. You wait and see. Your dad knows people...people who can help him get something to use against Jill. Even if they have to fabricate it."

"I don't care how they do it. And there's the money Mike found. That can't be on the up and up."

"No. And the right person can find out what the hell's going on with that. So hang in there, okay? Bryan needs you more than ever. So does your brother...you and Paul have to keep him at the cabin. I'll be home Saturday night. Be up there with you by Sunday morning."

"You mean you're not coming straight home?"

"No, Amy. And I feel terrible about it. But your Dad doesn't want to waste any time trying to derail Jill. We're going to put our heads together in Summit tonight."

Another lie, a wishful lie I wanted to make true, but a lie. Couldn't tell her the real reason, though, and the deceit would mushroom, making me appreciate every scrap of truth I could share.

"It's okay, Mom. I know finding a way to stop Jill and keep Bryan safe is the most important thing. You're for sure coming home Saturday night, though, right?"

"You bet. And like I said...be up at the cabin Sunday morning."

"I can't wait to see you. Things will look tons better when we're all together again...won't they?"

"Guaranteed. Well, better let you go, honey. Sooner you get up to the cabin, the less likely you'll run into Jill. I'll be in Summit soon and have coverage there. Call me when you're at the gate."

"Wait...did you make a motel reservation?"

"I'll do it right now."

"Okay. Talk to you soon, Mom."

As if aware we'd be setting a juggernaut of life-changing events in motion, there were a few seconds of silence before either of us could bring ourselves to say goodbye. Then, recalling what Phil once told me—when you have to lie, fortify it with as much truth as possible because it might be all that saves your ass later on—I did actually go to Summit.

Of all the places I could've said Phil and I were meeting, why had I blurted out that town? I decided it must've been a subconscious punishment for all my dishonesty. It isn't anywhere I'd willingly spend the night. I got there thirty-five minutes later without a reservation. My lousy information service had no listings for Summit, but it wasn't a problem. There were only two places to stay, and both adhered to the town's dusty, downtrodden, garbage-strewn theme, and both had vacancies.

I checked into the crème de la crap, an old place called the Freemont Inn, and laughed because it was indisputably a motel and a very bad one. The odor of cigarette smoke, urine, and a moldy bathroom met me at the door. Asking for a different cabin would've been an annoying waste of time—knew by the looks of the place they'd have all been like number eight. I retreated to my truck to wait for word from the kids, and exactly ten minutes later Mike called.

"Are you at the gate, honey? What did Jill say when you told her?"

"She just laughed and hung up...the bitch. And, yes, we're at the gate."

"Everything's okay then."

"Yeah...if you call having to hide your son from his own mother okay."

Like his dad's, Mike's hazel eyes turn brown when he's hurting. I could see them all too clearly, and it scalded my heart. Balm was the fact he and Bryan would soon be safe from Jill.

"Fair point...so *relatively* okay then. How's the little guy handling all the commotion in his life?"

"Hasn't bothered him one little bit. He's even sound asleep...in Paul and Amy's Jeep. Seemed safer. That way they could just cut and run if Jill was out looking and found me."

"Smart. But thank god you made it to the gate without seeing her."

"One weird thing, though. When Paul went to my house to get some more things for Bryan and me...I knew it'd be alright. Jill wouldn't have a prayer's chance of slowing him down and—"

"Can't argue with that."

"No. And anyway...someone showed up. Paul said they turned into the driveway right after he pulled out. But he couldn't see the driver. Windows were too tinted. But it was a flashy black Navigator. And I've seen it before. Just can't, for the life of me, remember where."

I didn't tell him.

"Never know, Mom. Maybe Jill has someone checking up on me. Paul didn't have time to wait and see if they hung around. Nobody followed us here, though. We made damn sure of that before we turned into the ranch."

"Good. Talked to your dad yet?"

His voice brightened a tad as he relayed what Phil told him, and it made everything better for a few seconds.

"Yeah, I did talk to Dad. And he finally told me a little bit about what he does. Said there'd be a real pro going after Jill by tomorrow afternoon."

Well that wasn't fair. Phil had been able to tell the truth when he lied to our son.

"You probably know more about what he does than I do now, Mike. And, see...what did I tell you? It's all going to be okay. You just stay strong. You've made it this far. And you'll get through the rest of it. I promise. And I love you."

"Love you too, Mom. But better get going."

Mike wasn't frantic anymore. Blind rage had turned to clear-sighted hatred. I hung up believing what I'd told him—we'd be okay—and tried to keep things on a positive note when I called Amy.

"Hi, honey. So you're all set to stay at the cabin?"

"Yup. And we could be there a month without running out of anything important."

I chalked that up to Paul's protective nature.

"That didn't have anything to do with your hubby, did it?"

Amy had me on speaker, and I heard Paul's deep chuckle. Having him for a son-in-law nearly made up for Jill. We depended on him for so much and could live to a ripe old age without having enough time to repay him.

"Hi, Paul. Good to hear your voice. What would we ever do without you?"

"Aw, hell. I'd do anything for Amy and the rest of you guys. You know that."

"I do. And it makes us luckier than we deserve. Guess I better let you get on up to the cabin. Love you both."

"We love you too, Mom...Paul's nodding his head."

At last, they were safe and where I wanted them to be. So why did it feel like I'd set them adrift in a lifeboat during a hurricane? I needed to talk to Phil, and only getting his answering machine left me hollow. I stared at the motel room door, painted a hideous shade of purple, envisioned a night on the other side of it then drove to the hardware store, bought three cans of Lysol spray disinfectant, six rolls of paper towels, five canvas tarps, and returned to the Freemont Inn prepared for cabin number eight.

After spreading four tarps over the filthy carpet, and down one can of Lysol, I attacked the bathroom and sprayed everything in that mildew factory, including the shower, even though I wouldn't have set a toe in the skanky thing. Then I used the motel's gray, but supposed to be white, towels to cover the dirty floor and put a roll of Bounty paper towels beside the sink on the toilet tank lid.

Next came the bed. I'd no intention of crawling between those sheets. I used the last tarp to cover the stained bedspread then, still coughing from air opaque with Lysol, went outside and fetched my sleeping bag from the truck bed toolbox. But the bag's campfire smell made me think of Geyser Mineral Springs where I could get the hot shower due me and a soothing soak too. I threw my sleeping bag on the back seat to keep it out of the room as long as possible, locked the cabin's awful purple door, and headed for the hot springs.

The squat building housing the hot springs was encircled by a parking lot stippled with puddles, and the old place looked like it had sprung a leak. I walked up to the counter and waited while a woman, the type to have been a lanky blonde at Woodstock, informed her sidekick about an imminent firewood delivery and took my money without actually acknowledging my existence.

After taking a nice soapy shower, I walked by the main pool, full of chlorine and high school kids going for a pre-kegger swim, and went directly to a walled-off area filled with steam and the pungent odors of sulfur and wet cedar. I had the smaller hot pool all to myself, too, and could really relax. The tourists in the campground next door were busy setting up their RVs and preparing evening meals. My supper would be the previous night's vending machine haul, and I'd laid everything out on the passenger seat before rummaging around in the duffel bag for my swimming suit.

Sinking into the steaming mineral water more than made up for a poor meal, though, and the only thing that could've made it better was Phil being there with me. Completely out of the question, so I made up my mind to enjoy myself without him and stayed in the pool a solid hour before getting out and letting gravity have its way with me.

Procuring two towels had cost ten dollars, same as the price of entrance, but they were nothing whatsoever like those I'd spread on the bathroom floor of cabin number eight. I'd have happily paid twice that to wrap up in those oversized rectangles of clean, fluffy, bleached white terrycloth after rinsing the sulfur water off.

Outside, the cool, piney air and smell of grilling meat stoked my appetite, but, after soaking so long, getting to the food and drink wasn't all that easy. My muscles were in such a stupor it took two tries to hoist myself into the truck. I immediately drained a bottle of juice then started my feast with the first bag to hand and kept right on eating when Phil called.

"What are you munching on?"

"Corn chips."

"Corn chips!"

"What's wrong with corn chips?

"Nothing...but you should get yourself a good meal. Nice steak or something."

"And where would I find one of those? I'm in Summit."

"Summit! What the hell are you doing there?"

"Like I said...eating corn chips."

He laughed and added music to my dining experience. Then I explained how the lie I'd told our daughter about why I wasn't going home, when I clearly should've and would've, had led to my being in Summit, and he laughed again.

"Anyway, Phil, the kids and Bryan should be eating supper at the cabin by this time. They were all at the gate about two and a half hours ago."

"That's a load off! They were just heading out when I talked to Mike. How's he doing?"

"Angry and bitter. But after he talked to you, a helluva lot calmer. Something's shifted."

A nebulous intuition that, put into words, coalesced into a frightening probability. I shivered and dropped the chip I was holding.

"Oh, Phil. What if he—"

"You don't think he's getting ready to do something stupid do you, Lynn?"

I thought he very well might be. I thought Amy and Paul might not be able stop him from leaving the cabin. I thought he might sneak away at night while they slept. I thought because he'd learned a little of how his dad made a living he might start liking the odds of getting away with putting a bullet in his wife's head. And I told Phil so.

"I didn't think he would. But now I'm not so sure. Maybe he's feeling more confident, and braver, after talking to you. What if he takes off tonight? And nobody misses him till morning? Without any way of knowing, we can't even—"

"There is one way, Lynn. We can leave voicemails. Tell him it's an emergency, and he needs to get ahold of us immediately. You know he would. And then we'd have a chance to stop him."

"That's brilliant! And, as long as he stays at the cabin, he won't get the messages till later. And we'll come up with some explanation then."

"Should work, Lynn. And anyway...it's all we've got."

"And I think it's all we need. Wish we really were meeting up here, Phil. That's why I called earlier."

"Been out working on the trailer. Must've had the grinder going and didn't hear the shop phone. Wish I could be there with you, too. And I'd head over in a heartbeat if not for this damn welding slowing me down. Not something you can do every once in a while and be any good at it. Won't be pretty...but it'll get the job done. When I'm finished, I'll put a few nicks in the plywood, rub in a little greasy dirt, and it'll look like it's been there since day one."

"I'm praying it won't matter...that no one but you and Jill will be seeing the interior of the trailer on Saturday."

"Big amen to that."

"Well, Phil, I'm here if there's anything I can do. And the kids have no phones, so I won't have to make up stories about where I'll be tomorrow."

"I'm sure you'll just be on your way home. The trailer will be ready tonight, and things should go like clockwork from then on. Oh, and you've got an ironclad alibi for tomorrow afternoon. No questions asked. You shouldn't need it...but better safe than sorry. These people live up the Skalkaho. And I want you go home that way so you'll know exactly what their place looks like, okay?"

"Is the pass even open?

"Yeah, I checked. You'll see their house off to your left not long after the gravel ends. Can't miss it. Big, white two-story on eighty acres. Make sure you're seen in Anaconda and in the Bitterroot too."

"Yeah. I'll have coffee, lunch, then more coffee, and use my credit card. I'll stop at Della's office in Stevensville too. You remember her, don't you?"

"Good lord. Is she still around?"

"Yup. And sharp as ever."

"I'll be damned. Anyway, sounds good. I'll call you in the morning."

Settling for the comfort of Phil's military certainty, rather than his embrace, left me feeling like a kid who'd found nothing under the tree on Christmas morning. After finishing off my snacks, I drove to the motel and thought I'd avoid the cabin a little longer by cleaning the truck cab. But soaking in the hot pool and eating all that food had sapped my energy. I'd done little more than gather up the garbage before, sleeping bag clamped under my arm and duffel bag in hand, I unlocked the door to number eight.

The scuzzy room reeked in a cleaner way at least and seemed a little more habitable. I spread my sleeping bag on the side of the bed closest to the door, barricaded the other side with my duffel bag, then put a bottle of water, a box of Kleenex, and my phone on the zippered flap. The bed became my little island of clean, and I told myself anything under the tarp would stay under the tarp.

Before turning in, I called Mike, felt relieved when he didn't pick up, and left the bogus voicemail imploring him to call me right away. It felt like setting a timer for disaster, and, more than ever, I wished for Phil's warm body to be waiting in that cold sleeping bag. Maybe then the gray silk lining against my skin wouldn't have reminded me of Marie's coffin, my forever loss, and Karl's sad face when he told me about the likelihood of Darlene having breast cancer. But, before the next vexing thought, I passed out, too exhausted to worry any longer about miles to go and promises to keep.

SATURDAY

The Freemont Inn had one thing going for it. It was quiet. There'd been no noise from the freeway, no stranger's head six inches from mine, and nobody trooping up and down a hallway. I'd slept sound for seven hours—and hadn't been bitten by anything after all. I left the tarps where they were, and the maid, if there was one, could think what she liked. A few miles down the freeway at Hunter's Meadow the mountains backed off but only exposed more dark clouds.

Phil hadn't phoned yet, so I called him. When he didn't answer, I figured he might've been in the shower but wondered why his answering machine wasn't on. Half an hour later, he still didn't answer, the answering machine still wasn't kicking in, and his cell, which didn't work anywhere near his mountaintop home anyway, went to voicemail. It was possible he'd left for Helena already and was between landline and cellphone coverage, but I didn't want to keep going without talking to him and pulled over below Evergreen RV Park.

It's not much of a park, just twelve dusty, rock-strewn campsites atop a barren hillside halfway between Summit and Butte, and in a corner of the property, a 1951 Ford pickup, paint nearly gone, weather-checked tires almost flat, and windows cracked, had been left to fall apart. I thought about driving up to the office and making an offer. We belonged on the windy prairie where the air is dry, the rhythm is slow, and a rusting body has a chance. A place where you can see what's headed at you in time to get out of the way. Ten minutes of daydreaming later the phone rang, and I laughed with relief.

"Phil!"

"Uh...no. Sorry. It's me."

"Oh. Hi, Karl."

"Sorry to bother you, Lynn. If it's a bad time I can—"

"No, no. Not at all. Any news?"

They hadn't heard anything about Darlene's biopsy results this soon, had they? I tried to focus on their valid concerns and forget my irrational fears of Phil lying unconscious in his shop, succumbing to an early heart attack, or being taken out by another professional—tried to be patient and listen like Amy would've.

"No, Lynn. Haven't heard a damn thing. Just thought I'd give you a call. Darlene didn't get home till nearly eight Thursday night. Said everything went okay. Not too painful or anything. I still feel like a piss poor husband...never should've let her go by herself."

"But she'd be the one feeling awful if you'd missed your mom's burial. And who knows, maybe she needed a little time alone."

"That's just what she said, Lynn. Kinda nice to be all by her lonesome and think things through."

"When will she get the results?"

"Doctor said he'd try and let her know today."

"On a Saturday?"

"Yeah...how about that? Said he didn't want to make her wait and worry clear till Tuesday on account of Memorial Day. Why is it these damn tests always end up being done at the end of the week. Same with Mom. Only her doc always made us sweat it out over the weekend."

"Glad this one didn't do that. And I'll be praying he has good news."

That last, wrapping-it-up, comment had slipped out despite my best intentions, and I felt bad because Karl hadn't missed it.

"Thanks, Lynn. Darlene said to say hi. She's napping right now. We're not getting much sleep."

"I'll bet not. Tell her I'm thinking about her. And please let me know as soon as you find out anything."

"I will. And thanks."

"Any time at all."

I meant it. Meant it when I'd said it on the way to the cemetery too, and regretted Karl hearing the disappointment in my voice when I answered the phone. But it should've been Phil getting back to me.

I tried him again, got no answer again, and wanted to turn around, drive to his house, and see what the hell was going on. But I put the truck in gear and kept it pointed toward Butte. Being in construction taught me it's always best to forge ahead—don't worry about what some other guy's doing and don't veer from the plan.

It had taken me a few years to assimilate that precept, but it was in Phil's nature not to second-guess himself or get distracted. He does what he says he will, when he says he will, and would never have willingly left me hanging. It was a big part of why I was so worried about him and an even bigger part of why I'd married him.

———

Lieutenant Phil Crandall, on his third tour in Vietnam, belonged to the Marines when we met. He'd come home to Missoula on a hardship leave because his parents and younger sister had been killed in a car accident. I worked at Burger Hut, and it was a bereft Phil who drove up to my window five times a day for three days in a row before finally asking me out. We only had a week together before he had to go back to Nam and spent nearly every hour together, then, after he left, we exchanged lengthy letters for seven months. What he wrote convinced me he was the good man Marie had described eight years earlier, and, like so many young women before and since, I counted the days till he'd be home.

Within hours of being stateside again, Phil called to propose, I accepted, and he didn't re-up. He'd already decided to take over his father's construction business if I agreed to marry him. He inherited everything else his parents had owned too. And everything else included three sections of bare mountainside with a cabin at the timberline and, far below, a ten-acre parcel of land where his boyhood home stood. I adored the glorious wedding-cake Victorian overlooking Missoula from the center of a grassy tablecloth, but Phil didn't share my penchant for old, drafty buildings. He wanted to sell the house, use the money to get his father's business out of mothballs, and save the life insurance proceeds for operating expenses.

I didn't protest. Not having a bank sucking away our profits took the sting out of losing that connection to my husband's childhood, and I didn't have to miss the old house for long. When it came time to build our own home on five acres with zoning that allowed a construction yard, Phil offered to replicate the old Victorian he grew up in, and so began my undying loyalty to him.

Marrying Phil at eighteen had removed the shackles slapped on me at conception, and, although I'd nothing but my virginity and enthusiasm for hard work to offer him, he didn't exacerbate my feelings of inadequacy to heighten his superiority as a lesser man would've. He did his best to erase them. Then he gently divested me of the false premise that dreams magically come true when you live normally and not the way my parents had.

Pulling me close in bed one night just to talk, he shared what he'd learned by osmosis. A good life isn't something you fall into. It's something you build bit by bit then maintain day by day. We were kept busy day and night doing just that, and I let it be the reason for Phil's lack of interest in his old pastimes. The golfing, skiing, fly-fishing, trophy-hunting version of Montana had never been anything but an unsubstantiated rumor in my world anyway, and having life revolve around the business suited me.

I was learning a lot about myself and discovering another world too. Without hurting my pride, Phil pointed out my rough edges and helped me smooth them. Then he shared the skill set he'd absorbed in the realm of well-off people and showed me how to break in—there are no invitations. He taught me about love, sex, business, people, power, and politics. Then he left me.

Phil confessed to wanting out of our marriage not long after our sixth wedding anniversary. It totally unraveled me, but he put me back together by loving me and staying until he'd finally convinced me his decision had nothing to do with anything I'd done. He simply needed the immediacy, camaraderie, and excitement he'd experienced in Nam to feel truly alive. From his point of view this acquired state of being wasn't a cross to bear or a problem to be solved. It was something he could market and have happiness thrown into the bargain. Because our Pygmalion relationship had served me well, because I owed him everything, and because he trusted me to understand—I finally did.

We divorced amicably, the kids coped well, and Crandall Construction stayed in the black. With every step away, Phil reassured me he'd be available to help with anything, anytime, and he worked hard to remain part of our world. He succeeded for the most part, too, even after moving onto a rugged piece of land in the Little Belt Mountains so remote bringing in power and phone lines had cost twice what he paid for the six hundred and twenty acres.

When Phil began teaching survival training, officially anyway, it was the mark of the man that he'd insisted on me becoming sole owner of our construction company. It streamlined operating the business and prevented the male bias in the financial sector from increasing his financial standing but not mine. Three years after our divorce, with Amy in kindergarten and Mike in second grade, I obtained my real estate license, and I started my own brokerage two years later. Owning symbiotic businesses proved lucrative, and running them kept me too busy for anything besides work and raising kids.

Now, for the first time in all the intervening years, I began to wonder if I'd missed out on something important by staying too busy to even consider a new relationship, much less have one. But I wanted no part of a dating game rigged against women—Mike's experience with Jill being the exception proving that rule. So much easier not to risk health, reputation, or safety and let the remnants of my marriage be enough. Phil had no time or wish for a full-time lover either, and we continued our undemanding relationship comparable to a perpetually engaged couple with grown children.

Our strange relationship benefited Mike and Amy, too, because Phil is a wonderful father. But, like God, he loves his children from a distance, and the view is always good from there. Not wanting to spoil it, Mike and Amy usually shared their problems with me. How telling of their frustration when they'd sought their father's opinion about how to survive Jill's onslaughts. He'd warned them to leave any fantasies about good guys always winning by the wayside and explained being on the white-hat side guaranteed nothing except having to work harder and smarter than your enemy.

They'd heeded his words and had the courage to fight Jill. But, too young to judge when to discard scruples for higher, though convoluted, moral ground, they would've lost. The savage ultimatum she'd just delivered to Mike proved they were no match for that woman and confirmed our right, our duty, to win the war she'd started by any means necessary.

Righteousness never overrules fate, though, and it didn't bode well to have the freeway whisk me past Butte without having heard from Phil. The Mining City is often and aptly referred to as Butte, America. Because, having more common sense and right-mindedness in one block than you'd find in the entirety of most states, it shouldn't belong to any of them and has nothing but geography in common with western Montana.

Phil thought I was joking when I'd suggested honeymooning in Butte. A happy memory overpowered by the unanswered ringing of his phone when I called him again, and disappointment cluttered my thoughts like the junipers poxing the hills west of town. I'd always imagined cutting down the graceless shrubs able to withstand the acid conditions created by Anaconda's copper smelter. But I would've gladly planted more to learn why Phil wouldn't or couldn't answer either of his phones.

I despised being left to guess. By the time the hills fell away and the highway suspended me above the Deer Lodge Valley, bleak suppositions were as deep as the snow on the towering peaks to the south. Those mountains are put in their place by the valley's imposing expanse of smooth foot-hills, though. And I enjoyed seeing a remnant of the open spaces I'd left behind for the foreseeable future—foreseeable being only a matter of hours as things turned out.

Sticking to my part of Phil's plan felt more counterintuitive than ever, but I exited onto the wide, unnecessary four-lane leading to the small town of Anaconda barely seven miles away. On its way there, the overbuilt highway brushes against the outskirts of the tiny community of Opportunity, or simply Opper to locals. It's as picturesque as it is unusual, and I slowed to gaze down Hauser Street.

The long, straight boulevard is roofed with arching tree branches, creating a scene as European as the village's original inhabitants who'd worked at the Anaconda Company copper smelter a few miles down the road. They'd built homes on the large lots offered by their employer to give their workers a taste of country life farther from the smelter. Not far enough, though, because livestock developed sores on their noses, and the cottonwood trees planted in Opper grew with strange, spiraling trunks and limbs.

Smelter emissions haven't drifted over the valley in years. But the stack, large enough to house the Washington Monument and rising to 580 feet, still towers over the surrounding area and remains one of the tallest freestanding masonry structures in the world. Below the stack, a gargantuan hill of black milling waste encroaches on the eastern side of the highway. The stuff can't be trucked away or economically contained because the metallic particles are so abrasive they grind invading machinery to a standstill within hours. Just driving through the blowing grit when the wind is howling will have you replacing a pitted windshield.

The unassailable mountain of waste brought visions of Jill. Was she going to win and evade justice because Phil's plan had fallen apart? I couldn't face hearing his phones go unanswered again without caffeine and something to call breakfast. The Korner Koffee Shoppe, despite its cutesy name, would provide both, and I'd be happy to stop in Anaconda.

The beautiful, complex, has-been town owes its existence to Marcus Daly who'd ordered it built, about a century earlier, to service the smelter that serviced the mines he owned in Butte. That city, flung atop "the hill" in response to the needs of mine owners and workers, had grown up rough and ready as a barkeep's daughter. Anaconda, nestled in a wooded valley after a well-planned birth, had enjoyed a genteel upbringing.

Nonetheless, the aristocrat was destined to meet the same fate as its bastard sibling, and Anaconda's grim new circumstances are nicely summed up beneath its welcome sign where a gigantic, rusty crucible ladles out marigolds instead of molten copper. They call it Black Monday—that day on September 29, 1980 when the smelter announced its immediate closure. Many, in shock, had simply refused to believe it, but the truth couldn't be avoided for long.

The company had left the town to live on pollution, poverty, pride, and the past.

All four are evident on the smelter-end of Anaconda they call Goosetown. It's chock-full of narrow clapboard or brick homes standing barely an arm's length apart, and, with front doors only foot-steps from the sidewalk, they hide behind glassed-in porches or cower beneath old spruce trees with branches long enough to spread over the neighbor-ing homes too. But some houses have no porches, no trees, and no grass where, behind hedges log-ger-pruned knee high, smiling children play in the worn-out, poisoned dirt like flowers blooming in a junkyard.

I glanced at a good-looking Harley with a *For sale* sign taped between the handlebars and exchanged nods with the owners, a young couple struggling to erect a swing set on a lawn not much wider while three preschool children watched intently from the porch. My attention returned to the street just as an emaciated, cigarette-smoking, teenage woman trudged in front of the truck without even a glance in my direction. I came to a screeching stop just inches from the woman, giving me that awful pins and needles tingling, but her gaze remained fixed on a point in space somewhere above the flimsy umbrella stroller holding her toddler.

The little boy appeared to be about Bryan's age. Might not have been a boy, though. I couldn't be sure.

The child wore nothing but a diaper on its thin body, would've been freezing, and alternately slapped or chewed the nipple of an empty bottle—about as nourishing as the rights of his unfit mother.

Our society no longer protects its neglected children, and individuals are helpless to interfere. Still, it felt wrong to evict the doomed toddler from my mind and concentrate on the one child I could save, the much-loved child who'd be waddling around the warm cabin with a full tummy while his auntie dusted everything in sight. Or maybe he'd be standing by the window watching Daddy and Unkie chop enough firewood to last through a long winter rather than a long weekend.

My grandson had been born into a better world than the little boy in the stroller, except for Jill. I'd wholeheartedly believed he'd be free of her that very day. The possibility he might not be after all couldn't be countenanced, and I let downtown Anaconda dispel that anathema. It's an uplifting, fascinating buffer zone between working class homes, old-money mansions, and rude, crude, wham-bam-thank-you-Uncle-Sam public housing.

Hooking a left at the Ancient Order of Hibernians building, I cruised by the Club Moderne, in all its 1930s glory, then the Hearst Library and, saving the best for last, the Washoe Theater. It's ranked fifth in the nation by the Smithsonian for its Art Deco interior, but the nondescript brick exterior gives no indication of the building's immense size or the splendor within. I'd been wowed speechless the day Phil took me there and still envy the people who can visit the theater every week for popcorn and a movie.

Anaconda has been lucky when it comes to architecture. I drove around the block, parked in front of the Beaux Arts-inspired post office, and just sat there for a minute, admiring its fluted columns and trying not to worry about Phil. Then, for some needed exercise, walked the three blocks to the coffee shop. After ten o'clock in the morning now, the rush had fizzled out, and the owner gave me her full, chatty attention for the entire time it took to concoct a latte, bag up a croissant, and run my credit card. Her good mood infected me, and I walked down the street smiling until a janitor flung open a door right in front of me and braced it open to air out an old bar.

Strolling into the stench from a hundred years of spilled booze and cigarette smoke brought unstoppable memories—fizzy orange pop served to me in a highball glass with two red cellophane straws, my parents making small talk with the bartender, and the dread of what would happen three or four beers later. Mom had always excused herself by saying good mothers don't leave their kids with someone else, and maybe she'd deluded herself into believing it. In truth, they couldn't have afforded to go to the bars every night if they'd hired someone to watch me, and she'd never have let my dad go alone. She didn't trust him any farther than she could throw him.

As a result, I'd accrued more time on a barstool by the first grade than most people do their entire lives, enduring hours of boredom and smelly old drunks fawning over me. Being polite to everyone at all times had been rule one. Anything less than quiet compliance meant being loudly chastised and humiliated by my inebriated mother, irony even a child could grasp. Ashamed of my parents and ashamed of myself for being with them, I'd despised every endless hour spent in those stinking dives.

I got through them by dreaming of freedom, of growing up and making damn sure certain no one ever again had the power to make my life hell. I'd succeeded too, until Jill slithered into my world. I couldn't tolerate her dodging her fate, and without one taste of the enticing latte or one bite of the warm huckleberry croissant, I phoned Phil again. Not getting an answer lessened the pastry's appeal, but I began sipping away at my jazzed-up coffee, that great elixir for banishing pessimism, before I got the truck in gear.

Anaconda's intrusive four-lane highway splits into a pair of wide, two-lane, one-way streets that mar the old town's grace. Then they, perversely, converge into a regular street with two-way traffic on the modern, western end of town. Here stretch the long blocks of ranch and split-level homes built in the sixties and early seventies when the smelter and union were going strong, and teenagers went to high school with twenty-dollar bills in their pockets.

Obsessively maintained and well preserved, with nary a blade of grass out of place nor an inch of peeling paint, the "lake end" of Anaconda would do a military base proud. The lakes are two reservoirs in the mountains nine miles west of town, and the highway leads to both—eventually. A twenty-five mile an hour speed limit extends well beyond the city limits and all reason. I broke the tedium by incessantly phoning Phil at home and on his mobile. This only increased my frustration, and, to ease it, I recited benign reasons for him not answering.

He might have still been working on the trailer and couldn't hear the phone, like the night before, or he might've been setting things up on Wedding Drive in Helena and left his phone in the vehicle, or maybe something came up with his work and he couldn't call me till later, or maybe he'd been in and out of the house and my timing was crap. As for his answering machine not picking up, he'd simply forgotten to turn it on—yeah right, and maybe Hell had cooled off too.

A few more miles out of town, cell coverage ended; maddening because, plainly, that's just when Phil would try to call me back. When the speed limit finally went to forty-five, slowly increased, then hit seventy, I reconsidered my options. Drive to Phil's house or turn around and stay in Anaconda until I got the go-ahead from him. Or, the bitter-pill third option, bury my worry and keep going.

The first two required deviating from the plan. Not a good move if things were going well for Phil and he just hadn't been able to phone for some bizarre reason. If that were the case, being in the Bitterroot establishing my alibis remained vitally important. But what if the savior needed saving? What then? The longer I traveled, the longer it would take me to get to him. In the end, I voted with my right foot, the truck surged into the mountains, and trees inundated the landscape like fire ants moving house.

Silver Lake appears first, and it lay flat and tarnished beneath the low sky, its waters deep, cold, and contained. But, only a mile farther, the highway narrows to squeeze through Georgetown Lake's swampy shoreline. This reservoir is forever striving to revert to the marshy meadow it was at the end of the previous century, before the Bimetallic Mining Company had Flint Creek dammed to provide them with more power. Cabins line its shore now, but locals, aware the oldest still have sewage pipes running directly into Georgetown, are circumspect about playing in the lake.

Others only know its shallow water freezes fast in winter and warms fast in summer. A seasonal mix of snowmobilers, fishermen, campers, skiers, swimmers, and boaters crowd the reservoir, and, nearly every Sunday night, the overgrown pond seems to overflow with toys as the weekenders drain down Flint Creek Hill. The hill, also called the divide or the grade, no longer inspires people to brag about owning a vehicle capable of making it over the top without overheating, but, call it what you want to, at around six percent it still demands your attention.

The highway switchbacks like ribbon candy too, and kept my mind off anything else until it unwound four miles later and I could glance at my cellphone again. When it gained two bars of coverage on the small rise beyond Porter's Corner, I pulled over and tried Phil's numbers again. Still no answer. So, figuring that stalling a couple hours wouldn't scupper the plan, I didn't turn west and cross into the Bitterroot where it would take several hours to get to Phil. I continued east and ten minutes later walked into the Sunshine Station, a mini truck stop surrounded by an excess of unpaved parking on the edge of Philipsburg. The restaurant serves good food, and the bar offers a free beer any day the sun doesn't shine, but they don't hand out many.

"Looks like they might be parting with a few bottles tonight."

The waitress didn't think so. She shook her gray braids and smiled.

"Naw. Ain't even noon yet. Sun'll be out long before the fishermen hit the bar."

I dawdled over my hamburger and fries lunch as long as possible then cruised into town, stopped at the famous candy shop, and took my time filling a few bags with our favorites. Across the street, someone had even opened an upscale coffee shop. My latte came with minimum conversation but maximum quality, and I savored it while driving around town to kill some more time.

Philipsburg's giddy silver-mining days hadn't outlived the nineteenth century, and the town had spent a hundred years in forced retirement. Then trout, scenery, sapphires, and one woman's dedication put the town on the map, and tourists put it back to work. Nearly all the buildings on Broadway were undergoing extensive restoration. You could almost smell the bright, fresh paint picking out every inch of ornate trim. The town was fast becoming a micro Missoula, sans loitering addicts and ubiquitous Subarus.

Time doesn't pass all that fast when you want it to. I visited the coffee shop again and ordered a second latte for the road. When another round of phone calls to Phil went unanswered, I gave in and returned to the Sunshine Station. I'd fueled up in Summit the night before and again in Anaconda, but I topped off the tank anyway then washed the windows and checked fluids that didn't need checking to burn up a few more minutes.

All the while, I'd been trying to clarify and classify the possible reasons I couldn't reach Phil. But categorizing theoretical outcomes to imagined events was like trying to organize a bathtub full of bubbles. I gave it up and arbitrarily decided Phil had been in some sort of accident. Unable to call Amy for the phone numbers of police departments and hospitals in White Sulphur Springs, Townsend, and Helena, I had to use my ridiculously inefficient information service—hands down the best time waster yet. And, for all my effort, I just irritated a lot of busy people and remained as bewildered as ever.

I started the truck and put it in gear but stopped to call Phil one last time, begging him to answer. Irrationally disappointed and hurt when he didn't comply, I slammed the accelerator to the floor and, trailing a cloud of dust and deep ruts, sped out of the parking lot like a jilted teenager. Even then, hope dictated sticking with the plan as long as possible, and I retraced the miles, this time with the Pintler Range in front of me.

But, before reaching Flint Creek Hill, I left that storybook land of bucolic foothills below forbidding Alpine mountains and headed west on the Skalkaho Highway. Designated a highway by sadistic mapmakers, it soon becomes a thinly graveled road that takes you across the Sapphire Mountains via the Skalkaho Pass at an elevation of 7,250 feet. You're nearly out of the mountains and in the Bitterroot before pavement reappears, without fanfare, apology, or explanation, as if twenty-five miles of washed-out, cliff-hanging dirt road normally happens in the middle of a highway.

The terrain misleads too, with irrigated pastureland quickly turning into dense forest. Being consumed by trees completed my transition from a fishbowl like Red Bend to being cut off from everyone—the kids, even Phil. I was operating in the vacuum Mother Nature abhors and feared a swift, catastrophic correction. A self-fulfilling prophecy because, preoccupied with what might happen, I hadn't noticed the cow moose trying to cross the road until—long lashes clearly visible above a massive brown eye—her head appeared in the passenger window as she swerved and began running beside the truck to avoid colliding with it.

I braked as hard as possible without skidding, and somehow she managed to keep her feet and race over the rocky berm till she could veer back into the trees. Her agility and smarts had saved my neck as well as her own. A deer would've made a suicidal, homicidal leap in front of the truck as soon as it got the chance. Damn close, though, and my hand shook as I turned the CD player off to better hear any oncoming vehicles. There'd be no dust to warn me. The road wasn't dry anymore.

They say the views along the Skalkaho will take your breath away—a permanent condition if you let them distract you for long. Like Jill, the pass hides its treachery beautifully, and the curves come at you hard and fast. As vantage points overlooking bright, unbroken vistas became fewer then disappeared altogether, I beamed a psychic message to Phil. *Please, please don't fail.* But my gut told me something or someone had blown his plan to smithereens.

Near the top of the pass, graupel began bouncing off the windshield. The same weird snow had speckled my lawn one afternoon when Bryan was only a few weeks old. A blizzard had blown in behind it, but bad weather wasn't what froze that night into my memory.

———

A phone ringing at two in the morning is never good, and the icy panic in Mike's voice took me from deep sleep to adrenalin-fueled alertness.

"Come get me, Mom. Fast as you can. I'm on foot about a block from home."

Minutes later, Mike stepped into my headlight beams. He had no coat or cap, only slippers on his feet, and held both hands to his chest. Was he in pain? Had he been stabbed or shot? I stopped the truck, ran to the passenger side, scooped everything off the seat, pitched it all on the floorboard in back, then turned around and saw *two* warm exhalations swirling into the blowing snow. He had the baby with him!

The hurt and humiliation in my son's eyes made me want to lash out at the woman bound to have caused it. But I held my tongue, got behind the wheel, and Mike, with hands too strong, too big, and too calloused for the job, tenderly delivered his infant child out from under his sweatshirt. Baby Bryan protested loudly, making it clear he preferred to remain against his daddy's warm chest.

"It's all right, little guy. Everything's fine. It'll all be okay, I promise."

Neither seemed convinced. I put the truck in reverse, backed into what I hoped was someone's driveway, turned toward home, and concentrated on the treacherous streets. Mike said nothing more, and Bryan fell silent too, one blockish fist pressed against his closed lips as if he'd nodded off before he'd quite maneuvered it into his mouth.

The minute we got into the house, I tossed Mike some of Phil's clothes, along with a pair of my oversized winter socks, then made him some hot, sweet tea and handed it to him after he'd changed. I had a drawer full of baby things at my house for Bryan, and, after making a warm bottle and changing his diaper, I settled into the rocking chair with him. Mike, hands wrapped around his mug of tea, paced the living room and explained why he'd walked away from home in the middle of the night in a snowstorm.

"Bryan didn't fall asleep until around ten. Jill wasn't home yet...not unusual these days. But, anyway, I didn't get to bed till about eleven and was dead tired. Got the lumber carried upstairs for the attic conversion in that big barn of a house on Marshall Street today."

"That would do a guy in, alright."

"Yeah...probably wouldn't have noticed someone crawling into bed with me anyhow. Not right away."

"What?!"

"No shit! Woke up to find this naked girl in bed with me trying to—"

"What do you mean *girl*? How old was she?"

"Not sure. Looked about fourteen...sounded a damn sight older, though."

"What the hell, Mike?"

"And it gets worse. She had a pair of handcuffs dangling from her wrist and some other S&M crap on the bed. Took me a second to figure out it wasn't a nightmare. Then I saw Jill standing there with a Polaroid camera."

"Oh my god!"

"Told ya, Mom. Anyway, I jumped out of bed and yanked it out of her hand. Told her she damn well better hand over the pictures, or else, and she pointed at the dresser. There were three laying there. I didn't fall for it, though, and checked the camera. Sure enough. Only four left out of twelve...five missing."

"The lying—"

"That's when I pinned her against the wall and found them in her pocket...thank god. By then, that girl had her clothes back on and took off before I could stop her. She was madder than hell. Kept yelling at Jill that she'd warned her to slip me more."

"Of what? Jesus, Mike!"

"I know. So, I slammed that bitch back up against the wall...let her know she better tell me what the hell was going on and what she gave me. But she refused to tell me. Just kept saying she wanted to make sure I'd never get custody of Bryan so I wouldn't try divorcing her. Why the hell she wants to stay married I'll never know. Anyway, that's when I looked at the pictures. And, holy Christ, they sure would've done the job. I grabbed my pants, got dizzy putting them on, and had to run for the bathroom. Couldn't stop throwing up."

"You alright? What the hell did she give you? And *how* did she?"

"Never know, I guess. She never would say. I ripped up the pictures and flushed them. When I came out of the bathroom, all that kinky sex stuff was gone, and, when I got downstairs, Jill was in the kitchen using the garbage disposal. Probably getting rid of the food she laced. I told her to pack her shit and get the hell out...immediately!"

My head came up, I stared at Mike, and he nodded.

"She went bat shit, Mom. Started throwing stuff. Screaming how she didn't have to leave and I couldn't make her. That's when the cops banged on the door. Bitch musta called them while I was puking my guts out."

"Never misses a trick, that one. You tell them what she did?"

"Tried. But they weren't interested. Wouldn't listen to a goddamn word I said."

"What! Didn't give you a chance to tell your side at all?"

"Hell no! Treated me like I'd just been released from prison for wife beating. But they couldn't get enough of her lies. The guy cop took her into the dining room to hear more. And the woman cop, a tall stocky blonde, hazed me into the kitchen. But every time I opened my mouth, she put her hand on the top of that stick they pack around and told me to shut up.

"She kept going on and on about options or something. Musta finally noticed nothing was registering, cuz then she got right up in my grill and started yelling. Said my wife had as much right to be in the house as I did, and if I thought I could throw her out I was sadly mistaken. Said I only had three choices. Stay and play nice, get the hell out of the house, or wind up in jail."

"But, Mike, Jill was the one breaking the law!"

"I tried to explain that, Mom. But what proof did I have? And they flat-out refused to listen."

"Well, Jesus Christ. What the hell's their problem? Sit down, honey...before you wear out the carpet."

Mike flopped on the couch and squeezed the life out of a throw pillow while he finished the story. And

I couldn't stop wishing he was relating a childhood nightmare that I could make fade away with a cuddle and leaving his bedroom light on.

"That damn cop. She wouldn't stop. She just kept at me. Over and over...'Stay and get along, leave, or come with us.' I'd already given in. But she was still at it on her way out...'Remember now. Get along, get out, or go to jail.' How's that fair?"

"It's not."

What happened to Mike brought a new kind of pain, the pain of being powerless to help him. I'd soothed little Bryan, sound asleep in my arms, but could do nothing for the man padding out to the kitchen for more hot water and a fresh teabag.

"Are you okay, Mike?"

"Yeah. Stomach's better now."

"Want something to eat with your tea? I could make toast or something."

"Not now...thanks. Maybe later. Where was I?"

"The cops finally left."

"Oh yeah. Soon as they were gone, I ran upstairs and got Bryan out of his crib. Had him in his carseat and everything before I noticed Jill's Lexus had me blocked in. She wouldn't move it, and wouldn't give me her keys...so I tucked Bryan under my shirt and started walking."

"You didn't really have a choice."

"No, sure didn't. But that really set her off. Started screaming stuff like, if I thought I could divorce her and take Bryan I was crazy. She'd find some other way to make sure I'd never get custody of him. And if I didn't come back, she'd call nine-one-one again and say I was threatening to beat her up for calling them the first time. And who did I think the cops would believe...a crazy guy walking off with a baby in a snowstorm...or her?"

Mike looked down at the pillow he'd mutilated, tried to reshape it, gave up, and threw it across the couch. Then, shoulders drooping, eyes searching mine to confirm the understanding in my voice, he forced the most humiliating part of the night into words.

"I sure as hell didn't want another run-in with the cops. And did feel like a complete idiot standing outside in a blizzard. So I headed back to the house. But when that bitch started laughing...like it was the funniest thing she ever saw...I knew I didn't dare get within throttling distance of her. So I took off again, called you, and hoped to god you'd get to me before the cops did. Don't think the bitch even called them again, though. Don't think she ever intended to."

His story finished, Mike relaxed a little and grabbed a fresh pillow. I feared his troubles with Jill were just beginning, but it certainly wasn't the time to tell him. And, anyhow, it would've been like some German telling a friend they thought Hitler might become a little intolerant.

"God how I hate that woman, Mom. And god how I hate not being able to get her out of my house...out of my life."

"You can't go back home, though. What's she going to try next?"

"Dunno. Can't leave, though. Just be forced to give Bryan to her. And he can't be left alone with that woman."

"Hell, no!"

"Going back home might be risky, but it's what I have do."

"No, Mike, it's not safe for you be around her anymore."

"It'll be okay. I'll figure something out."

"Maybe you could separate yourself and Bryan from her without actually leaving. You've already moved into the bedroom next to the nursery. You could turn the bar in the den into a kitchenette, use the other bedroom for a small living room, then you'd have a nice apartment. And the landing's plenty big enough for an entryway."

"Hey, Mom, that's not a bad idea. I could lock my door, keep my food safe, and never worry about her pulling this shit again. And, technically, I'd still be living there. Still have the whole house when she wasn't home, too."

"It would work, Mike. But it's a bad deal, you having to live like that."

"Gotta do what you gotta do, Mom."

"Yeah...but please don't move in till you can lock her out. I wouldn't sleep the whole time. You either most likely."

"Does that mean you're going to put up with Bryan and me living with you for a day or two? And feed us and everything?"

He didn't doubt it, of course, but he wanted to lighten the mood, and I smiled for him.

"I wouldn't mind if you moved in permanently."

"Thanks, Mom. But even staying for a couple nights might be playing right into Jill's hands. Paul and I better not waste any time. Won't take long to get the top floor closed off and set up the balcony for a fire exit, though."

"Isn't going to go over too well with her."

"Yeah. But there's not a damn thing she can do about it. And I'm really going to enjoy that. Oh, and thanks for getting there so fast tonight, Mom. Never saw you in your work boots and a robe before."

Our laughter was weak and welcome as winter sunshine.

In the months following that awful night, Jill honed her attempts to malign Mike until they'd become as impossible to avoid as the sharp rocks in the road over the Skalkaho were now. And, as Marie had warned me, if we didn't do something, the year and a half we'd just gone through would seem like the good old days. I couldn't let that happen and wished for the backup plan that had never materialized. Reaction is a hazardous substitute, but even checking out Marie's gun had to be postponed. The graupel had been replaced by dense fog, and staying on the road became my only concern.

When I reached Skalkaho Falls, the swirling air dispersed the fog, and I could've checked out Marie's gun there, but the crashing water would mask the sound of an approaching vehicle. Letting someone see me sighting in the weapon would've been stupid, and hiking through the deep snow to get away from the road didn't even merit consideration. I needed a fairly dry, south-facing road cut and found it where a kelly-humped skid trail joined the road.

I parked the truck at an angle with the passenger side toward the dirt bank, and it felt good to get out and stretch. The air had the leafy smell of winter retreating, but I yearned for the scent of sun-warmed sage and Karl. Still wondering if he'd seen me take Marie's gun, I slipped it and the ammo from the sleeves of my heavy work coat where I'd hidden them the morning of her funeral. The revolver was old, but the shiny silver box with a rider astride a galloping horse wasn't, and it contained all twenty .45 caliber FMJ cartridges. I dropped seven of them into my pocket and put the box in my duffle bag.

Then, pistol in my right hand, I released the thumb safety, pulled the slide partway open with my left hand, and checked to make sure the barrel was empty. Phil had included shooting in his tutorage, and each lesson included the old saying "Assume is making an ass out of u and me." The left side of the barrel clearly read UNITED STATES PROPERTY M1911A1 US ARMY. The stamped letters on the right side were too worn to read, but the information I sought, COLT .45 AUTO, remained visible on the bottom of the clip. It released reluctantly, but took the seven cartridges smoothly and gave a reassuring click when reinserted.

Listening intently for the sound of an engine and hearing nothing but a Steller's jay hoping for a hand-out, I gripped the revolver with both hands, took aim at a reddish spot in the bank, and gently squeezed the trigger. The gun fired with a nice quiet crack, not too much kick, and the bullet hit about an inch to the right of the small target approximately four yards away. Close enough to get the job done. I thumbed up the lock, settled the warm gun in my coat pocket, and got back in the driver's seat.

At the bottom of the pass, cellphone coverage returned with the pavement, and I braced for the devastating news that would explain the severed contact with Phil. But there were no missed calls and no new voicemails. Phoning him again brought the same infuriating results it had all day, and, other than the increased desperation in my voice, I left the same message too.

Watching for the place Phil wanted me to remember bolstered my faith in his plan, and it appeared around the next bend. At least thirty of the eighty acres had been cleared, leveled, and planted to grass, and the white-on-white steamboat of a house floated in the middle of an artificial meadow ringed by groves of quaking aspen. All those leaves shimmying in the breeze gave the place a dreamlike quality, and Phil had been right. I couldn't have missed it and sure wouldn't forget what it looked like.

I knew any details about the owners would be supplied if needed, and I never would get used to the strange work-world Phil inhabited. Who were these people, and why would they help us? Whoever they were, I felt grateful. I still hoped having an alibi would be important—that Phil going incommunicado didn't necessarily mean he couldn't meet up with Jill.

The longer I drove without hearing from him, the harder that was to believe. Then the trees turned to brush, the cloud ceiling seemed to rise as the world leveled out in the Bitterroot Valley, and my outlook brightened too. I lowered my window and reached into air at least ten degrees warmer than it would've been anywhere else that side of Montana. The Bitterroot Valley isn't called the banana belt for nothing, though.

Decades earlier, it's where Marcus Daly found the timber and grew the food he needed to keep his Butte mines and miners going, and he built a town here too, Hamilton. But the only thing connecting Butte, Anaconda, and Hamilton these days is the Skalkaho road. Latter-day robber barons left Butte's mines to fill with water, Anaconda's smelter stack is nothing but a monument to loss, and the fields surrounding Hamilton only produce houses—the new cash crop. I'd sold a few of them. Nearly impossible to avoid doing business up "the root."

Although Hamilton hadn't burgeoned like Missoula, it did have a gas station with a good automated car wash. Before getting out to fill the tank, I parted with Marie's gun and slid it between the files, notebooks, receipts, and ledgers in my office box.

I sprang for the most expensive wash, but the scoria dust I'd carried from Rimrock County turned the foamy soap orange and viscous as it streamed off, and I had to drive through again to remove the streaks and last of the bug parts. Worth it, though, because driving a clean, shiny truck made me feel more hopeful about the day's outcome. Then, like a gambler putting the money they've just won right back in the machine, I phoned Phil, and the unanswered calls left me spiritually broke again.

In no rush to get home, I stayed on the old road and avoided the constant irritation of Highway 93. It slits the Bitterroot Valley like a gutted trout as it takes speeding vehicles to Missoula then climbs to the Mission Mountains, Flathead Lake, Kalispell, and the touristy ski town of Whitefish. Along the way, it hosts so many wrecks that the Montana Highway Patrol took to displaying bumper stickers reading *Pray for Me I Drive 93*.

Taking the Eastside Highway was infinitely better—slower traffic and acres of farmland between the subdivisions—but the old route wouldn't be like that for much longer. I knew it, and so did the aging raven taking stock of a sprouting cornfield from his perch on the billboard map signaling the loss of his larder.

The valley was fast becoming unrecognizable, but Stevensville hadn't lost its identity, and my formidable friend, or as close to a friend as either of us had time for, hadn't moved her office to one of the strip malls out on 93. Della continued doing business from the main drag of old Stevi where she'd first put up her real estate sign. She has a figure like a Mack truck, and food stains on every blouse attest to her ample breasts, arthritis, and tri-focal glasses. But she never did give a damn about her appearance, her mind is still quicker than most twenty-year-olds', and there's not a better broker anywhere.

Before my time in the business, Della had kept her head above water during the hard years that bankrupted most independents, and she did it on her own without a husband's income keeping her afloat. Not long after starting her own company,

she'd converted an old bank building into an apartment in back and an office up front.

I walked in at three o'clock, Phil's zero hour, but I'd
begun to internalize his failure, and imagining Jill's hot
indignation over being stood up offered little consola-
tion. Visiting Della kept my spirits from hitting rock bottom, though. Her offer to buy me a cup of coffee and a
piece of pie was as inevitable as my acceptance, and we
walked across the street to a small cafe featuring home
cooking and the owner's oil paintings of bygone times.

"Well, Lynn, how've you been keeping?"

"Okay, thanks. How about yourself?"

"Tell ya, I'm in a constant state of amazement.
Getting crazier and crazier out there. Wish I could do
what you did. Get into the construction end of the
business."

"What a waste of talent that would be. And you'd
miss our double-dealing colleagues...and all the lying buyers and yelling sellers too."

Sellers are yellers and buyers are liars was the
warning she'd given me when I started out in the
business, and she laughed.

"I'm not so sure I really would miss it. Not anymore. Some guy came in this morning bitching
about how the men around here are too cheap to pay
thirty bucks for a haircut. Then he started hollering
about how the inflated property taxes this screwed-
up state expects him to pay make living here next to
impossible. Then he says, 'It's beautiful here but you

can't eat the scenery.' Like I don't hear *that* at least once a week."

It was my turn to laugh. It felt good, and I realized I'd do anything to make Jill retract her claws. I wanted my life back. Then Della continued, savoring her contempt as much as her next forkful of chocolate cream pie.

"He did finally get around to asking me how much his barbershop is worth, though, and I got the listing. When it sells, I'll get the listing on the house I sold him last summer too. That joke isn't wrong... what's the difference between a rich Californian and a broke Bitterrooter?"

"About a year."

I hadn't missed my cue, and, this time, we laughed together.

"But how would we ever get by without 'em, Della?"

"That's the conundrum, alright. So, Lynn, what brings you down my way?"

"Just thought I'd stop by. Heading home from back east and decided to take the Skalkaho. Never in a hurry to see Missoula again after being out on the prairie."

"Don't know what you see in that desolate country on the other side of the state."

"Please, Della. Call it anything but that. Saw a documentary about Fort Peck Dam, and, I swear, that narrator described the area as desolate at least a dozen times in an hour-long show. That's more than once every six minutes for god's sake. Journalists, screenwriters, novelists...they all use the same damn word to describe the plains."

"It's because they can't find a better one."

I grinned but had to defend the place I love.

"Well, Della...how about open, honest, sweeping, uncluttered, harmonious? I could go on."

"Please don't."

But she laughed, so I did.

"And that wind everyone hates keeps the deer-flies, tourists, and clouds at bay."

"Sorry, Lynn. The prairie just looks empty to me. Makes me kinda nervous too. Like there's nothing stopping me from getting blown off the face of the earth."

That would take *some* wind, but before I could come up with a kinder retort a mutual acquaintance pranced over and saved me the trouble. Her ample perfume, although not as offensive as Jill's, mingled unpleasantly with the aroma of coffee and frying food. The aging beauty, with coifed black hair and a flirtatious eyelid flutter becoming more like a tic every year, has an unrelenting sweetness that's as hard to stomach as a cheap box of cream chocolates. Della and I cut her questions short by giving all our attention to our food, and the saccharine woman soon melted away.

"Sounds like you really would be happier in eastern Montana, Lynn."

She made it sound so simple. Nothing in that sentence about the impossibility of leaving while Jill still threatened my family. Nothing about missing them. Nothing about not being able to watch little Bryan grow up. Could I really give up so much?

"Maybe you're right, Della. And I know just where I'd go."

"Where's that?"

"Up in the northeastern corner of the state. You won't have heard of the place."

"Try me. My parents came from Plentywood."

"You have got to be kidding!"

"Nope, we moved to Stevi when I was ten. Few months after a twister came through up there. Still remember hiding in the root cellar...scared shitless."

"Damn! I wouldn't want any part of those things either. But the area I'm talking about is west of that pothole prairie next to North Dakota. Closer to Opheim...and no tornados."

"Still sounds like hell to me. But everyone loves hunting up there, Lynn. Better watch out. Or you'll be putting up every relative, friend, and acquaintance within mooching distance."

"Maybe I'll have to live in a one bedroom house and get a big, stinky, really friendly dog."

"That oughta do it, Lynn. Oh, and as long as you're here, I've got this couple, burned-out commuters with four kids, who want to move back to Missoula in the worst way. They're already qualified and—"

"Can't help you, Della. Our houses are selling before we break ground. And buyers are trying to move in before we even have the damn sod laid down."

"Well, good for you, Lynn. You've come a long way since you had to wear a padded bra and a tight tee shirt when you went to the lumberyard so they wouldn't load all the other contractors ahead of you."

"Can't believe I told you about that!"

"Only after a few beers at a New Year's Eve do. Oh, and something else I wanted to mention. Do you remember that parcel of dryland scrub over by the Big Hole? They pulled it off a huge hay ranch about six years ago. And we thought the buyer was outright insane for paying almost a million for it. Well, guess who just bought that same piece of land for over *four* million."

"No way. Who'd be that boneheaded?"

"The great state of Montana, that's who! The university and Fish and Game to be specific. Wager last year's commissions the guy has friends in the right places and had a deal going with them before he even bought that land."

"Well, wouldn't be the first time...and won't be the last, Della."

"Sweet deal for those bastards, though. Nothing like being hired to watch the henhouse when you're a fox, is there?"

"Nope. Taxpayers buy the land, for way more than it's worth, and the only ones getting to use it are out-of-state hunters and guides. Working stiffs don't have the time, money, or vehicles to get to, or into, that kinda country."

"That's right...we both know how it is, Lynn. The rich gets richer, the poor gets poorer, and the folks in between pay for it all. Question is...what happens when they've bled the middle class dry? Oh, the hell with all that! Let's take a drive."

She hustled me into her Chevy Suburban and gave me a tour of her nearby listings. When we happened across anyone else's, they were deemed overpriced or shouldn't be touched with a ten-foot pole for some reason it wouldn't be fair to divulge. Her real motive for shanghaiing me came last. She'd recently acquired an unspoiled Arts and Crafts-style farmhouse on sixty acres of nice woodland and wanted it turned into a B&B with stables.

"I'd be grateful if you'd take it on, Lynn."

"You know how much I'd love working on something like this. And it's a great—"

"Yes it is. And you're the best there is at remodeling these old places without destroying their aura."

"Don't know about aura. And cut out the flattery... before I start believing you. Probably couldn't make it fly, anyway. Amy calls them my museum projects. Whenever there's talk of taking on another one, she starts relating the slim profits they've generated."

Della frowned, and so did I. I didn't like taking a pass on a place that unaltered. Most period houses, even those built as late as the fifties, sixties, and seventies, have been updated and remodeled beyond recognition. Unmolested homes of a certain age, similar to factory-original show cars, will fetch a good price, just not enough to offset the pain-in-the-ass factor. Old buildings are a hassle. But, to me, they're like lost, whimpering puppies. No matter the disease, style, size, or shortcomings, there's always something about them to love.

"Come on, Lynn. It'd be a real showpiece for Crandall Construction."

"Yeah, Della. It's a great-looking place. And, if you bought it, I know it's been kept dry and has good bones. But we'd still have to hire specialized craftsmen for stuff like molding repairs. And that'll only be the start of our headaches."

"That's what you're so good at, though. All those complicated details of making a place look just right."

"There you go again with the flattery. Oh, what the hell. Fax the details to Amy, and I'll run it by her."

"Thanks, Lynn. You're a pal. And I'd have my fingers crossed if I could still do that."

Della wasn't afraid to laugh at herself, and it was probably the secret to her longevity. She took a different road back into Stevi. And there it was—that black Lincoln Navigator—parked in the driveway of the newest, biggest McMansion on the block. And it didn't take long to find out who owned it.

"Look at that black SUV, Della. Wonder if they could find room to add a little more chrome?"

"Little gaudy, huh? Know who it belongs to, don't you?"

"I shook my head."

"That asshole down at Missoula OPG."

I didn't have to ask which one. Anyone in the business could identify *the* asshole at the city-county planning office.

"Ron Steadman, huh? That figures."

Good lord, Jill and Steadman. And we already had more reason than most for despising that man. Phil's buddy, a vet whose injuries limited his ability to work, had scrimped for years to save enough for the big down payment needed to build a rental behind his house The rent would pay off a short-term loan then add to his meager income.

The owner of the property next door had added a second rental only that spring, a modular home with zero setback, its foundation directly on the property line bordering the alley. When Phil's buddy was denied a building permit because he didn't have the required thirty-foot setback from the alley, he called the city and explained why it had to have been a mistake. But they said, no, there'd been no mistake and refused to comment on how the modular home came to be there.

I'd looked into it and wasn't surprised to find it belonged to Collins Modular Home Sales. Phil told his Marine Corp buddy what I'd found out, and he showed up at city hall demanding to know who'd signed off on those permits. When he got past the gals up front to Steadman, who said the information had somehow been lost, the vet didn't like being lied to, called him a few choice names, and landed in jail. He got out the next day, but being treated like that left him more despondent than Phil had ever seen him.

We told him not to give up on building the rental; we'd try forcing the city to grant him a variance and, failing that, would find another way to help him. But Steadman had accomplished what the punji sticks in Nam hadn't, and Phil's friend committed suicide before we could do anything. The note he left said it had come down to swallowing those pills or shooting the bent bastard in cahoots with Collins and taking away *his* dreams. We hadn't kept the incident to ourselves, and Della had no reason to question my interest in Steadman.

"Feel for you, Della. Couldn't have been any fun working with that SOB."

"Nope, but I had that overpriced pile of lumber listed for a year. And there's no one I'd rather have unloaded it on than him and his wife. Might've even sold it to our next governor."

"Not Steadman!"

"Good god, no."

Della rolled her eyes at the absurdity of Steadman running for that office and was still shaking her head at the idea when she began filling me in.

"Meant his wife. She's the one with all the money...an orthopedic surgeon. Specializes in sports injuries. The university loves her. She's pulling down over three hundred thousand a year. And her daddy's a big deal attorney in Helena."

"But isn't she going to have a tough time getting elected with a husband as hated as hers is?"

"Yeah, and she must've thought so too. Uses her maiden name. Not many will make the connection. And I bet Steadman will be kept so far back in the shadows he'll need a flashlight to know where he is half the time."

Della slowed in front of her office and steered the Suburban into the parking spot marked with a sign that simply read MINE. After grabbing the top of the steering wheel with both knobby fists to heft herself out, she paused and reminded me about her project.

"Appreciate you running my project by Amy. I'll fax everything to her. Mail some photos too."

"That'll help. The less she has to dig for info...the less she'll hate the idea. See you later, Della."

Should've guessed Jill and Steadman might've hooked up. And if his wife became governor, nothing would stop Jill from tearing our lives apart. The two women might even be friends; Jill's family had moved to Helena from San Diego before she started high school.

Driving back to Steadman's house didn't make sense—did I think Jill was visiting and would walk across the road in front me so I could run her over? But I was careful about being seen there and parked across the road a house down from theirs. I still had a good view of their driveway, and, a few minutes later, Steadman, handsome in a California newscaster sort of way, came out of the house, strutted over to the Navigator, then stood there admiring it like he'd bought it that day. I hoped he wasn't leaving, and, when he got in and backed out of the driveway, I cursed myself for being there.

When he took off in the opposite direction, I decided I'd pushed my luck far enough. But, before I could get away, one of the garage doors opened for the silver Mercedes headed toward it. The driver, a tall, thin brunette wearing the wealthy suburbanite's Saturday uniform of designer jeans, leather jacket, and high-heeled boots, got out and took quick, long strides to the mailbox. Busy scooping out an armload of manila envelopes, she didn't even glance in my direction. Then she walked back into the garage and the door came down behind her. The woman looked mighty capable of getting elected to me.

What a trio Mike would be facing when that happened, the governor, Steadman, and Jill. It made truly accepting Phil's failure impossible, and clinging to a defunct plan seemed better than my pitiful backup—having a gun that worked. But following his instructions to stay away from Missoula until at least eight o'clock left nearly three hours to agonize over his silence, and, for the first time in my life, I wanted to walk into a bar and drink it all away.

The appalling impulse frightened me into pretending things would be alright, and I tried to add weight to the fantasy by behaving normally and stopping to scrounge for vintage bath fixtures, light globes, doorknobs, and window latches at every junk store, thrift shop, and antique mall between Stevi and Lolo. But they were all closed, and, as I left the parking lot of the last one, my phone rang. It took tremendous constraint to look before answering, but I needed time to hide my crushing disappointment if it wasn't Phil. And it wasn't.

"Hi, Karl."

"You home yet, Lynn?"

"Not quite. Had some business to take care of in the Bitterroot and took a detour over Skalkaho Pass."

I already knew the outcome of Darlene's biopsy—Karl would've given me *good* news before I'd gotten hello out of my mouth. I made it easier for him.

"Not the best news, then?"

"No. It damn sure wasn't. Came back Stage III breast cancer."

"Oh my god!"

"And, know what, Lynn? The doctor came right out and blamed the fallout from those bomb tests. Doesn't matter, though. There's not one solitary thing we can do about it. It's the damn government."

"Jesus, Karl. Knowing the bastards responsible will never be punished makes it even worse."

"It sure as hell does. Doctor did say there's compensation money we can apply for. That's something at least. But nothing's going to stop what's coming. And after what Mom went through, I'm all too aware of the hell Darlene has ahead of her. So is she, and it's hard to take. And not being able to do a goddamn thing about it is killing me. Just wish...shit...I can't talk anymore. I'm sor—"

"It's okay, Karl. It's okay. Call me later. You know I'll be thinking of you both."

Poor man. Why was this happening to his wife and not my son's? Then I'd be celebrating instead of feeling bad, and two good people wouldn't be in torment. But there'd never been a time when I expected life to be fair.

I could only imagine Darlene's fear and dread but understood Karl's pain—the pain of being helpless to protect someone he loved. At least Phil and I could stop Jill, and not hearing from him didn't absolutely prove his plan had failed. He could've carried it out even though I hadn't heard from him.

It was only around six-thirty when I reached Lolo, Missoula's first bedroom community, so I stopped at the truck stop for a Coke. I'd nearly filled my cup with ice, and cubes flew everywhere when a voice boomed behind me.

"Well as I live and breathe! If it ain't Lynn Crandall."

"Jesus, Bob. You trying to give me a heart attack?"

"A little jumpy today, are we? How you been, anyway?"

"Okay. How about you?"

"If I felt any better...I'd be dangerous. Heard you're getting out of our racket."

"Yeah...had enough fun. And the construction business keeps me plenty busy."

I couldn't have run into Bob at a better time. He's cowboy charming, older than he looks, and his lightning-fast wit makes him a kick to be around. He likes testing people by dropping quips into the conversation. If they don't laugh, he's forewarned they're dullards or poor listeners. And his timing is impeccable. At some meeting or other, a group of us were talking about Steadman being a planning official half the town would cheerfully lynch and wondering why we'd been saddled with such a know-nothing blowhard. Bob had walked by and, quick as a bee sting, delivered his one-liner.

"If you gave that guy an enema before he died, you could bury him in a matchbox."

Bob's the personification of the old saw "It isn't what you've got; it's how you use it," and he had me laughing before he left for his small ranch up the Bitterroot. Returning to my truck brought me down like a trip wire, though, and I turned toward home with a festering awareness of failure.

After being away for five days, I'd have to get used to the trash and weeds lining the streets and roadsides all over again, and Missoula looked more crowded than ever. Like debris from the waves of newcomers, an odd assortment of continually changing small businesses had washed up on both sides of the four-lane. But none of them provided good paying jobs because industry had become a dirty word. Mills, logging companies, and manufacturing businesses were replaced by malls, casinos, and breweries, and Missoula began feeding on itself. The perfect venue for Jill to prosper after destroying us—a postwar outcome that, with or without Phil, had to be avoided. If he'd failed, maybe I could do something to stop her. I had a gun and a truck, didn't I?

But the smartest way to put them to work for me, that was the big unknown, and for once I didn't mind being waylaid at malfunction junction. The intersection is two busy streets meeting a third, even busier, street and was so ill conceived that, in 1973, a national magazine reported it as having the longest wait time in the country. As always, the light turned red the second I approached. It had postponed what the night could bring, though, and I was content to watch the plastic shards from a recent fender bender twinkle red, green, and yellow on the black, oily pavement.

Even after the infamous light turned green, I only drove a few blocks then parked and inspected the fish-belly sky hanging low over the city. Unable to parse out a plan of action in the stagnant clouds,

I was caught in a quagmire of indecision and tried to drive out of it by meandering through the heavily wooded university district. But not having Marie or Phil to talk ideas over with had me thinking in circles.

The irritations that came with being home didn't help, and I resented having to pull over and use eye drops not needed since leaving town. Blinking away the excess liquid turned a placard-carrying swami into a student peering around a large box as he stumbled along in his flip flops toward a moving van. The vacated rental, a Queen Anne—style home long since relegated to cash provider, stood with paint peeling, front porch sagging, and door agape—an old whore worn out from too many comings and goings.

It was a depressing sight and not a good place to park anyway. The aphids on the overhanging maple trees would soon cover my clean truck with their shiny, sappy excrement. Or did they sleep at night? Leaving seemed safest, and I drove past our Third Street project then stopped to straighten a wobbly sign but had to wait for a dog-walker to get out of the way. Faded and wrinkled as his clothes, the old man obediently shuffled along behind his sniffing toy poodle and looked on vicariously when it lifted its leg to pee on our sign. I got out, rinsed off the sign with a bottle of water, then got a hammer out of my toolbox and pounded its steel legs deeper into the ground.

Looking up at the 1930s brownstone showcasing some of our best renovating work, I knew I had to stop Jill from stealing what she wanted from us and poisoning the rest. But how to stop her without losing everything anyway? Fatigue and habit drew me to my driveway where I automatically hit the garage door opener and drove inside. No closer to having a plan and feeling defeated, I gathered up my bag, Bryan's toys, and the sacks of Philipsburg candy and took it all into the house.

It was the same as I'd left it. And it seemed life would be the same too, an endless, escalating battle with Jill. Unless—I approached the answering machine with a prayer on my lips, but found no message from Phil saying his plan had been a success and explaining why he hadn't called. There were only work-related questions and telemarketers, and I'd have smashed the offending machine underfoot if not for needing some of those messages when life returned to normal. Normal? Life would never be normal again. Not as long as Jill was alive.

I tried to reach Phil one last time, but dialing his number from my home phone didn't produce different results, just gave me the satisfaction of slamming the handset back in the base. I couldn't formulate one realistic hypothesis about what had subverted his plan. Something had, though, because he would never have gotten cold feet and backed out. I called his cellphone again, this time to leave a message saying I'd made it home, and Marie's words came back to me loud and clear.

"So, Lynn, what's the verdict? Better bite the bullet and do something PDQ. Or the regret will chew on you like maggots on a wire-cut sheep for the rest of your life."

Plan or no plan, it was time to find Jill—a somatic conclusion that left my mind playing catch-up. Gathering up all the advice Marie had ever given me, like a bouquet of her yellow roses, I returned to the cab of my truck. But turning the key would start more than the engine, and I just sat there staring at the workbench Phil built the afternoon we found out we were having our first baby. Sawdust had clung to his face, his neck, and the hair on his chest, forever linking the smell of freshly cut lumber to the tender passion of that afternoon.

I couldn't have saved my marriage, but maybe I could save my family from Jill. What she'd done when Phil hadn't shown up for their meeting was anyone's guess. If she'd stayed in Helena, I'd have little chance of finding her. She wasn't likely to answer my phone call and tell me where she was. But with any luck she'd come home. Only one way to find out. I turned the key, and the engine roared to life with all the confidence, energy, and enthusiasm lacking in me.

Mike had made a good point earlier. Jill should've been excised long before—before she'd given the family such compelling, public motives to want her dead. Bryan could live with the fact his mother had been killed and be better off without her. His grandma having been a suspect in her murder, maybe put on trial for it, maybe even convicted for it, would be something else altogether. And the odds of doing away with Jill and not getting caught weren't that great.

I didn't doubt my ability to kill, though. Hadn't I plunged a butcher knife into my dad's beer-bloated gut, pushing until his flesh resisted the hilt? Hadn't I watched him bleed out, feeling nothing but relief? And guilt's pugnacious face hadn't appeared until the next morning, when I'd been disappointed to find my father's death had only been a dream. There'd be no guilt at all about ending Jill's life, though—only the satisfaction of honoring a vow to protect my kids.

Driving the mile to Mike's house gave me time to pray his wife would cooperate for once in her life and be in the home we'd built years before he met her. He'd designed a lodge-style house and located it on two acres with three hundred feet of Bitterroot River frontage. The perfect setting. And his instinctive choice to eschew a lawn and tidy what nature planted not only saved time, money, and effort but further enhanced his large rustic home. He'd also inadvertently created the quintessential I'm-greener-than-thou residence. When it became a popular Parade Home, Mike had been embarrassed by the attention and irritated by the inconvenience until Amy pointed out all the buyers and free publicity it generated.

Adding even more beauty and privacy to the place, he'd wound the driveway through the old-growth ponderosa, but I couldn't see who might be at the house. So I switched off my headlights, turned into the dirt lane closer to the river, and parked behind the small garage full of rafts, floating tubes, coolers, and fishing paraphernalia.

Then, without allowing myself to think past the next second, I took the gun from my front seat office box, cocked it, thumbed up the safety, and slipped it into my jacket pocket. Still painfully aware of my recent clumsiness, I was glad the old pistol used a pin-lock system. It meant that, even jostled, bumped or dropped, the gun wouldn't fire unless someone pulled the trigger. But I planned to pull it.

The situation didn't trump the misery of living with the status quo. It came close though. But completely at odds with the task at hand, every step toward Mike's house released woodsy, riverbank, picnicking scents, welcome reminders of the happiness to be won. And there were no strange cars in front of the house. I thanked my lucky stars for that, pulled on my gloves, and tried the side door of the garage. But it was locked, and, with the windows set high to help prevent thieves from gaining entry, I couldn't tell if Jill's Lexus was inside or not. The house looked dark, and it made me worry she might not have come home after all. But the icy breeze blowing across my soul told me the woman was there.

I walked around the side of the house, past the outdoor fireplace that gave our family so much enjoyment before Jill came along, and intended to roust her with my best cop knock—bang, bang, bang, bang with the side of a gloved fist. But the back door stood slightly ajar. Remembering how Karl had swept me into a hug as I crept into Marie's dimly lit hospital room, I yelled into the stillness like a pissed-off drill sergeant.

"Jill! You home? Jill! It's me...Lynn!"

Silence. I yelled again. More silence. Opening the door slowly, I took tentative steps into the kitchen, saw a small heap in the middle of the floor, and switched on the light. Jill—motionless, curled into the fetal position. Placing a boot against her ribs, I rolled her onto her back. The long curls fell away from her face, and I must've unconsciously presumed her blood to be as black as her heart because the bright red liquid seeping from her nostrils and ears surprised me.

I knelt down beside her, but didn't check for a pulse because I didn't want to find one. Humming tunelessly to avoid hearing any sounds of life, I looked for a wound, saw no sign of one, then wanted to count my blessings and walk away. However, not discovering anything like a gash or bullet hole didn't rule out foul play. Even dead, or nearly dead, on the kitchen floor, she could generate more trouble than most people do in a lifetime. So, forever segmenting my life into before and after that instant, I stood up, went over to the wide-open back door, closed it, turned the dead bolt, and returned to Jill.

Getting rid of her body was one thing, but what if she wasn't a body yet and came around? She showed no signs of doing that, though, and I took a Kleenex from the box on the counter, twisted pieces of it into plugs, then shoved them into her ears and nostrils to keep blood off the floor. The cops would never have reason to examine Mike's kitchen if I could get rid of Jill's body, but he would wonder what had happened if he found blood on the floor. And I didn't want anything drawing attention to where she'd *really* died. The distance I'd painstakingly put between my whereabouts and where Jill was supposed to die had snapped back like a rubber band.

The kids were still okay though, if they'd kept their promises and stayed at the cabin. I called Mike and Amy, and Paul too, just to be safe. When their cellphones went directly to voicemail, I needed the comfort of letting myself assume it meant they were still up there. But Paul had once said he'd give anything to hear Jill take her last breath, and recalling that fact sparked a wildfire of foreboding. Easy to imagine the big man knocking on the door, following Jill into the kitchen, then taking off his jacket and dropping it over her head before pounding it against the slate flooring. And I could see him picking up his coat after she'd quit moving and walking out the door a happy man.

An enraged Mike or Amy might even have been responsible, or one of Jill's cohorts, or she might have died of an undiagnosed heart problem or aneurysm for all I knew. I wasn't about to bet my life or the kids' on those last two scenarios, though, and needed to come up with an idea of what to do next, other than getting the hell out of that room. Thinking clearer out in the hallway, I decided to make sure no one else—maybe even Jill's killer—was in the house. I took the gun out of my pocket and held it tight with both hands; then they only shook when I let go to open closet doors, check under beds, or wipe the sweat off my palms.

Blood surging against my eardrums and the voice in my mind screaming, "Get the hell out, you idiot," made hearing a doorknob turn or a floorboard squeak about as likely as catching a whispered remark during a dustoff. But no lover, friend, or murderer had hidden on the main floor, and Mike's second-floor suite remained locked. That only left the basement, saved for last so someone upstairs couldn't sneak out the front door while I was down there and because it frightened me the most.

No one had hidden behind the couch in the family room, or under the pool table, or in amongst the stuff in the storage room, though. And I'd gained a little composure by the time I reached the top of the stairs, or I would've tumbled back down them when my cellphone rang. In a frenzied attempt to pull a glove off with my teeth so I could wrest the phone from my pocket, I dropped the gun on my foot, and it bounced away.

"Hello? Hello? Phil?"

Dial tone. Damn, damn, damn, the ring hadn't been a ring, just a voicemail notification. How could I have missed a call? I'd had good coverage since coming off the Skalkaho. Delayed notifications had happened before though, and I'd cursed the cellphone company then too, just not with such visceral hatred. Someone had called at 2:35 pm, right about the time I'd been trying to phone Phil after checking out Marie's gun. I didn't recognize the number, and the possibility someone from an emergency room or police station had left the message constricted my lungs.

"Hi, Lynn."

Phil's voice—like morphine to a burn victim.

"I'm phoning from the neighbor's house."

His voice had a warning tone that told me they were listening and he couldn't say much.

"A freak storm hit my place around dawn. Dumped about ten inches of heavy wet snow. Took down the power lines and phone line and dropped a half-dozen lodgepole through the shop roof! So I can't even get to the chain saws. And the hell of it is, my truck's in there too. Along with your trailer and the four-wheelers. Thought I'd better hike out and let you know what's going on. I—"

He'd used up his time. Frantic, I checked for another message, and my heart didn't beat till I'd found it.

"Like I was saying...I won't be going to Helena today. What a hellacious mess! First mile of my road looks like a giant game of pick-up sticks. I'll have to get a logger with a self loader in here. Talk to you as soon I can. Crazy-bad timing, huh?"

Bad timing, or Mother Nature, another amoral bitch, had taken Jill's side. How frustrating to hear Phil but not be able to ask him what to do with her body or if he'd gotten hurt. He had to be okay, though, didn't he, to hike eight miles to his neighbor's place? Might've been a different story if the trees closer to his house had blown down—could've crushed him in his own bed or skewered him with splintering wood.

Thankfully, he'd been spared, and the riddle was answered at last. A goddamn storm had screwed everything up. Not even after hearing Karl's story about a low snow in May killing Lame Johnny had I considered it being what had stymied Phil. Life never lets you follow the course you've set unmolested. It turns you round and round, shoves you in the wrong direction, and you stagger forward as best you can.

After retrieving the gun from where it had landed five steps down, I went into the kitchen and nearly slipped in the puddle of urine next to Jill's body. Mike would certainly find *that* odd. Taking a roll of toilet paper from the bathroom cupboard, I unwound the entire thing in the liquid, slid it around with my boot, then bent down to scoop it up and noticed her face. All color had drained from her skin, leaving a mask of makeup, and her eyes were unnaturally dilated, large black holes ringed by attenuated green. I pressed my gloved fingers above her long, thick lashes and closed her eyelids. Not out of respect. I'd have flushed her body down the toilet with the soggy paper if it had been possible.

With that being out of the question, what could I do with it? And do fast. When my gaze fell on the door leading into the garage, I realized I hadn't checked the most obvious place for Jill's killer, if there'd been one, to have hidden. Certain the oversight would be the death of me, I took Marie's gun in both hands again, swung the door open, elbowed the light on, and tried to look everywhere at once.

Nothing moved. But someone could've taken cover behind Jill's Lexus, and I picked my way across the cement floor like it was a lake of rotten ice. Not smart—should've run and at least been a moving target. Luckily, there was no one hiding beneath, behind, or inside the SUV to take advantage of my ineptitude, and I could lean against a shiny white fender and try to determine the depth and breadth of the shit creek I'd drifted into minus that all-important paddle.

The thought of someone knocking on the front door terrified me, but a random visitor could be disregarded. They wouldn't have a key and, ignored, would go away. Excluding the unlikely disaster of the police breaking down the door, I had time to move Jill's body. I just needed the how. Solutions repeatedly broke rank, regrouped, tripped over logic, and scattered again. Phil, the consummate chess player, had come up with a foolproof plan, barring freak snowstorms. I examined it closely, looking for enough usable bits and pieces to cover my exposed keister.

The first four steps—meeting up with Jill, luring her inside the enclosed trailer, breaking her neck, simple, clean, and quick, then hiding her body in the false wall he'd fabricated in the trailer—weren't relevant. But the rest were. His next step would've been to load her Lexus in the trailer and drive seventeen miles south of Helena where he'd located a wide jayhole above a steep ravine on an old logging road. Then he would've positioned Jill's body behind the wheel, started the engine, stood on the running board, shifted into reverse, shut the door as he jumped clear, and the Lexus would've backed over the edge and rolled to the bottom.

Phil said vehicles crashing and bursting into flames happened in the movies but usually nowhere else. He'd have scraped away his truck and trailer tracks in the jayhole, but let vehicles traveling the road blot out the rest, and it might've been days before anyone noticed the wreckage. Of course, it would've been discovered eventually, and he hadn't overlooked giving Jill a reason for being there. Like Missoula, Helena's outlying area had homes for sale deep in the mountains. A few of them would've been circled in the local newspaper left on the front seat of the Lexus, and investigators would surmise Jill got lost then backed over the edge trying to turn around in the dark.

Making it seem like Jill was ready to leave Mike and move back to Helena wouldn't have struck a false note. She'd made sure of that herself. Phil's few hours of jeopardy would've saved us from a lifetime of purgatory, a great plan gone to waste. Or could the last steps be jerry-rigged to work for me? Maybe, if I could somehow get Jill's body into her vehicle, load it on a trailer, and find somewhere to ditch it. But going home then bringing a trailer to Mike's left the body unattended, and loading the Lexus at his house was a bad idea anyway—too much chance of someone coming around.

I'd no choice. I had to drive Jill's vehicle to my house with her body already inside, and I let the logistics of that operation slip by me. There were enough complications to deal with just getting her corpse to the garage. She didn't weigh much, but even a hundred pounds of dead weight was too much to pack around. Dragging her would've been easiest, if not for needing to lift the body into the driver's seat of a high-mounted SUV when I got it there. But the solution was right in front of me.

Always being enlisted to help someone move, Mike had confiscated one of our appliance dollies. I hooked a fistful of bungee cords across the handles and wheeled it into the kitchen. The problem now was, for Jill's body to end up face forward behind the steering wheel of her Lexus, she'd have to be face down on the dolly. Worried about the metal crossbars causing incongruous bruising, I found a long, thick scarf in the hall closet, wound it around her head to protect her face, then realized she'd have been wearing a jacket.

Getting her into a jacket was worse than undressing a passed-out drunk. And it made me question the feasibility of getting her body not just onto the appliance dolly, but in a face-down position. I came up with a plan, and, after lowering the unwieldy implement to the floor lengthwise against a wall, knelt down and shoved Jill's body across the floor into the side of it, then pushed harder and lifted as it collided, and her body flipped onto the thing face down.

It went far better than expected, and tightening the strap across her chest and crisscrossing bungee cords everywhere else went smoothly too. But I wasn't sure I'd have the strength to upright the dolly from a horizontal position. No one could've done it, though, without something stopping the wheels from skidding across the floor. I took the rubber mats out of the sink, used them to chock the little tires, then stood behind Jill's head, bent my knees, grabbed the curved handles of the dolly, straightened my legs, lifted, and lo and behold it was vertical. Good thing nothing went wrong during that first try. No way could I have done it twice.

Upright, Jill looked like the lead in a grade school rendition of *The Mummy*. Before wheeling her out of the kitchen, I put the mats back in the sink, found her Louis Vuitton purse, hung it around her neck, then tried to figure out what I'd do if the bungee cords didn't hold going down the steps into the garage. They did, though, and I hooked some of them under the handrail so I could let go of the dolly and set up the Lexus.

Fishing the gold key fob from Jill's purse with gloves on wasn't easy, and, although it seemed like a good idea, I didn't have to time to search through it. I had to keep my mind on getting out of there and went over to the Lexus, put the key in the ignition, then raised the steering wheel and lowered the seat. But it needed to be even lower. Scratching my noggin for an answer produced an image of Mike and Paul doing the same when they'd scoffed at the vehicle's adjustable height control mechanism.

If Jill had valued clearance over getting in and out easier and hadn't already set that gizmo to the low position, it could remedy my problem. I switched the button to *on*, then pressed the down arrow, and the chassis dropped enough to let the seat line up below Jill's scrawny ass. Why wasn't Mike happily married to a woman with big hips and an even bigger heart? He deserved a second chance not a murder charge. We both did. We all did. But I'd begun to question my ability to remove our familial fat from the fire.

Jill's body still had to be transferred from the appliance dolly to the driver's seat of the Lexus then to my house, and I'd already strained each and every muscle just getting it to the garage. Brainwashing myself into believing the rest of the job would be easier helped, and I got back to work.

Wheeling Jill closer to the Lexus, I leaned her back on the metal garbage can Mike used for wood scraps and carefully removed the straps and bungee cords. How to slide the can out of the way and move the dolly without fully uprighting it was the next hurdle. But, by taking all the weight to keep the thing nearly horizontal, then standing on one foot while pushing the can away with the other, I managed to wrangle Jill's body over to the driver's seat without dumping it on the concrete floor.

Now for the make-it-or-break-it trick. I jerked the appliance dolly upright, and, as I'd visualized, the back of Jill's knees hit the running board, causing her to bend at the waist and her body to plop across the seat. But I hadn't foreseen her feet kicking forward as she fell. And, when they did, my foot got knocked off the wheel brake and the dolly's axle shot backward, nearly breaking my shins. Goddamn woman—nothing but trouble even dead.

I danced around and rubbed my shins till I'd run out of cuss words, then took a deep breath, hobbled back to the dolly, uprighted the damn thing, and put it back against the wall where Mike kept it. Luckily, Jill's body had stayed where it landed. I grabbed a fistful of her jacket in both hands, yanked her torso off the console, slammed it against the seatback, then pushed her feet up onto the floorboard. Her scarf had fallen off, and, even though it had served its purpose, I took the time to rewind it tightly around her head. I couldn't stand seeing her face even when she was alive.

Once I'd gathered the bungee cords and hung them where they belonged, I went into the house to switch off the lights I'd left blazing. Limping from room to room grated on my last nerve but gave me time to realize Jill wouldn't have gone out of town without packing. I went back to the master bedroom, pushed aside the clothing filling the walk-in closet, and didn't have trouble identifying her suitcase from the others. It reeked of her perfume.

I threw it on the bed, started filling it, and found handling her personal belongings, even with gloves on, disgusted me as much as touching her lifeless body. I packed all sorts of makeup, toothbrush, hairbrush, birth control pills, nightgown, socks, and tortuous-looking panties I couldn't see the point of wearing. Then I added a pair of jeans and two cowl neck sweaters. Under the sweaters—that's where I found the photographs.

The woman with the whip had her back to the camera, and I didn't recognize the young woman handcuffed and collared to the wall, but the aroused man standing naked in the well-lit room was Ron Steadman. Could Jill have been the person taking those photos? It didn't jive. Granted, she'd taken those porn shots of Mike the night she drugged him, but that's the only time she'd been interested in a camera that wasn't pointed at her. It would've taken a professional or serious hobbyist to capture the ecstatic grimaces, drops of blood, and aberrant sex acts in these close-ups.

The glossy five-by-sevens were dynamite, and the newspaper clippings with them, dated two years previous, could light the fuse. All three of the *Independent Record* articles included a photo of the woman who'd been chained to the wall. The seventeen-year-old, repeatedly and erroneously referred to as a young girl to sell more papers, had been found dead in a barrow pit west of Helena where Vista Grande intersects Birdseye Road. A later story said she'd died of erotic asphyxiation, her death was being investigated as suspicious, and police were pursuing leads.

Did the clippings and pictures somehow precipitate Jill's death? I doubted it. If she'd been blackmailing Steadman or the unknown woman with them, they wouldn't have still been in the house. They were easy enough to find, right there with Jill's sweaters in a heavyweight white envelope labeled LIFE INSURANCE. She had a sense of humor, I'd give her that. And maybe the contents had only been for protection, but why hadn't she locked something like that away in a safe deposit box or hidden it better? Ludicrous to be pondering mysteries when I had a body to move, and I stashed the envelope in the inside pocket of my jacket.

But walking away from a nearly completed puzzle is difficult. I wondered if the photos and clippings had anything to do with the 20K Mike had discovered and if they'd been there when he found it. He might have just stopped looking when he found all that cash and missed the envelope. I squandered time locating Jill's scarf drawer. No money there anymore, though, just the silk rectangles of gold, pink, and green she wore to set off her red hair. I threw a couple of them on top of the sweaters, along with an indigo bottle of her perfume. Then I closed the suitcase, picked it up, and wondered what life would be like next time I walked out of Mike's kitchen.

I put Jill's suitcase in the Lexus, and the most repugnant job of the night started innocuously with me trotting through the woods to get my garage door opener from the truck. The cab looked so inviting—and nothing prevented me from driving home, sitting down in my living room, and pretending I'd never left. Nothing but knowing better. I slipped the opener from the visor and retraced my steps to the garage.

Hearing music when I opened the door brought me to a heart-thudding stop. When the tune ended with a beep, I realized it had only been Jill's cell-phone ringing and envisioned her laughing behind the layers of scarf. Snatching the phone from her purse, I looked to see who'd called, didn't recognize the number, and dropped it on the seat. Jill always kept it within easy reach.

The time had come to get her body to my house, but I wasn't ready and never would've been. It meant sitting on her lap—the only way to get her and the Lexus to the trailer in one trip without having to load her body twice. First into the passenger seat at Mike's then into the driver's seat after I got to my garage, an onerous undertaking that would've eaten up far too much time.

Like it or not, I'd be riding on a dead body, and dilly-dallying wasn't going make it any better. After turning off the garage lights and locking the side door, I reclined the seat as far back as it would go, stepped up on the running board, then took hold of the steering wheel with both hands and lowered myself onto Jill's cold, boney thighs like they were freshly heated branding irons.

Mike's garage door seemed to rise inch by slow inch, setting the pace for my macabre mission. I didn't dare speed. But not racing home when the cold from Jill's flesh began seeping into mine, like part of her infecting my being, revealed the true meaning of willpower, and waiting for my own garage door to inch open nearly annihilated the last of mine. But I scraped together enough to get off Jill's lap without dragging her out with me, a teenager's maneuver taking an exhausted, middle-aged woman forever to execute.

After a few seconds of trying to brush Jill off my clothing, I jogged through the equipment yard to the 1971 dual axle Ford pickup Phil had dubbed Tom Dooley. Amy had compiled a list of reasons for getting rid of the old truck, but it hadn't swayed me, and my old friend was still there to help me out. I slid my fingers along the top of the front tire, where the key had lain for a year or more, and thought about all the legitimate excuses our first work truck had for not starting.

Tom D never disappoints, though, and was soon kicking out enough warm air to soothe my knotted muscles. The cab smelled of dusty manifolds heating, exhaust fumes from an engine running a little rich, and the early days of Phil and me. Remembering those times and driving without a dead woman underneath me eased the tension, and my brain slipped into neutral—the sanity-saving break before a new fear shoved it into overdrive. I had a startling recollection of Phil's words that morning after. After we'd decided to get rid of Jill, after the gentle, re-connecting sex, after he'd come up with his brilliant, ill-fated plan.

His gaze had shifted from his plate of scrambled eggs to me, and he'd said he hoped there wouldn't be much traffic on that old logging road. Because if he had to wait too long and rigor mortis set in, a medical examiner would be able to tell Jill hadn't died from car injures. I tried to work it out. I'd gotten back to Missoula an hour or so before I'd wanted to and found her curled up on the kitchen floor right around eight. But, having no idea exactly when she'd done us all a favor and quit breathing, I'd no idea when her body would go rigid. The window of time for getting her positioned behind the wheel of her Lexus could slam shut any minute.

Nothing to be done about it, though, and at least there were no flashing police lights at Mike's place, another danger feeding on my moxie. I tucked old Tom in close to the shed, where he wouldn't be noticed for a few days, and I could, at long last, go back home in my own truck, hitch up the trailer, and get the hell out of town. That is, I could've if things hadn't gone directly and deeply south when a vehicle decelerated in the street and light beams swung through the trees. Might've been smarter to get in the truck and leave anyway, but who was this interloper? What if Mike hadn't stayed at the cabin like I'd begged him to? Or maybe Paul had come to check on things for him?

Slipping on layers of pine needles and slapping away branches, I cut through the trees, hid in a thick stand of chokecherry bushes, and turned off my phone. One panting breath later, motion detector lights came on as a man walked around the corner of the garage—Ron Steadman! What in hell was he doing there? Had he come to see Jill? He didn't go to the house, though. Stopping no more than twenty feet from my hiding spot, he tried to open the side door to the garage, and I regretted having locked it. The crowbar in his hand was obviously a mystery to him, and he used it like a sledgehammer. The doorknob clanked to the sidewalk and wood splintered. Then Steadman went inside, switched on the light, and began ranting into his cellphone.

"It's gone! I don't know...don't know. It's just fucking gone."

A second later he appeared in the doorway, pulled the phone from his mouth to throw his arms in the air, and began fervently pacing the sidewalk. When he stopped to swing the crowbar across the chokecherry branches sheltering me, my reaction wasn't exactly quiet, and he'd have heard me if he hadn't started yelling into the phone at that exact moment.

"Yes! I did exactly what you said. No broken skin."

So, Steadman had murdered Jill. I wanted to pin a medal on him—then beat him to death with that damn crowbar for leaving her body behind.

"Yes, I'm sure. And I am not going back inside that house no matter what you say. I just need to find that fucking Lexus, wipe it down, and get rid of a blanket. Or they'll find more than my prints. And I don't know where the fucking thing is!"

The crowbar came crashing through the bushes again, releasing a second cloud of pollen from the pendulous blossoms, and suppressing sneezes became nothing short of excruciating. If only he'd clear off. But the conversation continued, and the man never known to string two words together without being flippant sounded pretty damn sincere.

"Sorry! Yes. I should've thought of it before. Hard to think straight, though, you know...right after."

Then, at last, he resumed his pacing, tracing circle eights in the air with the crowbar as he went, and I could exhale and inhale again.

"Why the fuck would someone show up here and just take Jill's fucking Lexus? If they'd gone in the house, the place would be crawling with cops. It makes no fucking sense!"

The woman on the other end of the conversation, assuredly his wife, raised her voice loud enough for me to hear her, and the unintelligible words completely deflated Steadman.

"Alright, alright...guess it doesn't matter now. So, what in the hell are we going to do about it?"

He stopped pacing to stare into the garage, but his wife said something to set him off again, and he straightened his slumped body and screamed into the phone.

"Yes...*we*. If you think for one second I'd go down alone for this, you better cut down on your lines."

He'd found some mettle, and he adjusted his crotch with the hand holding the crowbar, like a gloved baseball pitcher, then swaggered back over to my chokecherry bushes and poked the tool deep into the branches.

Anger, more than fear, brought on the trembling; I didn't need another body on my hands. Clenching my jaw to keep my teeth from chattering and breathing quietly through my nose, I gripped the revolver harder and reminded myself to shoot right through the pocket. Phil said trying to remove the gun first might be the last thing you ever did. But before I ruined my favorite jacket, Steadman stopped molesting the bushes and turned his face toward the driveway.

"Fuck this! I'm getting out of here before someone shows up."

He took a few steps in the right direction, then stopped, refusing to simply walk away.

"Why does it always have to be like this with you? Fuck! Phone me when you finish up at the hospital then."

My legs had cramped from standing still in the cold, the bushes seemed to offer less cover with each passing second, and the bastard just would not leave.

"Okay, you might be right. I'll look there first."

Where? Where was he going to look first? But he closed his phone and finally took off, scraping the crowbar against the side of the garage as he went. What an asshole. As soon as his Navigator cleared the driveway, I switched off the garage light, pulled the needlessly mangled door shut, then raced to my truck.

If mine was the house Steadman wanted to check first, he'd take Clements Road there, so I took Alder Lane home and unlocked the wide gate at the rear of the property. Being aware of his arrival would've been impossible even if he misused the crowbar to break into my locked garage the way he had Mike's. The storm dithering above the valley had let loose, rendering me deaf and nearly blind.

Wishing to god Phil hadn't taken the enclosed car hauler, I backed up to the only equipment trailer we had left in the yard, threw my jacket hood over my cap, and got out. The temperature had dropped at least ten degrees, and the wind blew so hard rain came at me from every direction—cold, blinding water, stinging my eyes, dribbling over my nose, running down my neck.

Each turn of the trailer jack handle churned out a plea to the heavens that I'd get the ball under the hitch in one try. It took three, but the wiring harness didn't give me any of the usual grief, and Steadman hadn't come by. Not as far as I could tell anyway. I could barely see to unlatch the trailer bed, and when I made a running jump to get onto it, my rain-soaked pant legs stuck to my thighs, pitching me backwards. I landed on the muddy grass with the breath and fight knocked out of me and felt like staying right there and going to sleep. But visions of a shared prison cell goaded me into action.

Groaning and rolling over on my belly, I got to my hands and knees, stood up, then climbed carefully onto the trailer and walked the bed down. My legs, still shaky from the fall, nearly buckled when I tried sprinting to the dry garage, and I had to stroll there, getting wetter, and wetter, then even wetter while struggling to unlock the door.

Ignoring the frightful, yet comical creature behind the wheel of the Lexus, I used limited time and resources to dig out the two magnetic signs left under the seat of a dump truck we'd bought at an auction. The black lettering spelling out *Orville Sand & Gravel* was in the same script used to paint *Monitor* on the tail vane of Marie's windmill, and I'd planned to tack the signs up in the garage. I'd never gotten around to it, though, and, they were perfect for concealing the company logo on my truck doors.

I loaded them in the back of the Lexus, noticed the blanket Steadman wanted so badly, then went outside to check for headlights on Clements. Seeing nothing but pouring rain, I ducked back into the garage and hoped sitting on a corpse would be easier the second time. It wasn't a damn bit easier. But at least I didn't have as far to drive, and, after standing in the downpour again to slap on the signs, anywhere dry sounded good, even if it did mean sitting on Jill's cold, smelly body.

Being out of the rain didn't make getting on and off her lap any easier, though, and I had to do it more than once. Windshield wipers are no match for a torrent. I struggled in and out of the Lexus twice before getting it lined up dead center with the trailer. But finally I could shift into low and start up the incline. I had a secure grip on the steering wheel and was ready for the stomach-flopping moment when the bed pivoted down. But nothing could've prepared me for being unable to stop because Jill's right foot had bounced under the brake pedal.

She would've defeated me right then and there if the steel guard at the front of the trailer hadn't held until I could kick her foot out of the way and stomp on the brake pedal. Not before I'd heard the sound of rending metal, though. Fearing the worst and the torture of having to, yet again, fight my way off Jill's lap made me lose it. I raised my fists, ready to pound her lifeless body to a pulp, but the thought of leaving some very discrepant bruising stopped me, and I could only scream at her corpse.

"You are not going to win this war! Quit trying! You're dead! And you're going to stay that way! Damn you! Damn you back to the hell you came from! I hope you burn for eternity! How could you have a baby just to use him? Not love him. Not even a little."

Spent, I stood searching for a bit of starlight above the storm clouds. The rain running between my lips tasted of tears and sweat. I wanted to give up, but couldn't, and prayed the noise I'd heard didn't mean the end of my getaway. Before walking in front of the Lexus to take a look, feeling a little crazy for not trusting Jill even dead, I turned off the engine and set the parking brake. Nothing had been damaged except the trailer jack handle, not needed during the trip anyhow. Shouting, "Thank you, God," I wiped the rain off my face and got on with the revolting chore.

What a relief to find Jill's body hadn't gone stiff yet. Another disaster averted. I raised the seat then pushed her arms through the openings in the steering wheel to keep her from flopping over during the drive. Fastening the seatbelt across her chest made me think about buckling Bryan into his carseat, and I realized he'd only know what we told him about his mother now. We could reinvent her as a good person, and she could never alter that implanted memory or ever again neglect or hurt him.

That intoxicating new reality had me hopping off the trailer like a kid, and I couldn't shut down the manic laughter. It wouldn't let me focus, and securing the trailer deck then climbing into the back of the truck, unlatching the toolbox, and finding what I needed to batten down the Lexus took far too long. Choking on rainwater sobered me up, though, and just in time. The Lexus had to be chained down, and, for me, tightening the chains properly requires the extra leverage of a cheater pipe positioned precariously close to the end of the binder handles—where Murphy sits smirking and swinging his wee feet.

My luck and the pipe held, though, and everything looked good to go. Everything but a corpse being behind the wheel. Jill had to be concealed with something, and the handiest thing was that U of M football blanket. But getting it out of the back of the Lexus then draping it over her body produced cringeworthy thoughts about it being smeared with Steadman's semen. And, for all that, it only made Jill look like a deceased Griz fan. I gingerly rolled it up and tossed it on the back seat.

What the hell to do? I possessed neither the time nor the strength to tarp a loaded vehicle on my own, in the dark, during a rainstorm. Thinking about Bryan preserved my what-passed-for-sanity, and I remembered the multitude of sunshades that kept the back seat cool whenever we were out and about on a hot day. I got them out of the truck, and there were enough because only the front windows and windshield needed covering. Jill had tinted the rest nearly as dark as those in Steadman's Navigator, thank god. Getting the springy buggers to stay against the glass left my patience reserve in the negative, and my body was so cold and sore it felt like my bones had shattered when I jumped off the trailer.

Climbing into the warm cab of my idling truck was as close to heaven as I could imagine at that moment. And, if I'd had a way to do it and more energy, I'd have hugged that dependable, uncalculating hulk of metal and plastic. But a few seconds in a hot, enclosed space made me aware the smell of Jill's perfume and urine-soaked clothing had permeated my nostrils like the acrid odor of burning garbage, and I was glad I could open the window all the way. The wind had gone down, and the rain had dwindled to a steady sprinkle. But the fresh air carried the sound of a familiar engine. I toggled off the cargo lamps and made it to the gate just as Steadman's Navigator slewed to a stop in my driveway.

Unable to decide if the timing of his appearance had been good luck or bad, I switched off the cab's interior light and opened the door. Thankfully, I could get out while the engine was running without setting off a buzzer. The dealership owner disables them on our personal trucks to keep us buying the company vehicles from him, and I'd make damn sure we never took our business elsewhere. Being back out in the cold made me wish Karl could've been there to open the gate, but I instantly recanted it. Some ingrained wisdom told me subterfuge and escape are best accomplished solo.

I'd made it back to the truck without any indication Steadman had seen me, but there's no quieting a big engine pulling a heavy load, and the truck roared up the incline to the street, announcing my location to anyone smart enough to listen. I thought that might leave Steadman out and drove the mile to Spurgin Road without seeing him.

Then, at the sharp corner where Clements turns into South Third, the unmistakable blue tint of HID headlights appeared in my side mirrors. Driving under the security lighting around Hawthorn Grade School confirmed they belonged to Steadman's Navigator, and looping through the next subdivision proved he was following me.

I didn't like being the rodent in our little game of cat and mouse, but it was the truth that sank its fangs into me—even if it was possible to lose Steadman while towing a loaded trailer, which I doubted, it would only leave the family more vulnerable. Steadman and his wife knew how and where Jill died and might well conclude one of us had staged the car wreck. Would they keep quiet, blackmail us, or worry about what we knew and permanently shut us up? It couldn't be left to chance. I had no alternative. I had to lure Steadman on with the blanket he wanted and find a way to kill him, or we'd be trading one albatross for two.

People always stare when you're towing something, but now every glance meant Jill's body had slumped against the door, knocking the shade off the window and exposing her mummy-wrapped head.

Waiting at a light was agony, and I avoided most of them by crossing the river on the old, shuddering Russell Street Bridge where there were only two lanes of traffic. Steadman was directly behind me after we crossed Broadway into the old Westside, a respectable working-class neighborhood fighting drug addicts to stay that way and losing. When he lagged behind, I worried he was on the phone getting new instructions from his wife. But he closed the gap before we got to the Scott's Street overpass and stayed close as we passed over the wide expanse of braided railroad tracks into the much older Northside area.

I still hadn't made a decision about where to take Jill's body, but the interstate forced me to pick a direction or drive straight into the side of Water Works Hill. So, rustling the vagrants camped in their dusty nests under the freeway abutment, I poured fuel to the engine, roared up the entrance on my right, and headed east. As I leaned forward to peer in the mirrors at how the trailer was tracking, I felt the bulky envelope in my jacket pocket and wondered how Jill came to possess its incendiary contents—and when? If she'd only become aware of the photos and clippings recently, it might explain why she'd returned Bryan right after taking him then left town.

Maybe she was the one being blackmailed and not the other way round. It would account for the disappearance of the 20K Mike discovered in her scarf drawer. Made more sense too; no one could accuse Jill of being simpleminded. If she'd been the one doing the blackmailing, she would've given the envelope in my pocket to a lawyer with instructions not to open it unless something happened to her and made that clear from the get-go.

So, if Jill had been blackmailing the Steadmans, they wouldn't have wanted her dead. Unless her lawyer had betrayed her—but that didn't add up either. If that had happened, Steadman still would've torn the house apart to make sure there weren't any copies of the damning evidence or anything else she might've had relating to that Helena woman's death. No, Jill hadn't been squeezing them for money; they just knew her well enough to make a preemptive strike before moving into the governor's mansion.

And Steadman and his wife could've been aware of, if not actually in on, Jill's scheme to extort the land from us. Maybe she'd boasted about how she'd soon have us on our knees and they'd decided to murder her while there were still Crandalls around town to take the blame. But I didn't really care whether Jill was being blackmailed or intended to blackmail someone other than the Steadmans. I was just happy that someone had put an end to her.

I smiled over her bad luck, smiled again when Steadman followed me over the interstate at the sharply curved Bonner exit, and started believing the whole mess could be dealt with. Then I passed the truck stop where Mike and I ate lunch the day before

I'd left for Red Bend and remembered how certain I was, then, that his father's plan would work. So certain, I'd spent the entire hour telling him things would get better soon and, without providing a single good reason why, convinced him it was true.

Mike had believed me because he loved his family and wanted us all to be happy. Nothing demonstrated this more than the fact that, even though things had become far worse instead of better, he'd let Phil and I talk him into going to the cabin rather than doing what his heart and gut were to telling him to do. But would he stay there? Or had he become another person ready to drain the life from Jill's pretty face? Paul would be more than willing to help him, without question. What if they'd left the cabin? But if they had, Amy would've bundled up Bryan then gone down to the gate and phoned me. Not that I'd have been able get any calls during the past couple of hours.

Damn it, how could I have forgotten to turn my phone back on after shutting it off when I hid from Steadman? But there were no missed calls or messages, and that helped me believe the kids and Bryan were all still safe at the cabin. Of course, Mike or Paul doing something to botch Phil's plan didn't matter anymore. But alibis did, and more than ever. The three of them insisting they'd been together at the cabin wouldn't be the soundest. Better than none, though. And, if we asked them to, the folks at the ranch would swear no one had come through their yard. Thank god I'd checked my phone, or I'd have had to worry all night whether or not Amy had tried to call me.

Cell coverage would end soon, no matter which way I went, and where in hell *was* I going, anyway? When visions of an expanse of prairie rolling away from the Rocky Mountain Front northeast of Remount sprang to mind, I thought being slammed to the ground trying to jump on the trailer had addled my brain. But, no, the place must've been flashing like a subliminal message since I'd found Jill curled up on Mike's kitchen floor.

Those sparsely inhabited highlands were the perfect location for staging a wreck. Helluva long way to be hauling a body around, but every detail of those roads had been mapped into my memory and would unfold when I needed them to. We'd moved there the spring I turned twelve, stayed for nearly a year, and I'd traveled many miles over those roads, back and forth in a bus every school day and to a bar in Remount every night.

Finally having a destination and, therefore, an end in sight left me as gung ho and unwitting as a recruit on his way to boot camp, and I didn't hesitate to draw Steadman north. When I turned onto Highway 200, he must've thought I'd be stopping soon and started tailgating. It would've been damn hard to lose me in Bonner, though. The old company town could be resettled within the chain-link boundary of its giant plywood plant.

Vintage worker's cottages line the road, but I couldn't admire them. The hi-tech headlights of Steadman's Navigator were blinding me. I thought of adjusting my side mirrors to redirect the glaring beams into his eyes and relished the idea of him hurtling off the highway into the flood-stage river. Great if it killed him outright. But what if it didn't?

That's when the Steadman solution came to me. The dirtbag would have a fatal accident right along with Jill. With his prints all over her Lexus and his DNA on that blanket, their deaths could easily be construed as an ill-fated lovers' tryst—case closed. Just how to lead him into that situation wasn't what worried me. The plan's biggest flaw was the fact it relied on Lady Luck's cooperation. A bitch that will turn on you even quicker than Mother Nature—and look what *she'd* done to me. If not for a freak snowstorm at Phil's place, I wouldn't be trying to cover up one death with another.

Phil—what would he think of my reckless actions? Should I even tell him? Should I tell anyone in the family? As I weighed the drawbacks of sharing my ordeal against the release it would afford me, the Lubrecht Experimental Forest came into view and brought to mind the conversation Phil and I had on that exact stretch of highway twenty-two years earlier.

"Can you believe how tall these trees are getting, Phil? Seems like they were just planted."

"I try to ignore them. They're beginning to make me feel old."

"That's why the prairie's better, Phil. Grass is ageless."

He'd just smiled, conceding the point. It wasn't like him, but he hadn't been himself all day. By nightfall he'd summoned the courage to tell me he no longer wanted to be married. I liked the Blackfoot even less after that—and didn't like it much to begin with. It's where I'd first set foot west of the Continental Divide after being a flatlander for all my thirteen years.

My parents and I had packed our things and left the ranch northeast of Remount that morning, and they soon stopped to have a beer or two at a roadside bar. It burned to the ground some years later and, as always tends to happen, reopened in a better, busier location. The scorched foundation remained visible until development dollars blew all the genuine ranches apart and knapweeds engulfed it along with a few acres of prairie that had escaped the plow. I often wonder if I would hate the mountains quite so much if my first encounter hadn't been connected to losing my summers with Marie, the horse I loved, the place I loved—and if the valley we'd moved to hadn't made all that worse.

⚊ ⚊

Heidi-inspired notions of mountain dwelling held no warning that the entrails exposed on Rogers Pass, waves of sage gray, scoria red, wheatgrass tan, and alkali white, would be the last respite from a static, mind-numbing green. And, like those colorful, exposed rocks, the buttercups growing around the bar we stopped at never hinted at their scarcity. Their dewy yellow petals made me think things might not be so bad after all. A happy thought canceled by reaching our new home.

Dad's latest job was on a ranch twenty-eight miles west of Missoula in the narrow Ninemile Valley. Walls of dark forest hid the ground, the horizon, and most of the sky. Feeble breezes and soft showers did nothing to disperse the dead air, the ash from teepee burners, or the reeking emissions from a pulp mill located a few miles east between Missoula and Frenchtown.

Frenchtown—the small town where I resumed eighth grade at a school far larger than any I'd ever attended, riding forty-five minutes on a bus with unfriendly kids twice a day, then slinking off motion sick, homesick, and heartsick.

Six months later, we left that sorry excuse for a ranch, just a get-out-of-town wedding present for a rich, obnoxious Texan and his pregnant, teenage, socialite bride, and moved into Missoula. At least it was in a much wider valley, and, along with lumber mills and teepee burners, there were fields of hay, wheat, and sugar beets, and even a tiny patch of prairie.

While I learned to tolerate my new home, the timber industry cleaned up its act and a good portion of America fell in love with the place. The tiny farms disappeared, and car exhaust, road dust, and wood smoke soon created air pollution on a par with Los Angeles. The newcomers themselves spoiled the town in longer-lasting ways.

———

In the decades since, although I hadn't exactly fallen in love with western Montana, we'd become close, and I resented people like Ron Steadman and his wife who elevated the prevailing corruption and greed to a celebrated lifestyle. For them to go on living like that, Steadman had to somehow heist that incriminating blanket, and I doubted he'd stop following me no matter how long the journey. But, unaware I'd moved Jill's body to her Lexus, he must've been totally flummoxed as to why and where I'd be taking that vehicle so late at night in such rotten weather. Being without his phone probably rattled him more; he wouldn't like not being able to rely on his wife if things got dicey. Good thing the brains in that pair had been silenced by a lack of cell coverage.

Thinking about the resources that woman could've marshaled to help her husband made my left eyelid twitch, and so did the cars passing me. The rapidly falling temperature could turn the water on the road to black ice at any moment, and the deer-crossing signs where bedrock pushed the highway against the river were portents of calamity as well. You're more likely today than a thousand years ago to be taken out by an animal. There's always blood on the highway.

Making it as far as Clearwater Junction without mishap was something to celebrate. I watched for Steadman to pull off the highway for gas or a pee, but the Navigator's bluish headlights held steady. New worries piled up with the mile markers, though, and I was glad to feel Marie's gun in my pocket. But maybe Steadman had a gun too, or what if he got ballsy enough to try forcing me to pull over or deliberately did something to cause a wreck so he could try to recover the blanket before a sheriff or the highway patrol showed up? And what kind of spiel would get me out of that?

"Really officer...a body...I'd no idea! The trailer was already loaded; I just hitched on and took off."

I didn't kid myself. If Steadman tried anything, I'd have to outdrive him, or, as Marie would've said, I'd be in more trouble than a naked, short man climbing over a four-strand barbed wire fence. And, really, anything at all that brought the law around would be the end of my freedom.

That oppressive, sudden awareness got the adrenaline flowing, my neglected stomach didn't take it well, and each glimpse of Jill's shiny white Lexus instead of a grimy backhoe in my rearview or side mirrors made me flinch. I tried to relax by searching for my next waypoint. But darkness and rain obscured the incredible fractal image of a gravel pit containing mounds of rock which mirror the surrounding glacial moraines, which mirror the foothills, which mirror mountains in the distance.

The only thing clearly visible was the fact my unavoidable pit stop in Lincoln would provide Steadman a perfect opportunity to go after that damn blanket. What if the man became desperate enough not to care if someone saw him breaking into the Lexus? I didn't believe he had what it took to do that, though, and clung to the warm fuzzy that, even if I was underestimating his courage and overestimating his stupidity, Jill wouldn't be contaminating anything but the ground now. A second later, I felt the truck intermittently losing contact with the pavement.

Less traffic had allowed the rain to freeze—an icy lens focusing my attention on the road. And I'd reached the steep stretch of highway where it's one curve after another, where the shoulder protecting you from miles of marsh spawning the Blackfoot River becomes even less substantial. Then bluish headlights appeared beside the trailer and took me to the rim of panic where it's hard to keep your wits about you.

I feathered the brake and braced for impact—because why would Steadman only be trying to pass me? But why run me off the road where he'd have no chance of making it to the wreckage and even less of getting the blanket? If he did try forcing force me down into that black mire, I was going to take him with me. It wasn't the Navigator that pulled along-side, though, just some daredevil in a dark-colored Lincoln Continental with the same HID headlights. Another dose of adrenaline, a wave of nausea, and shivering that didn't stop until I reached the final landing on the rocky staircase to Rogers Pass.

A few minutes later I rolled into Lincoln, a small town squatting under some of the biggest pine trees in the state. It was named for its proximity to Abe Lincoln Gulch not directly for the president, but to me its name pays tribute to the can of Lincoln Logs I'd cherished as a child. Nearly every building there is made of logs. It enhances the deep woods, lumber camp veneer of the place, but, these days, you see more deer than logging trucks. In fact, you see more deer than anything. They wander the streets like stray dogs, browse in fenced yards, and make the deer ornaments decorating lawns seem like fantastically effective decoys.

I'd be spared that spectacle. The rain had changed to sleet and limited visibility to a few yards. Trusting the sunshades were still concealing Jill's mummy-wrapped head, I signaled then pulled in at the con-venience store burgeoning into a small truck stop, and Steadman followed suit.

My truck and trailer took up an entire line of pumps, and I didn't have to worry about him parking beside me either. The place was even busier than I'd hoped, thanks to the bad road conditions, and he had to use a pump at the opposite end. It left as much distance between us as possible, but I'd have liked even more.

I'd have liked a drier jacket hood too. It was still cold and heavy with rainwater, but I pulled it on anyway then leaned out far enough to peer up at the Lexus—ready to take off if the shades had slipped. They hadn't, though, and I went ahead and fueled up. I kept a close eye on Steadman too and nearly laughed when he refused to touch the pump handle until he'd raised his small hands to eye level and smoothed on thin leather gloves, like a woman in an old movie getting ready for the opera.

The gas tank had all it could hold, but I waited at the pump and watched through the glass doors until Steadman paid. He used his credit card then darted into the casino beside the store. I could only hope he was after a drink to steady his nerves and not for the Dutch courage to go after the blanket. Surely not, though. He seemed to have spent enough time in Jill's Lexus to be aware of its alarm system and wouldn't risk setting it off where there were so many people around.

I stretched the soggy jacket hood until it shielded more of my face then walked into the store with my emergency cash in hand. A person could be mistaken, but there would be no arguing with a bankcard statement. I kept my head down while paying the cashier and while walking back to the restroom. Using it was no longer optional, but wading through the aroma of Broasted chicken, warm doughnuts, and hot coffee was an endurance test.

Having pie with Della seemed like days before, and I had to quicken my pace and tell myself there'd be something to eat in the truck, the coffee would be terrible, and who needed caffeine when they were towing a dead woman around with her murderer following. And, more pertinent, the less time spent in the c-store, the less threat of someone remembering a grubby woman in a gray GMC towing a luxury SUV with sunshades in the windows.

I returned to the truck with a happier bladder, but angrier stomach, and Steadman had already settled into his vehicle. He was busy admiring himself in the mirror, though, and I couldn't resist taking advantage of the bright lights to check the trailer over. A big mistake. Some boozy guy at that age where they should drop the young stud act, but don't, got out of his yellow Jeep Wrangler and stuck his nose into my business with the enthusiasm of an AWOL hog in a potato patch.

"Snowin' in May! Jesus! Gonna get worse b'fore mornin' too. Accordin' to guy on the radio."

Enough of his license plate showed through the caked snow to tell me he resided in the Bitterroot.

"Say, hon. You pullin' that trailer all by yerself in this weather?"

I almost said, "No, the truck's a big help," but being a smartass would only lengthen the conversation and give him more reason to remember me.

"Yup."

"Think I'll jus' put up here t'night. Don't s'pose you'd happen to know a good motel?"

I did. The Tamarack Inn, with nice, quiet, modernized log cabins.

"Afraid not."

"I can jus' ask at the bar. Say, wouldya like to join me for a little drink?"

"Nope. Need to get home to Great Falls."

Then, with more energy than I could spare, I ran to the cab, hopped in, shut the door before he could open his mouth again, and hoped he was drunk enough to forget everything about me, the trailer, the Lexus, my Missoula county plates—everything except the lie about where I lived.

Driving away from Lincoln felt like removing my finger from a match flame, and Steadman had pulled right in behind me, but my nerve was disappearing quicker than the stale Snickers bar I'd found in the jockey box. Damn, why had I taken all that delicious candy I'd bought in P-burg into the house? I tried to replace clear visions of those bulging sacks with details of my Steadman solution. But they remained shadowy, and a plague of doubt descended, followed by an acute, unreasonable longing to return to that horrible motel room in Summit.

I wanted to go back to that night, call Phil to warn him about the storm, and stop the nasty carnival ride from ever starting. Failing that, the desire to get rid of the body, the Lexus, and Steadman, without delay, replicated like a virus until every neuron screamed for me to make it happen. I even began looking for the right place. But Alice Creek Road came and went, then Fletcher Pass Road, a paved corkscrew of no use whatsoever anyway, slipped behind me, and I drove right on by Mike Horse Creek Road, the last possible place before I hit the pass.

Stopping the game mid-play wouldn't have worked anyway, and the crushing impulse faded to the sound of the engine working to pull the Lexus over the Continental Divide. Engineering a rational plan and reaching my destination felt doable again, and seeing the *Record Cold Spot* sign atop Rogers Pass cemented my resolve.

At a nearby mine on January 20, 1954, Mr. Kleinschmidt woke to the sound of freezing pitch cracking the logs of his cabin and went outside to find the thermometer had broken at minus seventy degrees. Those were his *working* conditions. I only had one miserable night to get through and would spend most of it in a nice warm truck. How could I give up without feeling weak and inept forever after? And there were no shortcuts. The only way out of this hell trip would be grinding my way to the end.

My newfound determination was put to the test on the other side of the pass when the highway vanished. It wasn't snowing, but it had been, and a hellish crosswind blasted the powdery crystals across the road—a ground blizzard—reducing the entire world to a black sky above a band of swirling white.

Turnouts were invisible. I couldn't pull over and stayed on the road by steering to the feel and sound of the right front tire contacting gravel whenever it drifted off the slick pavement. Keeping my hands light on the wheel, my foot off the brake, and my speed up to twenty felt self-annihilating. But being nearly stopped on the highway would've guaranteed someone, most likely Steadman, would slam into the trailer and send us both over the edge.

The answer to combining Steadman's death with staging Jill's accident had just presented itself but didn't penetrate. My mind had shut out anything that didn't involve surviving that space-and-time-distorting wall of writhing snow. When I made it off the pass, the longest five miles I'd ever traveled, I wanted to get out and kiss the ground instead of taking on the rest of Highway 200. But things were better there; the wind had no snow to play with and returned the world to me. It seemed angry about it though, and gusted fiercely, causing the Lexus to strain against its chains, intensifying the push-pull of the trailer against the hitch as the truck dove in and out of the deep ravines.

The highway winds through the mountains on the west side of Rogers Pass, but it's a rollercoaster ride across the hills on the east side, and I'd lost sight of Steadman miles back. Had he decided he'd sooner face his wife than deal with that ground blizzard and gone home? As far as he knew, Jill's body was still on her kitchen floor. He might have convinced himself her Lexus would end up somewhere the police wouldn't check it then decided to take his chances and tell his wife he'd managed to get hold of the blanket and gotten rid of it. But she would know his weaselly ways and demand enough details to expose his bulldust.

Hopefully, Steadman wasn't too thick to work that out for himself. I had my freedom, maybe Mike's too, riding on him carrying out his wife's orders no matter how tough things got. But where the hell was the man? Had he driven off the road, soon to wake up in a hospital babbling about Jill and the Lexus? Before I could make myself crazy wondering how to defuse such an event, familiar blue headlights glinted in the mirror. Thank the lord. Steadman had made it and could die where and when I wanted him to.

Limp with relief, I could sense, as I always had, a lingering energy from the cataclysmic events that created this stark, beautifully crumpled landscape geologists call the Disturbed Zone. Humans had altered it more recently by installing a hidden Minuteman facility next to the highway—about as inconspicuous as Jill at a Tupperware party.

I'd first encountered the peculiar group of buildings as a child when my parents and I lived on a ranch north of Wolf Creek. We'd driven by them on our way to Great Falls, and, although surrounded by grain fields, the site failed to deceive even a seven-year-old. I'd seen right away it couldn't be a farm or ranch. The fences were too tall, the yard lights were too high, the lawn still looked green in September, the dirt yard around the buildings had gravel, and there weren't any animals. I asked Mom what it was, but Dad answered.

"It's a ranch. Doesn't it look like one?"

"No."

He'd laughed then told me about Malmstrom Air Force Base and explained we'd driven by one of the places where they hid missiles in gigantic underground silos. He said they were supposed to look like wheat ranches to keep the Russians from finding them, and it made me worry.

"They're not fooling anyone, though, are they? There's no combine, no plows, no tractors, no shed. And not even one *real* silo."

"Don't you think it might look like a ranch if you were flying way up high in an airplane, though?"

"Maybe...I guess."

Dad could be nice sometimes. We'd even stopped for lunch at a restaurant with no bar that day. When two young airmen came in and both had blond hair with buzz cuts, it made me wonder if the silly Air

Force thought they'd blend into the stubble wheat around the fake farm where they worked.

I wouldn't see that missile site, maybe empty, maybe holding bigger and better missiles, on this trip. I had to leave Highway 200. Signaling well ahead of time to let Steadman know my intentions, I turned onto 287 and continued trundling toward Remount and the highlands beyond. A nearby Hutterite colony had tripled in size over the years, and the industrial lights of their factory-farm buildings created an unsightly glow in the dark prairie. I promised myself, if I remained a free woman, I'd buy a ranch somewhere more remote and spend my days watching the wind sweep away anything dissonant or insubstantial. I'd done my time in the mountains. The kids could take over the business, and I'd move on.

Unfortunately, my happy retreat depended on a dead Steadman, one unable to tell tales. It also depended on me not shackling myself with remorse over killing him, but that wouldn't be a problem. He'd murdered Jill in her own home, knowing Mike would be blamed, and he'd had something to do with that young woman's asphyxiation too. He deserved to die, and I had a good chance of killing him without getting caught. Letting him live would be irresponsible and cowardly—not how my world spins.

No, killing Steadman wouldn't be what crimped my peace of mind; it would be worrying about what his wife would do if she thought Mike threatened her campaign in any way. You won't find a find politician sitting on the fence when it comes to tying up loose ends. But one problem at a time, and that answer about how to stage a fatal accident for two drifting around since Rogers Pass had finally docked. If the Lexus were to end up on the highway in front of Steadman, he'd plow right into it, especially if it happened at the end of a steep grade. Somewhere like Black Coulee, a deep, wide gorge cutting through the highland hills.

When we'd lived on a nearby ranch, the owner let me use one of his cow horses, and the bottom of the coulee was my favorite place to ride. Sun on my shoulders, tropical scent of milkweed in my nostrils, I would lope the big gelding, a blue roan savvy as Marie's mare Babe, to the coulee. We'd stop at the rim where I'd let him have his head so he could goose-step down the long, steep bank with his haunches under his belly. As soon as his hooves hit flat ground, he'd break into a gallop, and I'd gather the reins to set him on a straight course. Then, like drawing lines through a dollar sign, he'd fly over the meandering creek whenever it crossed our path.

I'd loved that gelding as much as I'd hated my life and plotted to take him, ride far away from Mom and Dad, and live off the land. To that end, I'd dismounted one day and chomped down on a wild onion. The putrid taste would gag a maggot off a gut wagon and had stayed in my mouth long enough to dissuade me from becoming a horse-thieving runaway.

How ironic to be revisiting the place with another, this time deadly serious, plan to fix my life—one I would carry out no matter how unpalatable it became. First, I'd have to devise a way to lose Steadman long enough to unchain the Lexus, but not so long I'd lose him altogether, and I needed to do it in the next few miles. I'd already reached the cottonwood grove surrounding Remount.

The town's streets were empty, its windows dark, its trees deathly still, and it could've been the ominous village in the first episode of *The Twilight Zone*, a milieu befitting the memory it unleashed. The acidic evocation had remained submerged when Mike and I were there Mike rescuing Bryan, but now it floated to the surface—as scum will do in a simmering pot.

———

There were no warning signs, just another night with Mom and Dad at the Mint Bar. I'd been studying the ugly side of a neon window sign for quite a while when an old man stopped on his way to the bathroom and slipped me a fifty-cent piece. My jubilant smile earned another one, and I was looking forward to standing in front of the jukebox for ages, flipping through songs, and shutting out the world. But you hear your name when it's mentioned, and I began listening to Mom and Dad's escalating fight.

"—take Lynnie? You can't even take care of your-self! Know goddamn good and well, if you leave, I'll be stuck with her!"

What a shock. I thought Mom cared and often wished she'd leave Dad. Then the two of us could live like other people, be home at night, and stay in one place for more than a few months.

"God dammit! Just said she's going with me, didn't I?"

Okay then, just Dad and me, no fighting at least. Would I have to cook? Could I get him to leave the bar and come home at night the way Mom always did?

"You? Why would you want to take her? So you could sell her for beer money...that's why! You'd have her out on a street corner. That's what you'd do!"

That didn't make sense. You can't sell people. Then—like getting a dirty joke—I understood. My knees went wobbly, holding back tears of humilia-tion choked me, and the roaring in my ears made me dizzy.

I pressed my pimply forehead against the transparent dome protecting the jukebox, and it didn't matter that the titles had become blurry be-cause I knew most of them by heart and pressed C-15. By the last refrain of *From a Jack to a King* I'd found the courage to turn around. Mom and Dad didn't notice me staring at them, but the bartender did, and the look on his face, pity and something repulsive I couldn't name, filled my soul with shame.

⸺

Hurt from the past lurks in your future, tripping you up when your step is uncertain. But I'd survived, burying what I'd heard that night and going on as if nothing had happened, and I'd survive this too. Snuffing out Steadman and moving on would be much easier than years of dreading something far worse from my parents than being dragged to a bar every night.

As though Steadman sensed my commitment to do away with him, he hung back and increased the distance between us. More likely, he'd begun questioning how long I'd believe we just happened to be traveling to the same place and was getting nervous. He'd never guess I'd been at Mike's house and knew who was following me, though. And the second thing in my favor was being able to visualize every detail of the next eleven miles.

Dad had never been in any condition to drive after spending a few hours at the Mint Bar, much less drive and argue with Mom at the same time. But he wouldn't let me behind the wheel out on the highway, so, hanging over the front seat, I'd stared through the windshield and nudged him on the arm whenever the car veered toward the barrow pit or drifted over the centerline.

Now those hair-raising trips were paying off. No way could Steadman know the area like I did. He'd assume I was heading to Chouteau, a fairly good-sized town farther north, a mistake that would let me ditch him long enough to lay a trap. But getting that far ahead of him would've been damn tough, maybe downright impossible, if Mother Nature hadn't switched sides. Monolithic clouds, heavy and dank, were banked miles deep against the craggy barrier, and, five miles out of Remount, the sky began dumping snow like shredded clouds.

The huge flakes tumbled into each other, filling every cubic inch of airspace, sidelining the windshield wipers, and reflecting the headlight beams back at me. Driving through a feather bed couldn't have been much worse, but every bloated, ragged flake increased the odds of giving Steadman the slip. Immediately after climbing out of the Sun River depression and topping the bench, I hit the odometer button, cut my lights, pushed the accelerator to the floor, and held it there for exactly two metal-testing miles—speeding blindly down the highway, praying it hadn't changed from where and how it was 1963. Not the most nerve-busting part of the stunt, though. That came last.

Taking my foot off the gas, I lowered the passenger window and watched for a change in the fence line. With all the snow and a strange absence of wind, scrutinizing the nearly invisible strands of barbed wire, just horizontal white behind vertical white, was my only chance of discerning the reinforced corner section. And I had to locate that corner to know where the fence turned east and where I had to make a suicidal turn onto the intersecting highway. All too soon, I spotted the diagonal corner post. Thought I had—hoped to hell I had—counted to three, then clenched my teeth, gunned the engine, feathered the trailer brakes, and made a hard right-hand turn.

I'd done it; I'd made the ninety-degree change in direction without jackknifing. The trailer, truck, and Lexus were still together and pointed in the right direction. But had I succeeded in losing Steadman? Yes! There was a faint blue glow behind me out on the main road. Steadman would eventually realize he'd been duped, though, then backtrack and locate the only side road I could've taken. He just had to. Everything depended on it.

Careening onto a highway only visible in memory had left me wired, and, just when I needed the precision of a rifle bullet, perceptions came like shotgun blasts. But muscle memory saved me. When I neared the gravel road leading to the ranch I had once called home, my foot came off the accelerator of its own accord, and I knew the highway would dive into Black Coulee a mile farther. So the steep grade shouldn't have taken me by surprise. But I'd been looking in the mirrors as much as through the windshield and couldn't slow the truck and trailer down fast enough on the snow-packed road.

I overshot the sweet spot and had to back the trailer to the deepest, flattest part of the swale. I pined for those lost minutes, too, while checking my pockets for the flashlight and gun, setting the truck and trailer brakes, and switching on the cargo light. Then, finally, I could get out and prepare for Steadman. The truck bed already held a few inches of the fat snowflakes hitting me in the face, hunting for my cheater pipe took way too long, and I didn't like the look of the trailer. That ferocious ground blizzard had plastered it with road grit and snow.

Beating the stuff off the binder handles then fighting to unchain the axles devoured even more time. Shivering with cold and cloaked head to foot in grimy, sticky snow, I looked forward to opening the door of the Lexus and sticking my face inside the dry space, but it smelled awful in there. And seeing how hard the big SUV must've rocked during that high-speed turn, I was astounded the chains hadn't snapped.

The sunshades had popped off the windows, the scarf I'd wound around Jill's face hung fashionably around her neck, and, as though she'd opened them in fright, her eyes were no longer closed. They weren't green anymore, either. A milky, light-absorbing film covered the lifeless orbs, and they were as iridescent as the coyote tobacco blooming along the pathway in Becky's lawn back when Jill's death was still a comforting dream not a nightmare on a stopwatch.

I gathered up the scattered sunshades, crammed them inside my jacket, then turned on the head-lights, heater, windshield wipers, seat warmer, and CD player to make it appear Jill had driven there. The illusion would have to be marred, though, because the Lexus couldn't roll off the trailer later if it was left in gear. Praying the inconsistency would be undetectable after the crash and pressing against Jill, for what I promised myself would be the last time, I shifted the vehicle into neutral, slowly released the emergency brake, then, very, very gently, closed the door.

One more quick task—and, despite my abject horror of the Navigator cresting the hill before it was completed, I did not try to hop off the trailer. I planked my butt down on the snow-covered decking and slid off. Even then I couldn't get a purchase on the icy road and went skating across it until my boots caught in the gravel on the other side. I'd come damn close to going right on over the bank, though, a brush with disaster that left me ill-equipped to deal with a frozen safety lock on the trailer. Close to tears, I stripped off my wet gloves and wrapped my hands around the icy metal.

My whispered curses were all that disrupted the cottony silence of falling snow, yet I couldn't cease glancing at the concealed hilltop for Steadman, and it seemed a sure bet my skin would freeze before the metal thawed. But the latch finally broke free, and the trailer could tilt when the Lexus rolled backward. Gathering up the cheater pipe, binders, and chains, I threw them in the truck bed then jumped in the cab, yanked the sunshades out of my jacket, tossed them in the back seat, and extinguished all the lights.

The trap was set. And just one more minute would've been too late. Before the cold could start leaching out of my bones, blue headlight beams shone behind the curtain of snow. I had to believe they belonged to Steadman's Navigator or couldn't have continued. Easing the truck forward until it gained traction, I pushed the accelerator to the floor and demanded everything the big engine had. The truck shot forward, the trailer bed tilted, and there was an almighty jerk as the Lexus obediently rolled off the trailer then the wonderful, explosive sounds of a collision and crumpling metal.

Cheering as though I'd engineered the first moon landing, I stopped the truck, turned on my flashers, got out to lower and re-secure the trailer, then eyeballed the results of my effort. But, in spite of the din, there wasn't much to see—just two trails of plastic and chrome leading toward the bank—and a single thought burned my conscience.

What if, against all odds, I'd dumped the Lexus in front of some unlucky sod whose vehicle also had HID headlights, someone like the guy driving the Lincoln that passed me earlier? Crossing my gloved fingers, I peered over the embankment. It was

Steadman's Navigator alright, about thirty feet down, on its roof, with blue headlights still shining, slowing rotating tires spouting snowflakes, and engine emitting whistling moans, like a beached whale.

I would've left right then if the possibility of the man surviving hadn't occurred to me. Now I had to make sure he was dead. And that slope would've been intimidating bone dry on a sunny day, so, snow-covered in darkness only allowed for a barely controlled, horrifically fast slide down to him. His arm hung from the crushed SUV like a mouse tail dangling from an owl's beak. I took out my pocket-knife, ready to slit his veins from wrist to elbow if I felt a pulse, but didn't feel the slightest throb.

I'd caught a break, but what about my finger-prints on his wrist? Could they be taken from skin? Not wanting to risk it, I struggled back into my wet gloves, scrubbed Steadman's pale wrist with snow, then turned around and took the first step toward home. I'd never felt such relief. My tragic opera had come to an end at last. But I was wrong—the fat lady hadn't even been laced into her peasant dress yet.

Like a brutal slap across the face, I remembered stuffing Kleenex in Jill's nose and ears to keep blood off the floor. It sure as hell couldn't stay there for a coroner to find. I began working my way farther down the embankment to the Lexus, jamming my boot heels into the snow with each step. Hard going, and my ankles had about given out by the time I got close to Jill's Lexus. It had rolled like the Navigator had, but landed upright then came to rest—until I tripped, sailed into a front fender, and started it plowing sideways down the bank again.

Screaming, "No, god damn it, no," I scrambled along behind as the Lexus ground its way toward the bottom of the coulee. Tires separated from their rims, black furrows formed in the snow, and the earth shuddered underfoot. But before I was well and truly done for, the bowed branches of an ancient clump of sagebrush sprang upright and stopped the mangled three-ton machine in its tracks. And I'd need that good luck to hold.

The only way to get at Jill's body was the driver's side door, on the downhill side of the Lexus, a place I did not want to be. But people don't run around with bloody Kleenex in their nose and ears, so, as if sneaking up on the homicidal wreck would help, I advanced very, very slowly. And when I reached it, careful not to touch or, god forbid, bump it, I dug down to dry clay with my boot heels to give myself a better chance of jumping clear if the damn thing headed for the bottom again.

Neither crash nor aftermath had caused the airbags to deploy, and Jill's head was encased in a helmet of steering wheel and dashboard. I swept the honeycombed glass from the edge of the window, reached for a fistful of long curly hair, wound it around my gloved hand, and pulled hard. But, when her head came free, my elbow slammed into the seatback, metal groaned, and some untapped source of adrenaline moved me ten feet away where, panting and sweating, I waited.

A minute and a thousand heartbeats later, the Lexus still hadn't budged. I held my breath, tiptoed back, then took out my flashlight and turned the beam on Jill's face. She was still recognizable—maybe—if you knew her really well. The wads of Kleenex I'd put in her ears offered no resistance even to my gloved fingers, but I needed my knife to fish out the pieces lodged in what remained of her nose.

I tucked the bloody tissue behind the bulky envelope still in my jacket pocket and thought harder about the photos and clippings it contained. For one reason or another they'd failed to protect Jill but, left with her body, might be good insurance for us. Evidence like that would take the heat off Mike and the rest of the family. And if the authorities dissimulated it to save Steadman's wife's gubernatorial campaign, so much the better—it guaranteed any other inglorious truths would be quashed as well. I slipped the envelope beneath the pile of glass on Jill's lap, eradicated the deep foothold I'd gouged in the ground, then said, "Good riddance, you evil bitch," and left her to the devil.

Covering my tracks wasn't worth the time. They're useless in clay, and any left on highway would melt away under the morning sun.

Something to be grateful for as, painfully over-stretching my legs to step from bunchgrass to bunchgrass for dry footing and clutching at sage-brush for balance, I began the long climb back to the highway. The ragged snowflakes stopped fall-ing as I neared the top of the bank, but, just before reaching it, I heard a vehicle and flattened my body against the melting snow.

A terrifying merry-go-round of possibilities whirled through my mind. And two were actually possible, a sheriff waiting to haul me to jail or an early-rising rancher stopping to gawp at my unfa-miliar vehicle. When adrenaline overcame hypother-mia, I identified the sound of my own truck idling. And, as well as clearing my thoughts, the hormone eased the pain of cold, mud-encrusted jeans sand-ing my thighs raw. I conquered the last few feet of the bank in seconds, then, chest heaving, sat down on the edge of the road. The eastern light creeping over the fresh snow created a beautiful, if grizzly, Christmas card scene about a hundred feet below.

I still couldn't see all the way to the bottom of the coulee, though, and I'd been lucky to have that sagebrush halt Jill's Lexus before reaching it became impossible. Then sheer stupidity almost did me in. I tried to stand up on the thawing highway with three inches of gumbo stuck to my boot soles, fell, and went sliding backward down the bank, jacket col-lar and waistband of my jeans scooping up muddy, gritty slush along the way. By the time I stopped my-self, rolled over, and got my head pointed toward the highway again, I had to repeat at least half the climb. I could've been laid out cold at the bottom, though, and tried to keep that in mind as I slogged back up that growing-ever-steeper bank.

My body seemed to have run out of adrenaline. I felt certain a sloth would've made it up ahead of me and didn't even consider trying to stand after drag-ging myself onto the road. I crawled to the center of the pavement and slowly worked myself upright. Loss of momentum had become the hypostasis of my being, and I felt in my bones what Marie had told me when she found out she wasn't going to make it past the cancer.

"Ya know, Lynn. We're like tops. Sooner or later something slows us down...we wobble till we stop... and then we fall over."

I'd sure as hell been slowed down and couldn't have been more wobbly. But the sun was slowly, ef-fortlessly returning color to the world, and freedom waited less than thirty yards away. I approached my truck like a starving coyote to a baited trap, cautious, steady, nose and ears to the wind, eyes on the prize.

Only one thing remained between me and a warm, dry cab—the impossibility of driving with that much clay on my boots. Scraping it off and leav-ing it on the highway would reveal to a person sharp enough to notice that someone had been standing near the embankment around the time of the wreck. So, leaning against the truck for support, I scraped some of the clay off with the edge of my gloved hand, deposited the gooey stuff inside the back fender well, and continued the process until I could feel my boot soles. Then I dropped the trashed gloves beside the toolbox and headed for the cab and sanctuary, but, as I reached for the door handle, someone or something appeared in the side mirror.

A fresh supply of panic juice assaulted me before I could recognize my own face, and trying to improve my image with a coat sleeve only moved the mud around. Wretched as an alley cat in a three-day blizzard, I dragged myself into the cab, put the truck in gear, then drove out of the coulee and into the rising sun.

My hand shook as I reached for the visor, and teeth-rattling tremors, blurred vision, and waves of nausea nearly overcame me. It would've been the first, and worst, time in my life to pass out. I turned into my old schoolyard, reclined the seat, closed my eyes, and took slow, deep breaths. The heater had been going full blast while the truck sat idling on the highway, and the cab had reached low oven temperatures, but it didn't stop my violent chills. Good thing too, because they were all that kept me conscious, and vulnerability gave rise to charitable thoughts about the grubby motel in Summit.

Without that one good night's sleep, I'd have been in even worse shape. And I was in bad shape.

It shouldn't have taken so long to know how thirsty I was and reach for water or taken three tries to get my hands around the bottle. And when I poured quicker than I could swallow, not even the jolt of liquid running under my shirt stopped the shivering. Hanging around was senseless and perilous but all I could manage. So, there I sat, staring at the gleaming white schoolhouse I'd left on a Friday afternoon in April thirty-five years earlier.

Exhaustion released the emotional responses put on lockdown to get through the last ten hours. They escaped en masse, and intense, insistent memories overcame pressing concerns of the here and now. Seeing the cozy teacherage reduced to a stone foundation made me cry. But, the next instant, I laughed with joy to see the weedy baseball field totally unchanged and saw my young self pitching hardball while listening for the teacher to ring the hand bell that ended recess. Or, if the wind happened to be blowing in the wrong direction, we watched for the youngest kids to go running in from the playground.

Then my gaze shifted to the empty flagpole, and my hands felt the weight of a full-sized flag folded into a precise triangle. Always fighting the wind and sometimes enduring below-freezing temps, we eighth graders had raised and lowered our country's ensign in pairs at the beginning and end of each school day. The chore dispensed excellent lessons in teamwork because the Stars and Stripes could never,

ever touch the ground—and even better lessons in conspiracy because it often did.

Hearing brass hooks clanging against the steel flagpole taxed my comprehension, memory or reality? But the wind had come up, I really was hearing that old chime song, and it was good medicine. I started feeling better and thinking about food. When I'd attended that school, it had one room, eight grades, and the best cook in the county to make us a hot lunch every day.

The slim, humorless, gray-haired woman had run a tight ship and happened to be married to the county sheriff. Sometimes, always in uniform, pistol and all, he would stop by at noon. The two of them would eat in the kitchen, and her threats to have her husband arrest us if things didn't stay quiet out in the dining hall only had to convince the first graders. The rest of us even speaking above a whisper had those little kids wide-eyed and squirming in their seats, and making them cry would've been the end of dessert for everyone.

Wondering how that old lawman would've reacted to the mess I'd left in his bailiwick reignited the urgency of leaving it far behind. I had things to do first, though, and slid my abused body off the seat to fetch a blowtorch from the toolbox. I cleaned the blade of my pocketknife in the flame, then burned the bloodied shreds of Kleenex from Jill's ears and nostrils to ash and gave them to the wind. Incinerating my coat, boots, and gloves would have to wait.

I had to get away from there while I could and headed for the warm the cab, but was startled, once again, by a glimpse of my face in the side mirror. I'd had enough of that. Scooping a handful of clean snow out of the truck bed and smothering thoughts of Steadman's pale, limp wrist, I scrubbed my face before climbing into the cab then finally hit the road.

The snow had receded to a few sparkling patches in the muddy barley fields rolling for miles in every direction, and the hypnotic scene turned my brain to sleep-craving mush. Scanning the highway for flashing lights was the only thing stopping me from nodding off, and when I passed a yard full of farm machinery, I thought how much easier it would be stay awake if I could call and talk to the kids or Phil. Impossible for many reasons, but being warm with slowly drying clothes made up for the isolation, and I felt safer too. I'd put a dozen miles behind me without seeing any law enforcement or emergency vehicles screaming to or from the coulee.

The likelihood of remaining free seemed even more likely when Fairfield came into view, but I didn't stop in the tidy little farm town. It seemed safer to cut south on a nearly empty tank and buy gas in Simms where my Missoula plates would go unnoticed, and the road ran downhill all the way there. Then there'd be the long trip over Rogers Pass and down the Blackfoot, but I wouldn't be dragging the Lexus through storms and over icy roads this time.

I'd be home in time to unload the trailer, take a quick shower, and still arrive at the cabin about the time I would've if I'd been tucked up in bed all night.

Feeling more secure farther from the coulee, I allowed the wrecked vehicles and bodies to infest my thoughts. Would noticing them intrude on someone's quiet Sunday morning, or would it be afternoon before they were discovered? No matter, I'd gotten away, and Bryan was safe, along with the rest of the family. They weren't aware of it, though. They were dreading Jill's next move and torn up over Mike's need to take his son and hide out in some lost corner of the earth.

A few words could stop all their suffering, but announcing Jill's death would generate unanswerable questions and hasty lies. I couldn't share the truth and burden them with a secret to guard forever. And what if it made them feel obligated to repay me somehow? Or what if they felt disappointed or appalled on some level? I didn't think they would, but couldn't be positive. Best not to tell anyone—well maybe Phil—about the past ten hours, but arriving at the cabin feigning worry and fear would be hell. And witnessing the kids' misery would be worse yet. They'd find out about Jill's death before too long, though, and could believe whatever story the authorities came up with.

I'd no idea how Steadman's doctor-wife had instructed him to end Jill's life so neatly. But, even if forensics disclosed she'd been murdered or the police somehow determined she couldn't have been driving when the vehicles collided, Mike wouldn't become a suspect. Not with the evidence I'd planted. And, with the cops already possessing those photos and clippings, Steadman's wife wouldn't have any reason to go after him either.

Events had worked out in our favor despite Mother Nature demolishing Phil's plan, and the most important thing remained. Jill was dead. I'd never call it a miracle, though. It was Marie. Her paradigm had served me well. A decent person never lets a dying creature suffer—or a dangerous one live.

Thinking about my absent mentor brought a delayed, overwhelming sense of loss. She'd enriched my childhood, moderated its wounds, and imparted her moral compass. Thanks to her, I'd had the courage to endorse Phil's plan and the strength to battle on when it fell apart. How bitterly unfair she couldn't share in the victory, or could she? Something to contemplate at the cabin while recuperating.

It had been a tough eleven hundred miles and sixty-eight hours since I'd gazed at Marie's body among that cascade of flowers. The only service Jill deserved was a stake through her chest, a coffin-less grave, and a sincere prayer of thanks for her death. Unfortunately, a more conventional funeral would be required. We'd have to be there too, for appearance's sake, but could think of it as a formal declaration of winning the war and try not to look too happy.

Sweet thoughts of being finally, indisputably, permanently free from Jill lingered as the grain fields turned to pastureland, and images of ranching and Karl drifted across the horizon. The two had entwined in some intangible way, leaving both more problematic yet, somehow, also more captivating. And, big or small part of Karl's life, I would be there for him. The only plan I needed now.